DEEPWATER

DEEPWATER

MATTHEW F. JONES

Matthew F. Jones (signature)

BLOOMSBURY

Published by Bloomsbury Publishing, New York and London.
Distributed to the trade by St. Martin's Press

A CIP catalogue record for this book
is available from the Library of Congress

ISBN 1–58234–059–5

First U.S. Edition 1999
10 9 8 7 6 5 4 3 2 1

Typeset by Hewer Text Ltd, Edinburgh, Scotland
Printed in the United States of America by
R.R. Donnelley & Sons Company, Harrisonburg, Virginia

Prologue

He finally stopped in the parking lot of an abandoned gas station in the middle of nowhere. He couldn't remember much of what he'd driven through. Good, he thought.

He ate a cold Big Mac and fries. He went to sleep in the car's backseat. He dreamed about planting seedling trees, the repetition of it: the digging, scooping, bending, filling, watering. At first light he woke feeling nearly all of a piece, feeling strong as an ox.

He ate his last Big Mac and started driving again.

One

Intangibles loomed large in Banyon's world. He put more stock in karma and gut feelings than he did in his five senses. One of his favorite mental pictures was of an Indian medicine man staring into the earth with his eyes squeezed shut. He believed that terrains were ruled by internal rhythms, which, in varying degrees, he could tune into as he drove through an area, thereby getting a sense of its overall temperament. Only rarely, as in these desolate mountains – appearing this high up untouched by man – did a place give off no vibes at all, at least none readily detectable to Banyon, who pictured the land as, far from lacking vibrancy, an aging but beautiful old maid struggling to hold in the great secret that had formed her.

Onto the Pontiac's windshield a light rain began to fall, though a small piece of sun was still visible. Banyon searched for a rainbow, but couldn't find one. Then the rain stopped. The clouds dissipated. The whole sun reemerged. Banyon opened his window. The temperate morning air was dampened only by a slight mist bearding the conifers to his right, from where the mountain dropped straight down for what looked to be a mile or more to a wooded valley interspersed by large, green fields and traversed north to south by a serpentining river. A sheer wall of blasted shale defaced the acclivity out his opposite window. Where the two-lane road started an even steeper descent ahead, a sign announced a town in ten miles. Banyon switched on the dash radio, but couldn't tune in a station. Entering a blind curve, he switched it off; from around the corner came a harsh screech of tires; a solid thud; the sound of a racing engine.

Lightening up on the Pontiac's accelerator, Banyon proceeded slowly through the bend to see a middle-aged Cadillac, its passenger-side wheels in the ditch, hugging the left bank a hundred yards in front of him. A beagle-sized animal, its back or neck apparently broken, flopped around in the road a few feet behind the car, the roar from which suggested its gas pedal was stuck to the floor. Banyon pulled the Pontiac onto the shoulder across from the one he'd been driving next to and stopped it thirty or so feet before the Cadillac. He stepped out and started trotting toward the disabled car, which appeared unoccupied. He was halfway to it when its engine abruptly quit. A head popped up from behind the steering wheel and a man's voice shouted, 'Halt right there.'

Believing he must have misunderstood the voice, Banyon ignored it. The sun reflecting off the car's windshield prevented him from seeing the speaker clearly. Blood marred the road beneath the wounded animal, which could now be heard mewling pathetically in its wrenching, half-paralyzed movements. The Cadillac's driver door opened and a stocky, white-haired man, maybe fifty, emerged; extending one hand coplike at Banyon, who was ten feet from him, he wielded in the other a large pistol. 'Don't come any farther,' he said.

Banyon didn't.

The man turned away from him, strode to within five feet of the wounded animal, which Banyon could now see was a fox, aimed his pistol at it, and shot it twice in the head. The fox stopped moving. The ceasing of its cries and the quieting of the gunshot's echo created a silence that seemed to Banyon even louder than the noise it replaced. The man shoved the pistol between his belt and pants. He faced Banyon. 'That acted rabid way it come out in front of me.' He bent down and picked up a stick near his feet. Realizing his hands were half-raised, Banyon self-consciously dropped them. The man approached the fox. 'See how its mouth's all foamed up?'

The question seemed not to require an answer and Banyon didn't provide one.

With one end of the stick, the man pushed the fox onto the gravel shoulder. 'A conservation officer will want to come out here and pick it up for testing before something else gets into it.'

He walked back to the Cadillac and nodded at its two right tires, which were flat. 'This here's changed my plans about heading over the mountain, wouldn't you say?'

Another statement dressed up as a question, thought Banyon, treating it that way. The man looked past him at the Pontiac. 'From out the area, I see?'

Banyon nodded, wondering when the man would ask a real question.

'Guess you're going into town?'

'I am if that's what's up ahead.'

The man chuckled almost boyishly. 'Was there when I left it a few minutes ago.'

'Probably still is then.'

The man seemed disappointed that Banyon hadn't found his joke more amusing. 'Got room for me?'

'Sure'.

The man pulled the pistol out of his belt. He smiled coyly. 'Won't need this, will I?'

'You won't to ride with me,' said Banyon, watching a tractor-trailer ascending inchmeal up the steep hill below them. 'Can't say 'bout after.'

The man chuckled again, then reached into the Cadillac through its open driver door, slid the gun under the front seat, pulled the keys from the ignition, withdrew from the car, and shut and locked the door. 'I sure do appreciate this, young man.'

'I'd of done the same for a lot of folks.'

'That's a fine trait to have.'

'I don't look at it as anything special, helping out someone. It's just the way I am.'

'By God, you don't hear that often today.'

Shrugging, Banyon turned and led the man back to the Pontiac. 'I'm Herman Finch,' the man told him over the car's roof, 'owner and operator of the Deepwater Motel' – he beamed – 'a rural hideaway.'

Banyon nodded, aware of the approaching tractor-trailer's tortured growl.

'And you are?'

Banyon reluctantly said his name, then climbed into the LeMans.

His shock of hair being mussed by the warm breeze blowing through the open windows, Herman Finch called out, 'I like how you handle a car, Nat.'

Guiding the LeMans at more than average speed through the sharp, downward curves, Banyon once more deemed a reply unnecessary.

'What year is she? '77, '78?'

So not to guess wrong, Banyon nodded evasively.

'At around your age, back in the dark ages, I owned a modified Chrysler – a real muscle car. Had a speedometer went up to one-forty and you could bury it in the shake of a dog's tail!' Finch looked into the rear seat at Banyon's bulging gym bag, then back out through the windshield at the lowlands ahead. 'Ever seen a valley so beautiful not up between a woman's legs, Nat?'

'It's a sight,' allowed Banyon.

'Twenty-five odd years ago I came here to shit or get flushed down the pot.'

'Which did you?'

Finch laughed. 'I'm doing all right, young man. Doing all right for myself.' He pointed a finger through the glass at a half-dozen or so vultures circling above a radio tower near the mountain's top. ' 'Pears one of our local DJs died on the air again.'

Banyon half-smiled, recalling how he'd been able to find just static on the dash radio earlier.

'What's your line of work, Nat?'

'A little of this, a little of that.'

'Well, you're young yet.'

'I got a want to keep moving.'

'Of course you do.'

Banyon didn't say anything.

'You need to see the world, right?'

Banyon wordlessly downshifted, chirping the tires.

'It's what I did instead of bothering with much school and it made me an educated man.'

'I've had jobs a plenty. I ain't afraid to take or leave one.'

'Mostly wage work?'

'I don't do it for free.'

Finch let out with his childlike laugh again. 'Which kind best suits you?'

'Kind where I ain't got a roof over my head, don't matter hot or cold. I planted twenty-five-thousand Christmas trees in North Carolina when it never went below ninety degrees and didn't much mind it for the heat.'

Finch whistled softly. 'That's a lot of trees.'

'I wouldn't put 'em in the ground again for twice the money.'

'Been there, done that, huh?'

'Was a bitch on the knees, but I didn't find out how big a one till later.'

Finch pulled a cigar from his shirt pocket. 'What do we learn of ourselves but through our labors, Nat?'

Banyon didn't offer an opinion.

'Any work you won't do?'

Banyon thought he detected a graver tone behind the light one in which Finch posed the question. 'Whatever might be harmful to my health, 'less it pays for the risk.'

Finch stuck the cigar into his mouth, but didn't light it. Banyon got the idea he was angling his way into a subject but Banyon couldn't guess what it might be. 'Sales is where I started out.'

'I tried my hand a little at that. Didn't much care for it.'

'Maybe it was the product.'

'That didn't strike me as entering into it.'

'Give me an example of what you were trying to sell.'

Banyon upshifted again, glancing suspiciously at Finch.

'If you don't mind, Nat.'

'Vacuum cleaners, furniture off a guy's truck, used cars for a while. The last thing was massaging chairs on straight commission to old people down in Florida.'

'Seeing how ninety-nine percent of those folks are on fixed incomes and figuring in what had to be the price of those chairs in relation to say Tylenol or Medicaid-allowed prescription pain killers, I'd be surprised that weren't a tough go.'

'A whole day's talking, which I ain't crazy over to begin with, more times than not netted me zero dollars.'

Finch's laugh was more a delighted giggle this time. 'You've convinced me that sales isn't for you, Nat.' He shoved the cigar back where he'd found it. 'And, to your credit, that you're honest about your shortcomings.'

Banyon slowed down the Pontiac as they entered the outskirts of a small, mountain-enclosed town divided by a sluggish river riding low in its bed amid a summer drought. 'I like knowing exactly what a job is and that if I do it right, I'll get paid regardless.'

Finch nodded as if thinking over that philosophy, but when he spoke next he brought up an entirely different subject. 'Cops around here will pull an out-of-state car over for doing as little as five miles per hour over the limit.'

Banyon, easing off the gas, nervously glanced left, right, and in the rearview mirror, but, to his relief, saw no sign of the law. Then he looked at Finch, who, acting as if he'd never mentioned the cops, directed him to take a right onto a metal bridge from which a barefoot fat woman in a halter top and bermudas fished. 'Like to treat you to a Deepwater breakfast, Nat.' He flapped his right hand several times toward the town center, indicating his destination was well beyond it. 'See if maybe two graduates of the school of hard knocks can't come together on some sort of a professional arrangement.'

Though having as little success tuning into Finch's internal rhythms as he was to those of the area in general, Banyon accepted the invitation.

Waving him into the parking lot of an L-shaped motel fronting six cottages and a small lake on a godforsaken stretch of highway eight miles from town, Finch announced, 'This is her,' as if not sure Banyon could read the sign out front. Needles from a canopy of white pine branches overhead covered the badly paint-chipped building's flat roof and the static, green water of a half-empty pool near the L's joint. Two cars and an old Indian motorcycle filled three of the cracked-concrete spaces facing the rooms. 'This is Herman Finch's Deepwater.'

An itch to light out hit Banyon, who'd stayed in a few worse places, but he was stopped from scratching it by another feeling that had to do with him being more interested in getting far away from where he'd been the day before than with where exactly he got to.

Finch had him halt the Pontiac before the office, the only part of the mustard-yellow structure with a rear attachment and a second floor, in which Finch, he told Banyon, lived with his wife. 'She's over there this time day.' Finch waved right of them at a dense patch of brushy woods, through which a dirt path led fifty or so feet to what looked to be a grounded submarine flashing a neon sign at the desolate highway. 'After I go in and call about having the Caddy and that fox taken care of, we'll go get a bite and you two can meet.'

Five minutes later he returned outside and led Banyon over to the Deepwater Restaurant/Gift Shop, a converted house trailer atop a concrete foundation in an unpaved parking lot. Three Mexican or Latino men filled the only occupied booth out of the six in the dining area. An old, sun-wrinkled couple drinking coffee had the counter to themselves. The sole waitress was a fading prom queen type around Finch's age, whom Banyon at first took for Finch's wife, but Finch introduced her simply as Pam, then ordered an omelet from her and asked Banyon what he wanted. Banyon ordered the same thing, plus toast and, since the meal was on Finch and only Banyon's second in 24 hours, a double stack of pancakes and Canadian bacon. 'By God,' said Finch. He threw a volley of shadow punches at Banyon, who, from the older man's technique, got the idea Finch considered himself somewhat of a pugilist.

'And he 'asn't a spare ounce on him,' Pam remarked.

Finch made a big show of eyeing Banyon's lean muscular build, prominent beneath his T-shirt and jeans, as if Banyon was hanging from a butcher's hook. 'Plenty of fuel must be part your routine for staying so fit, eh, Nat?'

Banyon, his face reddening slightly, readjusted himself without replying on the counter stool next to the one Finch was on.

Pam said, 'Have what you want to, honey. You can afford it.'

'You mean I can,' Finch corrected her.

'I'm saying he don't carry it on him, like a few others I know.'

'I never thought twice about it,' Banyon told her.

'A big appetite won't kill you, Nat' – Finch palm-banged his own midsection, which made a more solid thud than Banyon would have guessed from looking at him – ' 'less it's for the wrong things."

'From the horse's mouth,' Pam said tartly. Finch looked at her in a way Banyon couldn't fathom. Pam poured them coffee. 'Thanks,' said Banyon.

Pam didn't answer. A moment later she went into the kitchen, just as, in a petition left of the counter, a door on which a hand-printed sign declared Gift Shop opened. A woman who briefly took Banyon's breath away came out. 'Nat, my wife, Iris,' Finch said.

Banyon drank from his coffee to mask his surprise at Finch's good fortune, then said, 'Hi.'

'Hey,' Iris told him.

She was maybe five years older than Banyon and at once less and even more of a knockout than he'd at first taken her for. Her jet-black hair was gathered in a disheveled bun at the nape of her neck. She had thick, fleshy lips; broad, full hips; large, firm-looking breasts. Not fat, she wasn't a model type either. Something about her – Banyon couldn't put a word to it – got to him even more than stone cold beauty could. She wouldn't smell sweet, he guessed, but ripe, like plump, red, juicy strawberries. 'Nat saved me from a ten-mile hike off Highmore Mountain,' said Finch, 'after a rabid fox ran me off the road.'

'That was nice of him.'

'Yeah.'

'How's the car?'

Finch tapped Banyon's shoulder. 'She wants to know how's the car. Not if I'm all right, but how's the car.' He laughed while putting an arm around his wife's waist. 'If you ever get lucky enough to find a lady like this, Nat, marry her. Sew her up fast and don't think twice about it.'

'I surely will,' said Banyon, looking directly at Iris. She hesitated a second before lowering her eyes. Banyon pictured her naked, stretching her arms and yawning after a long sleep. She affected him that way, right from the get-go. A few times before a woman might have, but not that he could recall. Concentrating on not staring at her, he hardly listened as Finch told her about the accident. She didn't sit down, nor smile once at Finch. After less than a minute she slipped out of Finch's grasp. Banyon took her escape as an indication that neither Finch nor living at the Deepwater fulfilled her. When their food came, she returned to the gift shop. 'Nice to meet you,' Banyon said to her back, but she didn't answer him or even show that she'd heard him.

'Pretty good eats, huh, Nat?'

'Great,' answered Banyon, meaning it, though wondering why Finch made such a big deal of pointing it out to him. Then Finch started in on how hard it was to find reliable help in the area and on how for close to a year he'd been pissing up a rope in his attempts to hire someone to paint and spruce up the Deepwater at a fair wage, and, after a little more hemming and hawing, he offered Banyon the position, in exchange for free accommodations and five dollars and fifty cents an hour.

'I'll put it next to a few other irons I got in the fire,' replied Banyon, who had no irons in any fire and who ten minutes earlier, before he'd glimpsed Iris Finch, wouldn't have thought twice about tying himself to another job or locale just yet. 'Course painting's a god-awful bore and even more so at that price.'

'Don't forget you'd be sleeping on me and I'll even throw in free breakfasts at the diner.' Finch leaned forward, lowering his voice conspiratorially. 'It'd all be off the books, too.' He glanced around the room, waiting for the three men, who'd just settled up their bill, to leave. 'Tell me if I'm wrong, Nat, in guessing two, three days of my wages'd more than double your entire assets, not counting the LeMans'— he waved to indicate the LeMans obviously had no value in such a calculation, making Banyon wonder what Finch had surmised about the car — 'at present?'

He wasn't wrong, but Banyon didn't tell Finch that. They dropped the subject to finish eating. Banyon noted how well kept and clean the inside of the restaurant was relative to the outside. White, red, and yellow flowers, some with long stems and sweet smells, sprouted from boxes on sills beneath the east-side windows; tongue-shaped shafts of sun entered through the half-blindered rectangles of glass. Based on no evidence at all, Banyon credited Iris Finch for the diner's neatness and homey feel. Less from hunger than from on odd desire to see how Finch would react to it, he ate two pieces of peach pie for dessert.

'By God,' Finch said again, even more emphatically than he had before, letting go another round of air punches.

His wife reentered the room. Now out of its bun, her hair

fell halfway to her waist. Banyon suspected his presence was
what had prompted her to let it drop. She told Finch the
Deepwater's front desk bell, which evidently was rigged to
ring in the gift shop when it did in the motel, had gone off and
she was heading over there to see why. Finch affectionately
patted her behind and told her he'd offered Banyon a job. 'I
hope you decide to take it,' Iris Finch said politely.

Banyon gave her his best smile, worrying, based upon her
almost embarrassed reaction to it, that a piece of peach had
stuck to his teeth. She had on a white cotton skirt and a loose-
fitting pullover shirt. Her firm, rolling walk, thought Banyon,
watching it as she strolled to the restaurant door, was calcu-
lated to affect him. 'I'm going to,' he blurted out.

Not glancing back, Iris said, 'You've got your work cut out
for you.'

'Atta boy, Nat,' exclaimed Finch.

Since the early morning's enigmatic shower the sun had shone
unabated and Banyon, starting that afternoon on the room
nearest the road and proceeding wall to wall, worked with his
shirt off, in sunglasses and a backward-facing baseball cap.
Finch had instructed him to prep the entire concrete-block
structure – first with a scraper to remove the loose paint, then
with an iron brush on the more stubborn spots, and finally
with sandpaper to smooth everything out – before priming it,
and to avoid any occupied rooms, though as far as Banyon
could tell the motel only had two guests, both in rooms near
the register's office.

A giant Rottweiler, which Banyon estimated weighed over
a hundred pounds, showed up snarling beneath his stepladder
about an hour into the project and around the same time
Finch left on the motorcycle that had been in the lot. Banyon
scurried up to the ladder's top rung, where the animal could

have still easily reached him had it been so inclined, but it seemed satisfied to have put the fear of God in him, for it soon quit growling, ambled fifteen feet to the shade of a rhododendron bush, lay down, and placidly eyed the work. The dog's coming and Finch's going seemed somehow connected to Banyon, though he couldn't see why they would be.

Eventually he climbed down from the ladder and, holding out one hand, warily approached the Rottweiler. The dog rubbed its head in his palm. Banyon absently scratched behind its ears for several seconds. When he stopped the dog declined its head, picked a stick up in its mouth, and gazed up at Banyon. Banyon took the stick from the dog and flung it out into the parking lot. The Rottweiler looked at the stick, then back at Banyon. 'I don't know what you want,' said Banyon. He sat down and listened to some thrushes and juncos singing in the crabapple trees between him and the highway. He saw Iris Finch enter the far end of the parking lot from the restaurant trail and walk over to the office. She glanced at him but didn't say anything, and Banyon wondered if she'd tell Finch when he got back how he'd been sitting down on the job and he decided she wouldn't.

He got back on the ladder. His elbow hurt already and he'd only scraped half a wall. He didn't plan to leave Finch in the lurch, but neither did he plan to fuck up his arm for five-fifty an hour and no workmen's compensation, so he decided to quit planning period and just wait and see how things went. Iris Finch came out of a door near the office hauling a cart with a mop and some towels on it. She stopped before one of the rooms, opened it with a key, and went inside, pulling the cart behind her. Banyon couldn't believe Finch would have her doing maid service, but maybe that's what people in family-owned businesses did. Still, it didn't seem right, and Banyon's opinion of Finch lowered a little. In a few minutes, she came out of the room and went into the next one, which was one closer to Banyon.

She approached him slowly that way, one room at a time, for close to an hour. Banyon never caught her looking up at him, but guessed, just from how she moved, she had him in mind, as much as he did her. He figured they were the same in a way that counted more than any other ways and that she could see it as clearly as him. When she exited the room two down from the one he was working on, he called out, 'Iris.' Not a question, just a statement.

She looked up at him, flicking a strand of hair out of her face.

'Beautiful flower,' he said.

She made no response.

'I sure am parched,' said Banyon.

'He didn't tell you were the spigot was?'

'You mean your husband?'

'Who else would I mean?'

'I wasn't sure because I thought his name was Herman.'

'Did he tell you or not?'

'He did, and it's good cold water coming out of it' – Banyon smiled widely at her – 'but I thought maybe I could have something a little tarter.'

'Like what?'

'Have you got any lemonade down at your place?'

Instead of answering, she nodded toward an opening between two rooms halfway between her and the office. Tiny beads of perspiration rolled down her neck and into her open collar. Her legs, noticed Banyon, were muscular and smooth beneath her knee-length skirt. 'There's a soda ma-chine down there. I think there's lemonade in it. I don't know, though, because I don't drink it.'

Banyon slowly climbed down from the ladder. 'Think I'll

have me one.' He reached into his pocket and pulled out some change. 'How much are they?'

'Seventy-five cents.'

Banyon walked toward her, looking down while counting his change. A couple feet from her cart, he stopped. 'I got enough for two drinks, Iris,' he said. 'Can I treat you to a Coke or something?'

She looked directly at him. Her eyes were dark blue and as unreadable as the terrain she lived in. Banyon still hadn't seen her smile, and he decided that if nothing else, he'd see her do it before he left the Deepwater. 'Okay,' she said, 'I'll have one.'

'Diet?'

'No. A regular Coke, with sugar and all.'

'If I were married to you, Iris, I wouldn't let you clean out rooms,' said Banyon, walking past her before she could answer, if she had meant to.

She popped open the Coke he handed her a minute later and leaned back against the wall, drinking it. Honeysuckle vines climbing a stone wall behind the motel and the towering pines above it sweetened the air with their blossoms. A loaded lumber truck went by on the highway, its rear end swaying precariously. Banyon glanced at the Rottweiler, sleeping or resting with its eyes closed. Following his gaze, Iris said, 'It'd tear somebody's heart out if he told it to.'

'Has he ever?'

'Doesn't matter whether he has or hasn't. He would.'

Banyon reached out and loosely placed two fingers on her wrist. She didn't move or suggest he ought to take his hand away. Banyon could feel her pulse pounding in rhythm with his own. 'I can't quite figure out what it is you're doing to me, Iris,' he whispered, 'but you're doing it good and I'm giving it right back to you.'

'I'm just standing here.'

'You're a knockout, you know?'

'I'm pretty good looking,' she answered matter-of-factly, 'for around here.'

'No, no. Anywhere – even out in Hollywood – you're a knockout, I know. I been around some.'

'You been around?'

'Ever since I can remember, I been going round and round.' He lifted her wrist lightly above her head and spun her in a slow circle. She still didn't smile. He could hear her breathing strongly through her nose.

'You're more than a pretty good looking guy yourself, Nat. I mean what you got, you got all over in spades.'

'I figure it's what God gave me to make up for some things a lot of ugly people have got I don't.'

Her lips moved slightly upward at the corners as if they might decide to keep going, but they didn't. 'He went into town to pick up the Cadillac,' she said.

'When will he be back?'

'Soon.'

'How soon?'

'Too soon.'

'God, it's hot.'

'Ain't it, though.'

'I bet it'd be cool in one them rooms with the air conditioner on.'

Banyon leaned forward and tried to kiss her. His lips touched hers long enough for him to taste on them the Coke she'd been drinking, then she suddenly ducked away from him. 'I'm not anything like you guess I am, Nat. You've got the entire wrong idea about me, I think.'

She turned and walked back to her cart. Banyon stood looking after her for a few seconds, then returned to his ladder.

★   ★   ★

He tried using shorter strokes with less pressure and discovered they were nearly as effective, without being as painful to his arm, as the longer, harder ones he'd abandoned them for. Then he began switching his scraping hand every five to ten minutes and that was even better. He couldn't believe how small changes could make such a huge difference. He started envisioning himself as the master of his work, whereas earlier it had been just the opposite.

In the late afternoon Finch came back in the Cadillac, followed by a man on Finch's Indian and two others in a pickup truck. The Rottweiler, which had barely moved since lying down earlier, got up and trotted over to Finch. Finch squatted down and greeted the dog. They almost looked to Banyon to be conversing. The motorcycle rider got in the pickup and it left.

On his way into the office, Finch casually waved at Banyon with the pistol he'd shot the fox with. In a few minutes he came out again and went into the utility shed, which housed the pool's broken filter. Banyon heard him hammering away in there. Around four-thirty Iris Finch walked from the motel over to the restaurant. Banyon remembered how soft and wet her lips had been and the firm pounding of her heart against his fingers. Far from experiencing guilt over his desire for her, he felt as entitled to it as he did to the air he breathed. He tossed his tools into a bucket half an hour later and started carrying the bucket and stepladder to the cottage where he'd found them. Finch popped out of the utility shed and said, 'I think we'll paint her a blue shade, Nat.'

'A dark one'd be best you don't want the yellow to show through.'

Finch, smiling, seemed amused by the suggestion. 'You play poker, young man?'

'Enough to have learned I'm better off not to.'

'This it'd only be a dollar ante and a fifty-dollar-per limit pot.'

'What would?'

'There's a game at my place, around eight.' Finch put his hand up. 'But you oughtn't to go against your good sense.'

'I go against it all the time. It and me's always at it about something.'

Finch giggled, sounding almost girlish. He nodded toward the nearly three walls and doors Banyon had finished prepping. 'That's a good piece of work, Nat.'

'I know it is.'

'Feels good when you step back and look at it, though, don't it?'

'Like pushing away from the table after a good feed.'

'I could tell talking to you earlier you'd feel that way about it.'

'How could you?'

'I don't know how. It was just a feeling I had.'

'You'll get what you paid for from me, Mr. Finch. Pay me enough and I'll make your motel look like the Holiday Inn.'

'The officer who cut that fox's head off to send it to the state for testing told me it looked almost certain to him to be real bad diseased, Nat' – Finch wiped the grease from his hands onto his pants legs – 'and that my killing it was a favor to every unsuspecting creature might of come near it.'

A beat-up old station wagon noisily entered the lot and stopped before the office. Finch made a wavering line in the air with one hand. 'Now's about the hour this time a year they always start rolling in.' He began ambling toward the car. 'Come nightfall, we'll be close to full up with 'em, Nat. Just you wait and see.'

Two

A couple of kids staying at the motel came down, followed by the Rottweiler, and threw sticks in the lake. The Rottweiler swam out from shore fully submerged, rose beneath the sticks, snatched them in its huge jaws, swam back underwater, emerged, and dropped them at the kids' feet. Banyon, sitting on the needle-covered floor behind his cottage, had never seen anything like it. The dog acted as if it didn't have this heart-tearing-out side to it, as if it wasn't the canine Dr. Jekyll and Mr. Hyde that Iris had described.

Banyon suspected the Rottweiler was a dog genius, capable not only of communicating with certain people, but of fathoming their intentions while masking its own. Finch was a lucky man, thought Banyon. He had the obedience of this smart superpowerful dog. And he had the obedience of Iris. On the other hand he wasn't lucky at all, because Iris didn't love him, had nothing in her heart for him. Of that much Banyon was certain. How the dog felt about Iris relative to Finch, he didn't know.

The huge ball of descending sun tinged the conifer trees behind the lake orange. Horse- and dragonflies buzzed. Wood ducks floated on the water. Giant bullfrogs croaked. Sunfish and rock bass jumped sporadically. Squirrels chattered in the surrounding trees. A swampy smell mingled with the pines' scent. Banyon told himself not to play poker at Finch's place, not to go anywhere near where Iris and Finch would be together. In his mind's eye he saw Iris asking for straight-up Coke, not Diet, with sugar and all, and the clear beads of perspiration descending her milky, smooth skin.

Three or four helicopters went over, flying as if their occupants were searching for something in the deep woods to the west. Banyon fretted for a moment over the Pontiac, sitting out front where anyone passing by could see it, but given how few people traveled the road and the plates that were now on the car, he convinced himself he was worrying unnecessarily.

The Rottweiler got out of the water and shook itself, scattering the kids. Banyon stood and went into the cottage, which until then Finch had been using, along with the other five, for storage. Renters hadn't much liked them, according to Finch, because of the mosquitoes and din from the lake and their distance from the parking lot. Banyon had no complaints, though. The double mattress on his bed was good and hard and the toilet, shower, coffeepot, and cook plate worked. He got down on the floor and did a hundred push-ups, then a hundred sit-ups. Afterward he unpacked his clothes from his gym bag, putting them in a three-legged chest of drawers next to the bed. Around 7:45 he took a shower.

Banyon preferred not to look too closely at his life behind him, had taught himself not to. He feared that sort of backward examination might make him a pessimist about the future. Not that, as far as he recalled, he'd done anything terribly bad. He was sure he'd always been trying to make life a little better for himself at the point he was at. What he'd thought was a good move sometimes turned out to be. Other times he'd not been so fortunate. When things went awry he believed it was because he had followed the wrong instinct or ignored the right one. He viewed his remembered mistakes as honest miscalculations; the ones he suspected he had forgotten about he took no responsibility for at all.

The persistent tapping of a woodpecker greeted him as he left the cottage for Finch's in a clean set of clothes. He reminded himself to retrieve from the LeMans's glove box later his transistor radio so that he could use it to block out nature's night noises. In the dying light, he cast a long shadow through the trees.

He recognized in Finch's approach to the game the same passion he himself had for following hunches and intuitions, never mind the odds. Finch took a good-sized pot with a masterful big-balled bluff, then a few hands later lost most of what he'd won on a stinker. 'You didn't think you'd get away with that twice, did you?' asked the motorcycle rider from that afternoon. He was maybe ten years younger than Finch, looked part-Indian or black, had a long scar on his right cheek, thick horn-rimmed glasses on, and had been complaining all night that fate or some power beyond his control had it in for him. The pot he'd taken from Finch was his first.

'I wasn't thinking about if I'd get away with it, Earl. I felt like playing, not folding, so I did, and now that you've finally won your one hand of the evening you can go back to losing until you've lost every penny you came with like you always do and have to go home with only your dick in your pants.'

'Fuck you too,' said Earl.

'Do you enjoy the experience of just being here and participating in a game with real card players, Earl?'

'What the fuck is that supposed to mean?' asked Earl.

Finch gulped down some whiskey. Banyon guessed himself to be the only one of them not at least a little drunk. Iris had brought them drinks and snacks early on and after that had not returned to the living room where they were playing. Her body had brushed against the back of Banyon on her way by him, and Banyon had sensed she'd done it on purpose and had been sending him a message of some kind, but he hadn't been able to figure out what the message was. Finch said to Earl, 'I'm wondering if your being here is the best thing for you, is all.'

'The best thing for me? I'm here playing fucking cards – so I don't know what the fuck you're asking me, is it the best thing for me or what it has to do with anything.' Earl looked around at the other four men at the table to see if he'd gotten a laugh out of them, but nobody acted amused.

'You'd be doing yourself a favor if you quit coming by, Earl.' This from Walnut, a muscular bald man with a serious demeanor, who Banyon had never seen take his cards off the table. He just bent forward, lifted each one up by its corner, and peeked at it. 'You're no good at this, we can all see it, and it's hurting you financially and probably in terms of your self-respect too. I think, Earl, you ought to stay home and watch TV or read a book when we play.'

Earl made a disgusted snort.

Finch said, 'Everybody who thinks Earl ought to leave right now, raise your hand.'

Everyone but Earl and Banyon solemnly raised their hands.

'You all want me to leave for real?' Earl acted incredulous. Then he seemed actually scared. 'I can't fucking believe this!'

'Don't forget your winnings,' said Walnut.

The fifth player, name of Petersen, said, 'How's it feel to be leaving someplace with a little of your own money in your pocket for the first time in your life, Earl?'

Earl suddenly looked as if he might cry. 'You guys have made a huge fucking mistake about this,' he said.

'Have a good night, Earl,' said Finch.

Earl stood up and brushed the money sitting before him into one hand, then shoved it into his pocket. He glanced around at the other men once more to make sure they weren't putting him on, then hurriedly left the room. Banyon wondered how long the four of them had been friends.

'Whose deal?' asked Finch.

'Mine,' answered Petersen. He picked up the cards.

Banyon said, 'I gotta take a leak,' and got up from the table.

'Through the kitchen, Nat,' Finch told him.

He turned right out of the room, making the other men disappear. The blank corridor walls suggested to him erased blackboards, only off-white instead of black. He had no curiosity about Iris and Finch's life together, he realized. All he needed or cared to know about it he'd learned when he'd first seen them together. The kitchen smelled of baking brownies or a cake. The heat from the oven flushed his face when he passed it. A magnetized note pad containing a grocery list was stuck to the refrigerator door next to a calendar, with each day up until that one neatly checked off in red Magic Marker. BLESS THIS HOUSE said a plaque above the entrance to the next hallway. Soft music floated from behind a closed door at the corridor's end.

Banyon turned right into the bathroom. A mesh-covered jar of cloves sat on a sill beneath an open screened window in the outside wall. Cricket chirps entered on a warm breeze. Banyon peed, flushed the toilet, then viewed his handsome, chiseled face in the glass of the shower door. He peered into the enclosed stall and bath. A small plastic duck sat in the tub bottom. He opened the cabinet above the sink, saw all the usual things. He picked up a small perfume bottle, squirted it at his wrist, smelled Iris's scent from earlier that evening on his hand.

25

In the hallway a moment later, he stood and listened to the card players in one direction, the soft music in the other, his heart's frenetic pounding between them. He turned and stared at the closed door, picturing Iris on a bed inside, her hair lying loosely about her head on the pillow. He tiptoed down to the door; a dull light shone from beneath it. Banyon put his ear to the wood paneling. No lyrics accompanied the music. He seized the knob gently, then quickly let it go, wondering, what if he had been wrong? Had misread everything? He recalled how he'd been unable that morning to feel the area's internal rhythm. How, just before he'd happened upon Herman Finch, he'd felt as if he'd entered a karmic vacuum. He pictured the Rottweiler, tensed behind the door, inches from him, ready to spring.

He did an about-face and started tiptoeing back down the corridor. Suddenly the door could be heard softly opening. Banyon abruptly pivoted toward the sound and saw Iris, in a long cotton nightie, standing in the crack of the partially opened doorway before him. 'They threw that guy Earl out of the game,' he told her.

Her hair was in a bun as it had been at the diner when he first saw her. She touched it lightly with one finger.

Banyon nodded toward the bathroom. 'It didn't seem like it was about poker to me, so I went to the can. I could see if they'd cleaned him out, but he'd just won his first pot, taken a big chunk of your husband's money.'

'He's got plenty.'

'Then he oughtn't to have you working so hard, Iris. That's not right.'

'He doesn't like people to know he's got plenty.'

'People, you mean like the law, or the IRS, or who are you talking about?'

'Your ear was right up next to my door a second ago, wasn't it?'

'I couldn't have gotten it any snugger.'

Iris dropped her hand from the wall and centered herself on her strong legs in the doorway. 'You any good at cards?'

'I either win or lose big. When my heart says go for broke, I do.'

'What about what your brain says?'

'Situation like what I just told you it doesn't get a vote.'

She almost smiled. Banyon took a step toward her. Then another one. He could see her pulse fluttering in her neck, hear her breathing hard. 'Where's that big old Rottweiler?'

'Outside.' She flicked her chin to the right. 'He doesn't let it come in.'

Banyon took one more step, reached out, put a hand behind her neck, the other on her rump, and yanked her toward him. She came hard, then she came easy. He felt her bottom tense beneath his fingers. He put his mouth on hers. It opened wide and her tongue went into him. Banyon put both hands on her butt, half picked her up, and put her up against the corridor to the left of the door. She ground her hips into him and Banyon, grinding back, lifted the thin fabric of her nightie, beneath which the underpants over her genitals were drenched. He could feel the heat of her. She panted in his ear, 'I can't kid around. I'm past just kidding around with some smart guy . . .'

'I'm not kidding around,' whispered Banyon. He slipped a hand down the back of her briefs and glanced down the hallway toward the kitchen. 'Does this feel like I'm kidding around?'

'I don't know what it feels like, except it feels good, Nat. It feels god-awful good.'

He kissed her again. 'I can't even stand it.'

Suddenly she pushed him away.

'What?'

'Get away from me before you kill me.'

A creak sounded from the hallway beyond the kitchen, then Walnut's voice clearly said, 'Two Budweisers, right?'

'Go!' she whispered.

Then she was inside the room behind the closed door, as if she'd never been with him at all. Banyon rapidly tiptoed down the hallway, hoping Walnut wouldn't notice he was breathing hard or smell her on him. He'd been back at the game scarcely twenty minutes when the man named Petersen abruptly stood up, announced he'd had enough for one night, and left almost as quickly as Earl had.

Three

An Isuzu Trooper carrying two upside-down bicycles on its roof circled the lot and stopped next to the wall Banyon was scraping. Banyon approached it. Its front passenger window glided down. Rock music came from inside. Banyon bent toward it. Electronically cooled air tantalizingly touched his heat-flushed face. A girl his age, or maybe even a little younger, inquired if there were other motels in the area. Banyon understood her to mean better ones. He told her a Ramada Inn was in town and more places too, probably, he wasn't sure. The guy driving asked if he knew where some bike trail was. Banyon said he didn't. The girl said, 'Gosh, it's beautiful around here and so, you know, in the middle of nowhere.'

Her boyfriend, or whoever, said, 'Everyplace is someplace, which means no place can be nowhere or in the middle of it.'

'Oh, you know what I mean,' said the girl. It was as if they were drunk on describing their location and had forgotten Banyon was even a part of it. In the severe midday heat the birds had stopped singing much. The shrubbery's wilted leaves gave the impression of begging for rain. Banyon wished for it too, so he could quit early. In the field across the road, cicadas buzzed. 'God's country then, okay?'

'Remote would be a more accurate description,' the guy told her.

Banyon got tired of hearing it. He left while they were still arguing and walked to the portico housing the soda machine. Iris and her cart had just entered a room three down from him. She hadn't come near Banyon all day. He imagined her wrestling with her urge for him, while he battled against his desire for her. The Isuzu roared onto the highway. Banyon bought a lemonade. He heard the pool filter start, sputter, stall, then Finch, tinkering with it, curse. Banyon sat on the portico's relatively cool concrete floor. He slowly drank his lemonade. Finch emerged from the utility shed. 'Goddamn contraption'll eat me up, won't it, Nat?' he hollered over to him.

Recognizing another one of Finch's statements disguised as a question, Banyon only waved.

Finch strode to the portico and bought a Coke. 'Mechanical things, Nat, make me feel numb-nutted.' He squatted next to Banyon. 'I never been good with 'em, but I swear I'd sooner fill in the pool with cement than pay out my ass to make one run.'

'Give you less a headache if it disappeared sounds like.'

'On the other hand I hate to, because a motel, Nat, seems to me it ought to have a pool.' Finch drank half his Coke in one swallow and placed it between his feet.

'Does it make you any money?'

'I don't know if it does.' Finch shrugged. 'People like to paddle around in it.' He lifted from his shirt pocket into his mouth one of the cigars Banyon had never seen him light. 'Picture a bar without a pool table, which for my dollar makes it less of a bar, Nat, and you'll understand my feeling on it.'

Angling to escape the sun longer, Banyon said, 'I could maybe take a whack at it for you.'

'You got a knack for making 'em go?'

'Takes patience mostly and a good ear.'

Finch put away the cigar and reached for his soda. 'You did all right for yourself last night, young man.'

Banyon glanced warily at him.

'My tallying made you out the evening's big winner.'

'Well, I won't be leaving my day job just yet, Mr. Finch.'

Finch giggled. 'Boys and I enjoyed playing with you anyway.'

Iris came out of the room she'd been working in. Her warm, wet smell returned to Banyon as if she were up against him right then, rubbing it all over him. Finch gave her a hello and she helloed him back. The thought struck Banyon that Finch knew all about the thing between them if only because he could read it plain as day on Banyon's face. Then he told himself that if that were true he, in turn, would be able to read Finch's face, which he absolutely couldn't. Iris vanished through the next doorway in line.

Finch said, 'Guess you were wondering about that whole Earl thing?'

Banyon shrugged to indicate if he was he wasn't the sort to ask about it.

'Earl wore out his welcome. Didn't just happen all the sudden like it might have seemed.'

Banyon drained his lemonade.

'Would have been just as easy to keep taking our own money back from him, but there's things worth more than money and not having to listen to Earl and his always harping on how fate or anything but himself accounted for him being such a loser is one of 'em.'

'I had kinda got it you all were friends.'

'I expect Earl was under the same misperception until we voted him out.' Finch stood up. He nodded toward the enclosed filter's engine. 'Think you can save her?'

'Depends on how far gone she is.'

Finch flipped his empty can in the garbage and started for the utility shed. 'She still whines, bitches, and farts when you try her, Nat, whatever that's worth.'

The engine was surrounded by haphazardly scattered tools. Finch told Banyon he'd leave him to it. Less than half an hour later Banyon determined that what it needed most, besides two cotter pins and a new drive belt, was a thorough cleaning, which, with rags and gasoline, he spent close to two hours giving it. With the new parts, he knew it would run like a top. He felt good for the work he'd done on it, same as he had when he'd finished planting those twenty-five thousand Christmas trees.

The still hot, early evening sun ricocheted off eight or nine cars of recently arrived guests as he carried his paint-scraping tools across the lot, stored them back in the equipment cottage, then walked to the office in which Iris tended the front desk before the open residence door. Banyon said, 'I lack ten bucks' worth of parts from having his pool back in business.'

'That'll make him happy as a clam,' she flatly replied.

'Couple little pins look like miniature bowties and a belt's all that's holding me back.'

'Guess you're some tinkerer.'

'Don't a mechanism exist I can't rev up.'

Iris didn't even remotely smile.

Banyon winked at her. 'He'll have to drive to town for 'em.'

Iris jerked her head behind her. 'Tell him your own self, why don't you.'

Banyon inclined at her, whispering, 'I didn't sleep a wink last night, Iris, from the pain I was in.'

She banged a hand on the bell, bringing Finch out pretty quick from the living quarters. Banyon gave him the poop on the filter, to which Finch, loosing at him another flurry of shadow punches, announced, 'By God!' Mostly to show off for Iris, Banyon shuffled, bobbed, and whistled several quick jabs a fraction of an inch past Finch's right ear, prompting Finch, not even flinching at the barrage, to declare, 'You've had some training, young man.'

Banyon shook his head. 'I was born with that there. Like I was with my flat belly.'

Finch danced friskily, feeling something inside. Banyon wasn't sure what. 'Can you take a hit or just throw bombs?'

'As good as the next man I reckon, though I've never much cared to.'

'Ever gone at it in a ring?'

'Mostly the kind drunks make standing on a sidewalk.'

Iris said, 'Herman fought for money out in Missouri thirty years ago.'

'Only I never made much, even when I won and was supposed to.' Finch fired three hooks in the air space left of him. 'Be interesting to see how we match up sometime, Nat.'

Iris said, 'That's crazy talk or I've never heard it.'

'You worried your husband's too old and fat to, Iris' – Finch feinted at Banyon – 'or Nat's too young and pretty to?'

'I don't care what you do,' said Iris.

Banyon was about to tell Finch he wouldn't get in a ring with a man over twice his age no matter what when an old guy in a Fifties-style fedora came through the front door and asked where the reservation casino was at. Finch told him twelve miles up the road. The old guy said okay, give him a double room with a lake view. Iris said he could only have that from the parking lot. The guy complained about misleading advertising, then took a room anyway. As Banyon left,

Finch told him, 'Tomorrow, lunchtime, Nat, I'll run in get those doohickies you need.

Pam and Banyon were two of three people in the diner. The third was a drunk Indian trying to snatch flying houseflies barehanded. Pam told Banyon the cook had gone home and that meatloaf and perch were his dinner options. Banyon chose meatloaf. Pam went back to the kitchen, warmed some up, then brought it to him. She complained of the heat and said she'd read that bad impulses get acted on most often in real hot weather. Banyon said he couldn't see how the temperature would factor into it. Pam didn't know why it would either. The Indian declared, 'Everything goes up with the mercury.'

Banyon went out and drove the Pontiac up the highway fast, loving how it handled and responded for him, though nonetheless feeling uncomfortable in the car, which reminded him of how he'd come by it. In two more days – three tops – he told himself, he'd sell it or, if he had to, dump it. Iris wouldn't leave his head, even at a hundred miles per hour, and Banyon couldn't figure out how she'd become so tightly lodged in it in the less than two days he'd known her. He ought, he knew, to keep driving, but he understood himself just well enough to know he wouldn't. He sped back to the diner.

'That was quick,' said Pam.

Banyon ordered a peach pie wedge and coffee. 'My carburetor was acting up on me. I wanted to check it out.'

'You got the problem fixed?'

Banyon indicated that he had for now. He asked Pam what sorts of gifts were in the gift shop. 'Locally made crafts and pottery, that sort of thing,' Pam told him.

'Artifacts of the red man,' interjected the Indian.

'Do many people buy them?' Banyon asked Pam.

'You'd be surprised what people spend money on.'

'Some people even pay other people to tell them bullshit,' the Indian announced gravely.

Pam said that in half an hour she was going to go home, strip naked, and sit in a cold bath with a glass of iced whiskey and that her tub could easily accommodate two adult bodies. The Indian glanced hopefully at her, but she said she wasn't talking to him. She left to clean up the kitchen. Banyon placed a nice-sized tip on the counter and slipped out before she came back.

He sat in front of his cottage until around ten, watching the moon hitting and bouncing off the lake, as impressive a sight of its kind as Banyon had ever seen. Birds, animals, and insects lived loud in the water and surrounding woods. He tried sleeping later, but the night was too noisy and hot. He remembered about his transistor radio, still in the LeMans, and went and got it. At the portico afterward he bought his sixth or seventh lemonade of the day. While he was drinking it a hairy little Spanish guy wearing only boxer shorts came and filled a bucket with ice. He and Banyon took a shot at conversing in their respective languages, but they couldn't make it work. The guy left. Banyon tried the radio, but the batteries must have been dead.

He walked over to the empty register's office, then around behind it. A light was on in the room outside of which he and Iris had kissed. He got all revved up again inside. He wondered if her ear had been against the door in the bed-room, listening for him, as his had been against it in the hallway, listening for her. He leaned on a tree twenty or so feet from the window, which a thin yellow curtain covered. He couldn't recollect having been a peeping tom ever before and couldn't fathom why he was being one now. His good sense seemed to have left him at the top of the mountain thirty-six hours ago. A disturbing sensation of being watched suddenly struck him. He pivoted his head gradually and saw two eyes not five feet from him. A low growl emerged from beneath them. Banyon backed slowly away from it. The Rottweiler just sat there, eyeing him. Banyon turned and hurriedly returned to his cottage, not once looking back.

Four

'Show me your hands, Nat.'

Banyon turned from the wall he was wire-brushing. 'What?'

'Your hands.' Finch extended his own hands palms up at Banyon to demonstrate what he meant. The Rottweiler, which had accompanied Finch from the office, watched placidly, loudly mouth-breathing in the sweltering noon air. 'Hold 'em out.'

Banyon placed the brush on the stepladder. Sweat rolling from beneath the blue-checked bandanna around his forehead entered and stung his eyes, slightly blurring his vision. His forearms and shoulders hurt. The irrational thought occurred to him that his hands carried evidence, which would be detectable to Finch, of their having touched Iris. 'Why do you want to see them?'

'Come on, Nat.' Finch flashed a coy grin. 'A fighter ought to be proud to show off his tools.'

Banyon held his hands before him, slowly rotating them. Finch whistled admiringly. 'Those are some hands.'

Banyon shrugged, not sure where Finch was headed. Finch angled his fingers up perpendicular to the ground. 'Put 'em up against mine.'

Banyon placed his palms flat against Finch's palms, proving them to be wider than Finch's and his fingers to be at least a half-inch longer than Finch's fingers, though not as thick. 'That's an extra large set of hands, young man' – Finch dropped his arms to his sides – 'or I'm not standing here looking at them.'

The encounter made Banyon feel self-conscious, as if a doctor had just handled his genitals. He wasn't sure how to respond to it, or if he should at all. He glanced down at his hands to see what Finch might've noticed on them, but only his calluses stuck out. Finch said, 'What else do I have to get for you?'

Banyon just looked at him.

'Besides the drive belt and doohickies?'

'Some WD-40 maybe, case her insides gum up again.'

Finch nodded. He reached out and patted the Rottweiler. 'What about for you personally?'

'For me how?'

'Anything I can pick you up in town?'

Banyon pushed at his drenched headband. 'I could use some batteries for my radio.' He started to reach for his wallet, but Finch waved at him not to.

'What size?'

'Double A.'

'How 'bout some provisions for your cottage down there, chance you don't always want to eat in the restaurant?'

'Probably do better picking those out myself.'

'I want you to be happy, Nat. Are your accommodations all right?'

Banyon realized he couldn't read Finch even a little bit. 'My only complaint is not having a television.'

'I can't help you there. Those cottages aren't cable-ready and you wouldn't get anything but a snowstorm on a set if you had one.' Finch pulled a twenty from his shirt pocket and handed it to Banyon. 'For staples in your little home.'

Banyon thanked him.

'I'll only take it out of your wages, Nat' – Finch headed into the parking lot – 'if those parts don't do the job you think they will.'

Banyon hoped Finch would bring the Rottweiler with him, but he didn't. Right after the Caddy left, the dog disappeared. Banyon guessed it went out back searching for shade to lie down in, though he had the uneasy feeling it was watching him from wherever it was.

Around one Iris walked from the end of the restaurant trail over to the office. Her hair was somewhere between being in a neat bun at the top of her back and free-falling down it. She wore black jeans and a snug yellow jersey. She didn't acknowledge Banyon, who hadn't expected her to. He watched the firm roll of her hips until he couldn't anymore, then he went and got a lemonade. A blubbery pipe smoker in an unbuttoned bathrobe wandered from the second to last room on the L's long side, looking lost or stoned. A second later he went back inside. His rusted Chevy Nova, a Buick Skylark three spaces right of it, and Banyon's LeMans were the only cars in the lot. Heat waves shimmered above the concrete. The cicadas were the loudest life forms about. Iris brought her cart out of the laundry room next to the office and into the first guest room on the aisle. Banyon crushed his empty lemonade can and tossed it in the trash. He let ten minutes pass by his watch, then strolled down the walkway, slipped into the open doorway Iris had entered, and shut the door behind him.

'Hey,' he said, not seeing her.

She came out of the bathroom. 'You're bound you'll get me killed or hurt bad, aren't you?'

39

'I don't think he would,' said Banyon.

'You don't think he would. You don't know anything if you think that.'

'He loves you, that's why.'

'He loves me is why he would.'

'But you don't love him.'

'Mr. Einstein, the motel painter, knows all about me in less than three days.'

'I knew all about you in three seconds and you did about me.'

She tossed the soiled towels she held in her hand into the cart.

'I like your hair that way, Iris.' It was completely out of its bun now. 'You ought never to tie it up again.'

She shook it, both freeing and tangling it further. 'You're following some kind of path in your mind, is that it?'

'Your spell's what put me on it.'

She made a disbelieving sound. 'My spell?'

'It's like that song, Iris — I can't eat right, I can't sleep.'

She harrumphed. 'I've seen how you eat.'

'I can't stop being hungry's what I mean.'

'You don't know what you mean.'

She cut her eyes to the window left of him. Banyon reached out, twisted the blind shut. Then he locked the door. 'I'm all hot and sweaty, Iris. Maybe I ought to jump in the shower.'

She pulled her jersey off over her head and threw it at him. 'There's no time for that.'

Suddenly Banyon was laboring to fill his lungs and the sound of him trying to seemed to dominate the room. With Iris's shirt he wiped his face, not just inhaling but swallowing her odor, then his naked chest, his belly, the back of his neck. He dropped the jersey on the floor. Iris unclasped and let go of her bra. Banyon used every once of his self-restraint not to move, just to stand there and look at her. She unzipped her jeans, pushed them down her legs, kicked her shoes off, stepped out of her jeans and underwear, and walked to him in just her socks. Banyon struggled to undo his pants. Iris yanked them down to his knees. 'Just keep us off those clean sheets I just changed, Nat.'

Banyon picked her up and she put him into her about an inch. Then she eased down on to him all the way, wetly exhaling in his ear, and Banyon gasped, 'Dear God in Heaven, that feels good, Iris!' He turned them around and, avoiding the freshly made bed, backed her up to the near wall. Iris wrapped her legs around his waist, panting, 'Don't hold back any, Nat, for fear of hurting me!'

'I'm not anything like you think I am, Nat.'

'You said something like that the other day.'

'I mean it, that's why.'

'I'm not much for thinking, period.'

'I wouldn't want you to get the idea I'm what I might seem to you.'

'I get feelings, is all, that I follow or don't.'

'What one have you got now?'

'I don't know how to put it into words – like this here, what we got, is a piece of work done perfect after it's been fucked up about a thousand times.'

'A piece of work?'

'A beautiful one, like stand back and marvel at it knowing no matter how long you live you'll never make, find, or luck onto a better one.'

'Just please don't shine me on, Nat. I've had enough shining on for a lifetime.'

'If I am let a lightning bolt strike me dead this second.'

'For me it feels like . . .'

'What?'

'I better keep it myself so you won't get cocky about how you've got to me.'

'Want me to guess?'

'You can guess if you want to, but that's all it'll be.'

'Like you were in a deep sleep and didn't even know it until you suddenly got this woke up.' Banyon closed his eyes and groped at the air in front of him like a blind man. 'The reason I know is I seen you sleep-walking before.'

She smiled, a sight as beautiful as the rest of her to Banyon, who said, 'That's the first I've seen of that.'

'Of what?'

Banyon showed her what he meant on his own face.

She flashed another one, back at him. 'It's the first I've felt like it in a while.'

'Tell me about it if you want to.'

Instead of telling him about it, she said, 'You won't get your fill of me then just disappear, will you, Nat?'

'I'm not going nowhere till this motel's painted.'

'Then what?'

'That won't be for a while.'

'The time'll come, though.'

'We can talk about it now, if you want to.'

'As long as I know it's in your mind, is all.'

'It's in there.'

'We'll talk about it later, then.' Rolling Banyon onto his back on the rug-covered floor, she said, 'Right now do to me again what we're both better at than talking 'fore you have to hurry up and leave in about ten minutes.'

Five

By noon the next day he had the filter running. Finch, grinning ear to ear, stood next to the smoothly purring engine. 'That's some sweet music, Nat.'

Banyon felt pretty good about it too, both for fixing it and for pleasing Finch in doing so. 'What say we put this swimming facility into triple-A-rated shape, young man?'

Banyon nodded, thinking that sounded preferable to scraping paint. With a long net Finch handed him, he fished from the turbid water several branches, two dead mice, six or seven frogs, and a good-size box turtle, which, with the frogs, he released into the pond. Later he spent close to two hours cleaning the deck, while Finch vacuumed the pool and then put several quarts of chlorine into it and a running garden hose to slowly fill it up. Around five they lugged a dozen or so pieces of patio furniture from one of the storage cottages to the deck. Nodding in satisfaction at the rising, still green water, Finch said, 'By God.'

'Uh huh,' responded Banyon, knowing exactly what he meant.

Finch got from his refrigerator a Budweiser six-pack, which the two of them drank in lounge chairs around an umbrella-topped metal table. 'She'll be blue as the ocean couple days, Nat, with little kids splashing in her.'

'Weren't that much amiss with her really, Mr. Finch.'

'You call me Herman, Nat.'

Banyon nodded. 'Just a couple little things, Herman.'

'I couldn't see what they were, though,' – Finch tapped his Budweiser can against Banyon's – 'and you could.'

A cloudbank had taken away the sun's direct sting, though hadn't lessened the heat. Iris came out to the pool fence and asked Finch if he was going to eat dinner. Finch told her not straightaway and to join them for drinks, but she went back inside. Though dying to catch her eye, Banyon didn't dare try to. Rather than easing his want of her as he'd hoped it might, his having sex with her had only heightened it. His over-whelming urge to have her, and knowing he could never fully satisfy it in their present states, frustrated him and, for reasons beyond his immediate grasp, frightened him some too. 'You ever been in love, Nat?'

Wondering if he might be in it with Finch's wife, Banyon replied, 'I never been a hundred percent sure I was or not.'

'Did any of 'em make your heart swell as much as they did your balls?'

'That's part of what I ain't sure about.'

Finch looked at him strangely. 'You want to drink more, Nat, or have you had enough?'

'I could drink some more, Herman, and look at this pool for a while.'

'Me too.'

Finch got up, went to his residence, and shortly returned with another six-pack, a quart of Old Grand-Dad, two tumblers, and a tape deck playing Tanya Tucker love songs. Listening to the music, they drank boilermakers and pridefully stared at the pool as if, instead of having just repaired and cleaned it, they'd built it that day. Five or six travelers checked in for the night. Three cars left after entering and circling the lot. The sky further darkened. A light rain started to fall. Finch backed out from under the umbrella and, saying something about 'God's long-delayed mercy,' turned his face upward. Then Banyon did, opening his mouth to the warm drops, trying to imagine the distance beyond their source, a void he equated with eternity.

'What are your plans regarding that Pontiac, Nat?'

Banyon abruptly leveled his gaze to see that the Rottweiler now sat to Finch's right as if it had taken shape there while Banyon was studying on the hereafter. 'If you don't mind me saying so, young man, you're asking for trouble leaving it out in the lot that way much longer.'

Banyon stared flatly at Finch and his dog.

'Don't tell me you hadn't considered the problem?'

'What problem?'

'Maybe the reason you didn't know it's a '79, not a '75 or '76, and why it's got plates from one state and dealer decals from another and somebody else's initials engraved on the glove box is because you just bought it?'

Banyon didn't say if he had. Finch reached down and scratched behind the Rottweiler's ears. Thunder, unaccompanied by lightning, rumbled placidly. 'I no more believe that every person who's broke the law is a criminal, Nat, than that human situations are carbon copies of one another, which I know for a fact they aren't. The more important question is, what's in here?' He placed the tumbler against his heart. 'What's in yours, Nat?'

Increasingly edgy over the conversation's direction, Banyon swiped at the water on his temple. The tape deck clicked off, making audible to them the peepers and cicadas across the road and two sweatsuit-clad women at the portico vending machines discussing whether the salt in potato chips or the sugar in Twinkies was worse for them. Finch put on a Waylon

Jennings cassette, once more muting the sounds beyond their immediate surroundings. Banyon said, 'I was hoping to find the right sort of buyer for it.'

'Going about that in an area unfamiliar to you strikes me as a tad reckless.'

Banyon didn't counter the opinion.

'What were you looking to get for her?'

'She's worth forty-five hundred easy. But I'd take some less.'

'I know a fella – mind you, I've got no connection with the business he's in and am telling you only because my hunch is you don't much either – 'd give you half a grand for it.'

'That wouldn't buy me even a four-wheeled shitbox to replace it with.'

'I know it wouldn't, Nat, but, with the risk he'd be taking, that's what he'll give you.'

'I'll put it next some things.'

'Know why I'm asking, Nat?'

Banyon shrugged.

Finch touched his tumbler to his chest again. 'If I thought you was of a certain type, Nat – a black heart – I'd of never even gotten in your hot rod, 'd likely have called the cops with your tags, and I damn straight would not have taken you into my employ.' He splashed more whiskey from the near-empty bottle into their glasses; ran a hand back through his snow-white hair; farted distinctly. 'Take cover,' he said.

Banyon chuckled confusedly, as befuddled by Finch as he was by his feelings for Iris. Finch let another one go, put a hand to his eyes, announced, 'They're all around us, son.'

While knowing he was best off not liking Finch, Banyon couldn't help doing so, though he didn't exactly trust him; but then, no one, including himself, who so often acted against his own best interests and intentions, did he exactly trust. The

Rottweiler began a low-volume growl at Banyon's half-laughter, prompting Finch, smoothing its rising back hairs, to remark, 'Dog and me don't always agree on an individual's merit, Nat. Course too, I think it sometimes just gets jealous.'

'It got a name?'

'None I gave it. Don't know 'bout if anybody else ever did.'

'It weren't you who raised it?'

'Dog showed up here just like you're looking at it.'

'Materialized in front your eyes, you mean?'

'Don't get mystical on me, Nat.' Finch gestured with his half-full tumbler toward the lake. 'Was sitting round back like it was watching over the place one morning I strolled out to the cabins. I figured somebody'd come asking after it, but . . .' He drained his glass. 'Afternoon of that same day Iris walked in the office wanting a few days' work for food and lodging and' – he raised his eyebrows at Banyon – 'three years later guess you might say both of 'em's still at it.'

He found the diner closed and found Pam heading for the road in her Escort. At Banyon's wave, she stopped the car next to him. A slight quiver moved through her lips. Banyon asked if he could get something to eat. Nodding through the trees toward the motel in a way that made him uneasy she snapped, ' 'Bout anything you want looks like, but not in this pit stop.'

Banyon tried smiling at her, but she just huffed and gunned the engine, so he asked her if she was mad at him to which she replied, 'Why in hell would I be?'

Banyon shrugged.

'I went home the other night and took a soak with Goddamn Joe Littlefeet.'

'He that fly-catching Indian?'

Pam nodded. The quivering in her lips, Banyon decided,

came from her working on them with her teeth to keep from crying or screaming, he wasn't sure which. 'Fucker passed out in my tub.'

'He seemed pretty lit,' allowed Banyon, pretty much that way himself.

'I got up to wait tables next morning like I'll probably be doing till I die and Juicehead Joe Littlefeet's sleeping naked next to me. I feel like finding a new goddamn apartment or hopping a train west or something.'

Mischaracterizing the root of her misery, Banyon inquired if the Indian was still at her place.

'No, he ain't. What's that got to do with anything?'

'I thought maybe you needed help getting rid of him.'

'I don't have any problems getting rid of the likes of Joe Littlefeet. Where I needed help was not bringing him home in the first place.'

Banyon, still hungry, tried changing the subject. 'Just coupla bread slices round some cold meat would do me.'

'You'll be a lucky son of bitch you don't get old.'

Leaning a hand on the Ford's roof, which was dewy from the rain that had quit before getting very serious, Banyon felt at once as dense as the fog blanketing the field across the highway and as thin as the mist coils floating in the lot. 'The grill wouldn't even need firing up.'

'I was plenty *as* good looking at your age, stud, as you are now.'

'And you're a damn sight better than just half-bad sitting here.'

'Oh, Jesus Christ' – Pam jerked the car in reverse – 'hold on let me park.'

She made him a turkey breast sandwich as thick as his forearm and microwaved him some frozen corn fritters, then sat across from him in the kitchen, drinking a beer while he ate. The rain started again, harder than before, and pounded loudly on the trailer's tin roof above a block of country-western songs about broken hearts playing on a radio next to the sink. Banyon was impressed with the kitchen's cleanliness and how it smelled, as a diner ought to but seldom did, like good homemade food. He thought about Iris showing up at the Deepwater three years before and marrying Finch and realized he didn't want to know why she had or where she'd come from anymore than he cared to know the histories of the many areas of the country he had stayed in for short periods of time. Only the here and now interested him and sometimes he even believed that people and things existed only coincident to his awareness of them. Pam stood up and invited him to dance. Banyon complied by wrapping his arms around her, inelegantly shuffling his feet so as not to step on hers, inhaling her scent, which seemed to spring from the same source as the diner's. She nuzzled his neck and rubbed his bottom, and Banyon, wanting to make her happy again, made no effort to stop her. They danced two slow ones, then Pam pushed away from him, went back to the table, and, breathing heavily, retook her seat. 'You're quite a worker, I guess.'

Banyon shrugged. 'It ain't hard, just tedious.'

She gave him an odd look. 'You're talking about what? Scraping paint?'

'Ain't that what you asked me about?'

She smiled. 'It was an open-ended question, honey, for you to take wherever you wanted to.'

'How long you been at this job?'

'Close to two years.'

'You like it?'

She laughed. 'Ask a fish if it likes to swim, know what I mean?'

'Sure. Okay.'

Banyon put some money in front of her for the sandwich, but she shoved it back at him, then waved in the general direction of the water. 'Anybody told you the rumor 'bout our lake, Nat?'

Banyon shook his head.

'You ought to ask somebody to.'

'How 'bout I ask you?'

'At least one dead man looks up from its bottom. That's what they say.'

'Who do they say it is?'

'Fella was a dealer at the casino couple years back, stayed here on a month-to-month basis, then one day he weren't anywhere to be found. Him or his car.'

'Why do they say he ended up in the lake?'

'For crossing or, depending on who you ask, getting in the way of his landlord, who fools people into thinking he's a teddy bear when he's really a grizzly bear.'

Banyon said, 'Sounds to me like a guy got bored with the action round here and pushed on.'

Pam got to her feet again, leaned forward, and softly kissed his cheek. 'I hope so, honey. I hope that's exactly what he did.'

Watching through a thin curtain the shadow of an embracing couple moving lazily to the wordless sort of music he'd heard from that room the night he'd first kissed Iris, Banyon assured himself the two dancers only looked to be in love, as the moon, spectrally visible through the dispersing clouds, only seemed to be creating light and the earth only felt as if it was standing still. He wondered if the Rottweiler was concealed nearby beneath the same fog to his waist and if his life was a narrow, one-way path, over which he had no say, leading to now. He told himself that was crazy talk, that he'd chanced onto the Deepwater and could leave it anytime; only he didn't want to leave it, not without Iris, and wasn't sure he could make himself go even if his good sense told him to.

He pulled off his T-shirt, lay it on the ground, which was still damp from the earlier rain, and sat down on it, vanishing to the world more than four feet from him. The room light soon snapped off, but music kept floating out through the screen. In the fog crickets chirped. An owl hooted arrhythmically. Drops of moisture fell from the overhead pine branches onto Banyon, who waited several minutes for the light to come back on or for other evidence that the room's occupants hadn't fallen fast asleep in each others arms, but he didn't, to his dismay, see either. With a soft click, the music stopped. Banyon stood, picked up his T-shirt, dangled it around his neck, and walked slowly back to his cottage.

Six

A sheriff's cruiser pulled into the lot and stopped next to the office at midafternoon. Two cops stepped from it, put on their hats, glanced at the LeMans, three spaces left of them, and at the other four vehicles in the lot, then walked back across it to where a shirtless Finch, in a battered Stetson and bermuda shorts, was mowing the thin grass strip before the highway with a small gas-powered push mower. Feeling or imagining their eyes on him, Banyon didn't turn from the portico wall he was sanding until the mower quit running and they were facing Finch at the lawn's edge. The three of them stayed there maybe five minutes, the big cop seeming to be asking questions, the smaller one watching the other two with his arms folded on his chest, and Finch punctuating whatever he was saying with nods or shakes of his head. Then they all walked together back to and into the office. The cops came out shortly after, got in their car, and left.

Banyon, who'd squashed a strong impulse to hightail it into the woods at their appearance, dropped his sandpaper into the bucket that stored his tools and bought a lemonade. He drank it leaning against the portico wall facing the road, on which two buzzards, sporadically interrupted by passing cars, picked at a woodchuck done in that morning by a minivan. He tried not to think about the LeMans, a possible dead card dealer in the lake, or, especially, Iris and Finch dancing and falling asleep together. An old one-armed-bandit junkie wearing gloves as white as her hair exited a room just to his right, struggling with a plastic pail full of coins, which she asked Banyon to carry to her car. Banyon did, then helped her into a mid-Seventies, three-tone Dodge Dart with undersized tires. The casino-bound crone tipped him a quarter.

Banyon told her he'd call his mother with it and let her know where he was, then, feeling bad for her, said, 'I hope you break them Indians, ma'am.'

Iris, looking at her feet instead of at him, made her way from the end of the restaurant trail over to the residence as Banyon was finishing his break. He wondered, intelligence wise, where he stood relative to the rest of the world and why the question had posed itself to him. Thankful for a definitive task to engage in, he resumed working. Cooled only briefly by the previous night's rain, the torrid air once more began to thicken and feel oily. A slow-moving cloud-bank partially obscured the western sky. A repainted, purple Oldsmobile Eighty Eight arrived around three. Finch popped out of the office as if he'd been expecting it and got in behind the car's two front-seat occupants. The Eighty Eight idled there a half-hour or more before Finch climbed back out of it, followed by Petersen and Walnut, who'd been at the wheel. Finch led the others over to see the pool, which was close to being filled with water only a few shades from aqua-blue. They all waved to Banyon, who had the idea they were talking about him. A few minutes later Walnut and Petersen left in the Buick and Finch, sweated up from the heat, his pigment-scarce skin a roseate color, ambled to the soda machine, bought an Orange Nehi, and, nodding approvingly, surveyed the portico Banyon was about finished sanding. 'Looks as if I'll be buying paint sooner'n I thought, Nat.'

'In three, four days, I'd guess' – Banyon peered at the nearing storm – 'the weather holds.'

'She ain't going to today.'

'Not all of it she won't.'

Finch pointed his Nehi at the walls. 'Be a temptation to a lesser worker than you, Nat – maybe even to most folks – to dog it an hourly wage job this kind.'

Recognizing Finch's snaky way of approaching an as yet-to-be-revealed subject, Banyon only wiped sweat from his temple with his forearm, then, reaching into his pocket for change, headed to the soda machine.

'Plenty of other people wouldn't even blame 'em for it.'

' 'Spect they wouldn't.'

Finch pushed the Stetson back on his head. 'Don't make you for the car thieving type, Nat.'

'I took that one from needing it bad, then got to liking too much how she handled.'

Finch seemed to be waiting for Banyon to further explain his motivation, which Banyon didn't do. 'I don't know about you, Nat, but those deputies driving in made me awful nervous your account.'

Banyon put three quarters in the machine and banged the lemonade button.

'Thank God for you, Nat, they come about Earl, not the LeMans.'

Removing his can from the dispenser, Banyon gazed at Finch as dispassionately as he could manage.

'Seems nobody – not even Earl's wife or kids – has seen or heard from him since the night of our card game.' Frowning, Finch wiped his brow on his shoulder. 'I'd feel real bad – so would Petersen and Walnut – if we played even a little part in

Earl's deciding to just up and take a powder on his family and responsibilities.' He looked at Banyon. 'Tell me – Gospel, Nat —you think we were too hard on him?'

Momentarily experiencing an odd sensation that Finch was not just to his right, but all around him, talking at him in various inflections from four different faces, Banyon, recalling how Earl had fairly dashed from the room in what seemed to be a scared state, replied, 'I didn't know the history of it.'

'Earl's refused forever to take responsibility for anything, including owing a bunch of folks in these parts more money than he could possibly earn in ten of his sorts of lifetimes, but, until lately, was always being cut slack because, well, basically, he's a likeable weasel far's weasels go.'

Banyon snapped open his lemonade.

Finch took off his hat and slammed it against his knee, sending sweat flying into the air. 'Well, I suppose he'll be back when he runs out of money or maybe he'll con himself into enough of it to stay gone for good.' Nodding at Banyon, he put his hat back on. 'Point is, far as I'm concerned, Nat, much better they come asking after Earl the errant weasel than after the best hired hand I've probably ever had.' He pulled a cigar from his shirtpocket.

'Think I'd like to take what your man is offering for the Pontiac, Herman,' Banyon said, imagining he'd just been skewered with invisible needles, 'if he still is.'

'Consider it done, Nat, and that particular mistake behind you.'

Banyon nodded.

Finch slid the cigar between his lips. 'Young man, I had an extraordinary night last night.' He smiled at the open room Iris was cleaning near the office. 'I just wanted you to know.'

'Know what?'

'About the romantic night this old man had with his wife of

56

the kind we hadn't had in too goddamned long.' Feeling all hollowed out inside, Banyon recalled the dancing shadows he'd seen the night before. Still smiling around his cigar, Finch raised his fists and started firing near-misses past Banyon's ears. 'Reason I want you to know, Nat, is I suspect all this pep me and the missus suddenly got has something to do with the sort of young energy you've brought to this place, and this aging cocksman needs you to understand he appreciates it.'

Banyon grinned weakly at him.

Finch dropped his hands. 'Guess I ought to finish that lawn 'fore the rain starts in.'

'Probably be a good idea.'

Banyon chugged his remaining lemonade as Iris, wheeling a maid's cart out of the room she'd been in, returned Finch's big looping wave with her own less dramatic gesture, before she opened and disappeared through another door. A topless Jeep crammed with teenagers playing high-volume rap music roared by on the highway. Banyon suddenly felt as if he'd stumbled into a dark cave inhabited by he didn't know what. Putting away his cigar, Finch started walking sprightly toward the lawnmower.

'You want to take that Pontiac out for one more drive, Nat, better do it soon, 'cause I'm going to need her keys 'fore sun-up.' Not looking back, he raised his hands in mock surrender. 'Only if you get stopped for speeding, whatever, old Herman Finch don't even know ya.'

It began lightly misting as Iris pushed her cart into the room before the one he was working on. Responding to her polite nod, Banyon waved, praying the rain would hold off until she'd entered the next room. He mentally replayed every movement and gesture she'd made when they'd been to-gether two afternoons earlier; recalled every word and sound she'd uttered; every place he'd touched her; the way she'd touched him; her body's powerful, hypnotic grinding; her natural, pungently alluring scent becoming over those twenty-odd minutes increasingly prominent. Then, against his will, he pictured her with Finch exactly as she'd been with him. That she sometimes had sex with her own husband oughtn't to bother him, he told himself. But it did. And troubling him as much was an intuition he had that Finch somehow knew it bothered him and had been aware of Banyon's presence beyond his and Iris's bedroom window last night. But how could he have been? Banyon thought of the Rottweiler, the way the dog seemed to him to possess abnormal powers. He told himself to stop thinking before it made him crazy.

He kept working even as the mist became a drizzle. His wrist and arm muscles, adapting to the new demands he'd put on them, scarcely hurt him anymore. His stroking motion was beginning to feel as second nature to him as breathing. He couldn't pinpoint exactly when he had decided to give Finch, even more so than he had to his past employers, a job superior to what he'd been paid for, a finished product that would lead Finch to unleash a punch flurry the envy of Mohammad Ali. 'You're going to get wet, looks like,' remarked Iris, approaching the door immediately right of where he was sanding.

'This is killing me, Iris,' blurted out Banyon, louder than he'd intended. 'We might's well be in a monastery.'

'Shhhh,' she cautioned him.

'You two had a great night, I guess.'

She scowled at him. 'He told you that?'

'Long those lines.'

'For Christ sake, Nat, he's my husband.' She stepped into the room, shoving her cart before her. Banyon glanced at the office, where Finch, if he wanted it, had a clear view of the entire motel. The window directly in front of him could be heard creaking open, then Iris saying through the screen, 'I married him, case you were wondering, because he was nice to me when I needed somebody to be in the worst way and what he was offering seemed like an awful lot from where I was looking at the time.'

'I like him too,' said Banyon.

'Who said I like him?'

'Don't you?'

'Less and less, and I didn't nearly enough even when I said yes to him.'

'He's been good to me.'

'He's good to everybody till he finds a reason not to be, and we've handed him a damn good one he gets wind of it.'

'Biggest thing on my mind right now, bad's it sounds, is when we can hand him another one.'

'I told you, Nat, I'm past just fooling around.'

'What's that mean?'

'Means if he doesn't find out about us over one thing, he will over another.'

'What are you saying?'

'I don't know what I'm saying. You're not just a kidder, are you, Nat?'

'I never felt this way over nobody. When I get done doing what he hired me to do, I'll go and you'll come with me.'

'Just like that? Just hop in your fancy Pontiac and go?'

'We'll go all right, but not in the Pontiac.' Banyon tried to see her through the screen, but it was covered by an open Venetian blind, so he tapped lightly on it instead. 'You crazy on me enough, Iris, to hear the truth?'

'I'm crazy about you sure enough, but I haven't heard the truth yet.'

'I grabbed that Pontiac off a Greenville lot on account of a strong feeling told me if I didn't want to get wrongly blamed for a bad situation happened down there I'd better clear out fast. I wouldn't a took it but from necessity, don't plan on taking one again, and this one's gonna be off my hands by morning.'

Banyon heard what he took for a sheet being briskly flapped in the air. He stopped sanding, put his mouth up next to the screen, hissed, 'Iris? Did you hear me?'

'I heard you.'

'I'm not a thief mostly. I just got in a jam.'

He heard the sheet flap again, or another one, then saw the wind it created ripple the blind. 'The five hundred I'm getting for it with what I'll make doing this here ought to buy me something runs good enough to start us down the road.'

Only the noise of her smoothing the sheets atop the mattress came back to him. 'Ain't you going to say anything, Iris?'

'Starting down the road's no trick, Nat. Sticking our thumbs out we could do that, only where would we get to?'

'Someplace together. Why's it matter?'

'Last time I thought that I ended up at the Deepwater.'

'Ain't that what we were talking about? How you still are at it.'

'I could leave anytime in somebody's jalopy with a few dollars' pocket change if that's all I wanted.'

'Thought you wanted to be with me.'

'Enough to do 'bout anything, Nat' – he heard her voice right up next to the blind – 'except go back to hand-to-mouth life on the road.'

'Long's I don't get scared a hard work and can stay away from playing bad hunches, I can make a buck. We both can.'

'A buck and then another one to replace the one we just spent, only they never add up to more than gas money to the next buck-paying job.' As if God had thrown a switch, the sky suddenly opened. To get out from under it, Banyon stopped working and squeezed in tight to the window beneath the roof's two-foot overhang. Through the blind's open louvers, he felt Iris's warm breath against his face. 'He's got a big stash of bills he thinks I don't know about in a floor safe in his workroom closet, Nat, which if it showed up missing he wouldn't rush to fill the cops in on.'

She pulled aside the blind and pressed her mouth flush to the wire mesh. Banyon, less than an inch from her full, moist lips, wanted her more than he ever had and wished like hell he didn't. 'You're talking about what, 'xactly?'

'About the two of us starting out on that road with a piece of what I've rightfully earned working here the last three years and haven't been paid.'

An eastward breeze pushed water pouring off the eaves against the back of Banyon, who was cognizant only of tires wetly hissing out on the highway and of Iris's hot, intermittent exhalations warming him. 'Guess he wouldn't let you leave with some of it?'

'No more than cut off his right arm and tell me to with that.'

'How 'bout without it?'

'It's the same diff' to him.'

' 'Nother words, no chance he'd give you his blessing regardless?'

'Far's that goes I might's well be part of those stashed bills.'

Wondering if she might not have even brought up the safe had he not got her thinking he was a thief, which, though he was technically, he didn't view himself to be generally, Banyon said, 'We could wear ourselves out talking, Iris.'

'Day after tomorr – Saturday nights he goes gambling with Walnut and Petersen.'

'Night after tomorrow's a long ways off.'

'We get lucky he'll up and run into town before then.'

'Two minutes after he does, I'll come hunting you.'

'You won't have to very hard.'

'You're a sorceress, a powerful something, Iris, I'm pretty sure of it.'

'Hush up about that, Nat. You're love struck, is all – same as me.'

'Get out the rain, young man,' Finch's elevated voice called, ' 'fore you drown!'

Banyon glanced at Finch, from the office doorway energetically gesturing him off of the job, as Iris fast closed the window. He waved to Finch, after which Finch returned inside and Banyon picked up his tools and sprinted to the portico. He sat down with his back to the candy machine, studying on the rain, enthralled by the miracle beyond his comprehension of a wall of water fracturing into harmless drops on its earthward descent.

Appearing at first only as a shadow in the near-dark, the Rottweiler, moving remarkably fast from what seemed to be scant effort, charged through the dusky woods straight at Banyon, sitting on his cottage stoop. Tensing involuntarily, Banyon remembered Iris saying the dog would tear someone's heart out if Finch told it to and Finch later revealing that Iris had arrived at the Deepwater mere hours after it did. Ten feet from Banyon, it abruptly halted, shook a spray of water from itself, suggesting to Banyon it had recently come out of the lake or from rolling on the still rain-damp forest floor, lay down with its head between its front feet, and through eyes dark as its pelt and as unfathomable to Banyon as a foreign language, starkly gazed at him.

Moderately drunk on brandy he'd had in his gym bag,

Banyon suddenly suspected the Rottweiler knew more than he did about his thoughts and what they might lead him to. He pictured its penetrating stare divulging his subconscious intentions. He imagined it had been shadowing him from birth, was intimately acquainted with every moment of his life, and, unlike himself, knew exactly what he would do next. Then he told the Rottweiler it was just a big, black dog and, from what he'd seen, not even a particularly smart one. He went inside, lay on his bed and, finishing the brandy, listened to a talk show about bass fishing on his transistor radio. He fell asleep and dreamt that something he couldn't see was chasing him.

He woke in blackness, grabbed his flashlight, went outside, saw the Rottweiler still lying there. The dog didn't so much scare him, he realized, as make him feel uncomfortable. He envisioned it as the embodiment of his conscience. Mostly he was tired of being watched by it. He asked the dog if it wanted some meat. The Rottweiler just kept looking at him. From the cottage's mini-refrigerator Banyon got a roast beef sandwich Pam had made him earlier at the diner, brought it back to the stoop, tore a hunk from it, and tossed it at the Rottweiler. The Rottweiler picked it up in its huge jaws and ate it in about five seconds. 'Not bad, huh?' said Banyon.

He threw it another piece, which the Rottweiler seized and, not even bothering to raise its head, devoured. 'Come on,' said Banyon, stepping off the stoop. 'You want more?'

For no reason he could identify, he began walking backward toward the mostly unlit motel, holding the rest of the sandwich out in front of him. The Rottweiler stood up and slowly followed him. Twice Banyon flung it decent-sized meat chunks, which the dog gobbled up as if they were breadcrumbs. He backed across the parking lot to the LeMans, unlocked and opened the driver door, climbed behind the wheel, tossed half the remaining sandwich onto the passenger side of the backseat, then opened the door opposite it. Standing at the opening, the Rottweiler glanced at Banyon, then at the sandwich, then back at Banyon, who told it, 'Hop in have a bite.' To his total surprise, the Rottweiler took him up on the invitation.

After devouring what Banyon had given it, it sat, facing forward in the middle of the seat, looking as if it wanted more. Banyon tossed it the food he had left. The dog ate it and stayed where it was, as did Banyon. Having taken off his watch before lying down earlier, he had no idea what time it was. He half-believed he was sleeping still. Marred by the dark shadows of lunar mountains, the full moon filled half the rear window. Bats knifed through the warm air. Banyon told the dog, 'You can get out if you want to,' but it didn't move. A few minutes later, Banyon reached back, pulled shut the door, and rolled down the window nearest the dog. Then he started up the Pontiac and took it out on the highway.

Even redlined, at a hundred twenty miles per hour, the car didn't make an unordinary tick, leading Banyon once more to marvel that such a gem had come from a trade-in lot and to regret his having to part with it. On a straightaway, he took his hands from the steering wheel and the LeMans scarcely wandered an inch. Then he slowed to sixty and just cruised. Looming in the rearview mirror, the Rottweiler turned its eyes from him only to occasionally gulp air entering through its window. Banyon wondered if it was loyal first to Finch, Iris, or the Deepwater and whether this ride had been more its idea than his. At a 7–11, leaving the dog in the car, he bought a week's supply of beer and staples and two sixteen-ounce porterhouse steaks, put the groceries in the trunk, gassed up the LeMans, and took off again, headed west, through Indian-owned lands.

Just past the reservation he turned onto a single-lane road traversing a small mountain. Hairpin turns hugged wooded hillsides on which houses had been sporadically wedged onto small, half-cleared plots. Fog patches, like dropped articles of clothing, dotted the ascending pavement; alongside of it, blasting had created patches of bare granite walls. The moon and stars rained light on the tops of leafy deciduous trees at the land's highest elevation, from where it again descended, this time through strip-mined woods, looking as if they'd been clawed by rapacious giants, into a valley of scrub conifers and abandoned pasture too rocky for farming or mankind generally, but rich, guessed Banyon, with game.

He pulled the LeMans onto a needle-covered pathway that petered out five hundred yards into a stand of sizable pines, cut the engine, stepped from the car, took the porterhouses from the trunk, tossed one twenty feet from him and the other fifteen feet beyond it. Then he opened the door nearest the Rottweiler. The dog promptly hopped out, lifted a leg and pissed on the Pontiac's left rear tire. A moment later, it trotted up to the first steak, pinned it to the ground with its front paws, and went about devouring it. Banyon jumped into the LeMans and slammed both doors. The Rottweiler, the blood-dripping meat dangling from its jaws, turned to him. Running water and a coyote's mournful yapping sounded somewhere. A mosquito swarm hovered around the Rottweiler's face. 'This ain't personal on my part,' Banyon told it out his window.

He started up the LeMans, turned it around, and headed it slow down the pathway toward the road. He glanced at the odometer, which said he and the dog had traveled fifty-plus miles together. Still holding the porterhouse, the Rottweiler trotted after him. It kept coming even after the car had reached the road and started up it in the direction from

65

which they'd come. Then it broke into a gallop. His heart pounding loud in his ears, Banyon stepped hard on the LeMans's accelerator, not easing off on it until he'd rounded the first curve and lost all trace of the Rottweiler.

At the Deepwater an hour and a half later, he parked the Pontiac in what had become its usual spot, then dropped its keys in the office checkout box. When he got up in the morning the LeMans was gone and in his message slot near the front desk was an envelope with his name on it containing five fifty dollar bills.

Seven

'I'm twice as poor this morning I ought to be, Herman.'

Looking up at Banyon from his late breakfast in the near-empty diner, Finch said, 'That merchandise last night, Nat' – he blew on his fingertips – 'hot, hot, 'cording my source.'

Banyon angrily slid into the seat opposite him. 'That's why he was only going to give me the chicken feed for it you said he was going to, and didn't.'

'Fella told me I over-estimated how much chicken feed by half, Nat, but, like I told you, I'm an amateur comes to it, and, so' – he shrugged – 'sorry.'

'Sorry?'

Finch pointed to a basket in the table's center. 'Help yourself to a corn muffin, young man.'

'I don't want no kind of muffin. I want what's due me.'

Finch frowned. 'S'pose I could see 'bout getting the car back for you, though he'd likely want a little something for his trouble.'

Ignoring the suggestion they both understood to be off the wall, Banyon said, 'Your man, whoever's, gon' get rich on her, that's for sure.'

'Other hand he's probably got overhead like the rest of us, Nat, plus a big fat downside a deal of his goes in the crapper.'

'I feel like I brung my clothes in to be cleaned, Herman, and only got back my underwear.'

'You tell me exactly what troubles you most about how things stand, Nat' – Finch gravely nodded – 'and I'll study on it best I can.'

'I just did tell ya. Top which, I got nothing to drive.'

'I regret now, then, I stuck my nose at all in her, even though I only did to try and keep out of jail the best goddamn worker I ever employed and' – Finch solemnly crossed a finger over his heart – 'a young man reminds me of myself at the same age.'

Nonplussed once more by Finch's embarrassing gush of affection toward him, Banyon brusquely grabbed and bit into one of the muffins he'd been offered, understanding, if nothing else and without comprehending exactly who to blame for it, that two hundred fifty dollars was all he would ever see for the LeMans. Said Finch, 'What say, young man, we go about putting you into some legal transportation?'

Banyon eyed him suspiciously. Finch opened his hands in a gesture of generosity. 'Herman Finch does for and to others, Nat, as they do for and to him.' He smiled at Banyon, but Banyon couldn't decipher the emotion behind it. He wondered if Finch had missed the Rottweiler yet and, if he had, where he figured it had got to and how it had got there. 'You want more to eat first?'

Banyon tossed the muffin back where he'd found it. 'I don't guess I need to right now.'

'Have you got your take from the LeMans on you?'

Banyon, for an answer, solemnly touched the cash-containing envelope in his shirt pocket.

Finch reached over and clapped him on the shoulder. 'By God, then, let's go fit you with some wheels.'

Thick woods interspersed with farm fields being harvested on a pellucid day, by growling John Deeres and Massey Fergu-

sons hauling balers from which cubes of sweet-smelling grass
and timothy flew into trailing wagons, lined the hollow road.
'Nice thing is, Nat, you already know Walnut, so it's not just
me vouching for him.'

Finch honked the Caddy's horn at an old huckster couple
peddling vegetables, live bait, and stenciled T-shirts from a
pickup truck's umbrella-covered bed.

'I bought this here vehicle off'n him couple years back, after
he'd sold me two before it, so that just shows you terms of
quality and customer satisfaction.'

'Where's he get 'em at?'

Replying indirectly Finch said, 'Walnut'll encourage you
put a microscope to 'em you want.'

'He'd take my note?'

'Way that'd hafta work, Nat, I think, given the circum-
stances, 'd be me fronting you against your paycheck and
whatever minimal interest we agree on.'

Two horses, each burdened with a teenage girl in cutoffs and a
halter top, trotted through a meadow in which a hugely en-
dowed bull humped a heifer in the shade of an expansive oak
tree. Banyon suddenly envisioned himself dangling puppetlike
from a giant pair of hands; a suspicion struck him that everything
he'd done since arriving at the Deepwater had been by the design
of a force outside of himself; he couldn't, though, penetrate to
the root of the thought or point to specific evidence to sub-
stantiate it; like most of what drove his behavior and preceded his
actions, it resulted mostly from a strong feeling he had. 'Maybe
you ought to bring me see the other one.'

'Fella relieved you of the Pontiac, you mean?'

'I wouldn't mind having a word with him.'

'He'd never allow you to in a way you'd know it was him,
Nat.' They whizzed past a yard full of crippled chairs and sofas
surrounding a hand-scrawled sign offering ANTIKES for sale.

'See, he's got a legit business on top the other and is real particular about keeping his second identity under wraps.'

Near a dilapidated barn, which adjoined a house's burned skeleton, Finch put on the Caddy's right blinker. Half a mile later he entered the driveway of a rambling, brick rancher. At their approach, a mountainous woman with her hair up in banana-shaped rollers stood up from a loveseat suspended from the porch ceiling by two chains and went inside. 'Walnut's wife, Frieda,' said Finch. 'She's people shy.'

A dozen or so buffed cars and trucks formed two rows behind a red-white-and-blue plastic strip on a lawn patch right of the residence. QUALITY USED ONES declared a flag-shaped banner flying from a pole atop a long, modular metal building behind the vehicles. Walnut popped out of a side doorway in the house basement. Waving at Finch and Banyon as they stepped from the Caddy to follow him, he headed for the automobiles as if he'd been expecting them, though Banyon was confused as to why he would be. 'Hot enough?' Finch greeted him at the lot.

'I expect I am,' answered Walnut, whose lime-green golfer's shirt clashed with his Scotch-plaid bermuda shorts and peeling, sunburned pate.

'Told you about Nat needing a car, so here he is.'

'You told him I did when?' asked Banyon.

'Last night, Nat' – Finch raised his eyes conspiratorially at Banyon, who was caught off guard by the admission – 'after your brother come and took his back from you.'

'Got left in the lurch, did ye?' said Walnut, around a thick chaw puffing out one of his cheeks.

Banyon didn't say if he did.

'Was the brother's car to begin with,' interjected Finch, 'only 'ccount he wrecked his other one he had to have the LeMans back quicker'n he'd planned on.'

Banyon suspected Walnut neither bought nor gave a shit about Finch's brother story, that he knew damn good and well why Banyon was suddenly in the car market and that Finch, for a reason Banyon couldn't fathom, had spun the yarn solely for Banyon's benefit. Walnut spat tobacco juice into the grass. 'Understood you to be looking at the low end of the market.'

Banyon said, 'I got two-fifty on me and a hundred and a half more to put toward one.'

'That won't hardly wipe a dry ass these days.'

'Plus another thousand on top of it from me,' said Finch.

'You sure you want to do that for this boy, Herman?'

'I'm sure.'

Walnut spit again. 'That still ain't much more than enough to pinch a small loaf out on.'

'Long's it runs and has a little pep to her,' said Banyon.

'Whyn't ya look this here over.' Walnut tapped an early model Ford Escort parked next to him.

Banyon said, 'I'd sooner walk or crawl as own a four-cylinder go-cart calls itself a car.'

'Ain't got but eighty thousand miles on her and never been in a wreck I can see.'

'I won't drive a machine bitches on a hill. I couldn't feel right about myself.'

'What about that Newport, Walnut?' Finch nodded half-way down the row at a late-sixties Chrysler sedan, with a silver-black paint job. 'What's running her?'

'A twice-rebuilt 440 cubic eight.' Walnut led them over to the relic, rolling his chaw into his opposite cheek. 'You want one that'll get up and go, she's it.' Banyon lay down and looked at the car's undercarriage. 'But I ain't taking no fourteen hundred for her' – Walnut fired another loogie, this one dangling nearly to the ground from his lips before he broke it off with his index finger. 'I'm telling you right now, 'fore you get too interested.'

Metal strips were welded to its floorboards where they'd probably rusted through, but the frame looked plenty solid to Banyon, who couldn't detect on it any Bondo or active rust. He heard Finch pull up the hood and say of the engine, 'Looks pretty clean.'

Banyon got up and peered in at the monstrosity. From what he knew of car engines, not much was visibly wrong with it. Finch said, 'What would you have to have for her?'

'Two large,' answered Walnut.

Banyon slammed the hood shut.

'Now tell me what you'd take from somebody ain't just in off the street,' said Finch.

'The boy can have her for nineteen hundred' – Walnut absently kicked the Newport's front driver-side tire – 'only 'cause I ain't give to no charities yet this year.'

Banyon said, 'Nineteen hundred don't talk to me no louder than two large did.'

Walnut fished from his pocket a chain attached to three or four keys, peeled one off, and tossed it to Banyon. 'How 'bout, son, you see if humping her into the redline don't 'bout make you shit yourself.'

Banyon shrugged. 'Long's it won't cost me nothing.'

'Time's all, son, and whatever you ain't crapped out yet.'

'While you're doing her, Nat, I'll whittle way here some at Walnut.'

Banyon opened the driver's door and slid in behind the wheel. The vinyl seats were spottily stained and, on the passenger side, had a big tear in them patched with duct tape. A dirty rabbit's foot dangled from the rearview mirror. The whole car smelled of Lysol. Banyon turned it on. 'Vrrroomm,' Walnut mouthed to him through the windshield, just before Banyon peeled out, digging up dual clumps of the salesman's lawn.

72

He chirped the tires going from first into second on the hollow road, squealed them again, at plus-sixty, shifting into third, before, half-hoping she'd drop her transmission so he could watch Walnut's reaction to hearing of it, he threw her back down into second, burning more rubber, after which he goosed her five or six times. Then he took her onto the highway and sat on her. She made one-ten in under fifteen seconds and nearly wore Banyon out keeping her between the lines. He backed off of her, then cruised at around seventy, the Newport yo-yo-ing like a son of a bitch on its beat-to-hell shocks and whenever Banyon even loosened his grip on her swerving hard to the right. She was all over the place, a regular rodeo bronc and just as juiced. Banyon perspired from his efforts with her while experiencing a muscular sort of tingling in his loins, and, against all reason, found himself wanting more from her. He stomped on the breaks, put her into a power slide, spun her around, and punched her hard again. Back at the lot, Walnut asked him if he'd dropped a load in his pants.

'She's sloppy as goose shit,' Banyon answered him.

'I bet she got yer dick hard though, didn't she?'

'I couldn't hardly make her go straight.'

'She'll make ya eat your Wheaties is what she'll do, boy.'

'Ain't nothing to her but speed and guts.'

'What else does a wet-behind-the-ears, balls-out son of a bitch like you need in one?'

Banyon mentally tagged Walnut as an asshole, then realized he'd already done that at the card game.

Finch told him, 'I got Walnut down to seventeen hundred.'

'Carved on me like I was a big tom turkey while you were dicking the Newport,' said Walnut.

'Looks to me,' Banyon told him, ready for Walnut to make something of it and to cold-cock him if he did, 'like he left most of the fat and feathers on you.'

Walnut, though, only spit again. Finch said, 'You want to own her, Nat?'

'I don't know if I do or not.'

'Vrrrroooom,' a straightfaced Walnut once more mouthed to him.

'If you do I'll front you what you don't got, Nat,' said Finch, 'long's you understand you'll be in my employ till we're square.'

Still high from the Chrysler's death-defying, life-enhancing spin, Banyon told Walnut, 'Fifteen-fifty.'

'Sixteen,' came back Walnut, 'only because a blind man could see you won't be worth a squirrel's shit to Finchie without her.'

Paying no mind to the same internal voice he'd ignored when he'd played in Finch's card game and involved himself with Iris, Banyon, only vaguely aware of or concerned by indenturing himself to Finch for the immediate future, pulled the wad of fifties from his pocket and slapped it into Walnut's hand, telling him, 'Ya ought to buy a hat with some of it.'

Finch, banging Banyon on the shoulder, informed Walnut he'd give him the rest tomorrow night.

'That case, let's go get Tarzan here his paperwork' – Walnut headed them toward the house – 'so's he can hump in his new heartthrob down to the local DMV and make her his.'

From instinct or for a specific purpose, nocturnal creatures loudly spoke outside the cottage in which Banyon woke with a start, unaware of what voice had caused him to. It was lost to him now, whatever communication had made his heart begin to rapidly beat and him to perspire through his underwear. A vehicle could be heard roaring in or out of the lot. His radio's fluorescent clock face said one-thirty. He got out of bed, took a beer from the refrigerator, walked out front to the edge of the moonlit lake, on which a tern pair sat statically, dangled his dick out his drawers, and pissed onto the shore's mossy rocks. He shook his dick dry, then put it away.

He traced with a finger the outline in the cloudless sky of the Big and Little Dippers, the only constellations he'd ever learned. Wisps of white gas, similar to the mist coils lying about in the woods, floated in the Milky Way. A star fell. He remembered being told once by someone, who, like most people in his life hadn't impressed him enough to remember specifically, that dying stars were sparks flicked from God's cigarettes. He thought of Iris then, how she was already permanently in his memory – her eyes wide open; her hair brushing his face; her hands pinning his to the floor above his head as she was suddenly humping him slowly, relentlessly, after she'd had him ride her fast and violently, her muscles, in excruciating spasms and spurts, keeping his orgasm at bay, until he couldn't stand it anymore and she knew it and hollered for him to shoot her. Banyon had never been completely taken over by another person that way. He pictured their minds and bodies as opposite halves of the same individual. He concluded now that he must be in love with her because thinking about her, which he did most of the time of late, eliminated for him the possibility that he'd ever loved anyone else. If not for her, his life and behavior in the last five days would make no sense at all.

He tossed off his beer, crushed the can in his hand, went and got another one. He walked back out to the stoop, sat down, and considered how in less than twelve hours he'd traded a primo car for a fast bomb and a twelve-hundred-fifty-dollar-plus-interest debt. Though he understood how it had happened and that it wouldn't have without his consent, he had a bothersome feeling he'd been taken on the deal, though he wasn't sure in what manner or by who. He recalled how Finch had steered him first to Walnut, then to the Newport. And that out of all the keys he must have possessed, Walnut had been carrying the Chrysler's key in his pocket. Part of him suspected that Finch and Walnut, for whatever reason, had been on the same page regarding the transaction from the beginning; another part told him that thanks to Finch he was well rid of the LeMans, which hadn't been his to sell at any rate, and now owned the Newport, which, with all its faults, gave him an even bigger rush at full throttle than had the Pontiac.

Probably the same owl he had heard every night at the Deepwater hooted off in the pines. A mosquito bit his thigh. He killed it, smearing the blood it had taken from him onto his skin. He longed to see Iris sleeping, to watch her dream, to slowly open her eyes with soft neck kisses, to mount her, enter her to the hilt, and, at a snail's pace, pull nearly completely out of her before she was fully conscious and, once she was, to keep going back into her hard and coming out of her easy that way until they both exploded, her with a harsh bark, after which he would put her back to sleep with a soft, hypnotic grind. A gust rippled the lake, causing one of the terns to rise up; it fluttered its wings, then acted dead again. Another eighteen hours, Banyon told himself, maybe even less, before he would have her with him for nearly a whole night. A door closed loud at the back of the motel. Shortly after a voice called out into the woods and, when it did, Banyon recognized it as the voice that had woken him. 'Dog!' Finch hollered. 'Dog! Dog! Are you out there, Dog?'

Eight

Daylight found him keenly aware, in the Rottweiler's absence, that nothing outside of himself was monitoring his every move, or his thoughts, and feeling at once liberated and vaguely frightened, as if he was in the Newport coming fast as hell around a blind corner. Charged with unfocused energy, he got down on the floor and did push-ups until his arm muscles trembled and he couldn't anymore, then he went outside and, for fifteen minutes on the needle-coated ground before the mist-shrouded lake, furiously jumped the weighted rope he carried with the rest of his belongings.

Beneath bluejays raucously chasing each other through the pines, he sat, cooling down, on the bank, across from a man fishing out of a rowboat three-quarters of the way to the far shore, and imagined himself as two people not that well acquainted with each other, both of them clueless to the other's thoughts or intentions. He pictured the first person flashing a series of images – Iris throwing her shirt at Banyon; Finch punching the air around Banyon's ears; the dancing shadows in Iris's window; Walnut mouthing 'Vrooom' through the Newport's windshield; the Rottweiler running hell-bent-for-leather after the Pontiac – to the second one, who found them disturbing, mostly because they struck him as being disjointed and out of context.

Back in the cottage, Banyon dumped onto the bed the entire contents of his gym bag – his dirty clothes, toiletries, bags of candy, boxes of crackers, the Bible he always carried and had never read but a few paragraphs of, a gold-plated harmonica he'd found on a Greyhound bus seat, a snapshot of him and a girl he'd spent a couple of days with holding up their winnings before a Reno craps table, his switchblade, a Yo-Yo, a blank postcard displaying a man wrestling an alligator, a few cheap souvenirs (painted ashtrays, little statuettes) of places he'd stayed at. Looking at his meager belongings made him painfully aware of the holes in his life for which he had no mementos or pictures at all. He carefully repacked the bag, showered, and changed into his work clothes.

He finished prepping the last room on the L's long side in the mid-afternoon, after which, at Finch's request, he put up the pool's diving board and ladders, a string of buoys between the shallow and deep ends, and on the wrought iron gate in the fence surrounding the now crystal clear water a sign that warned FOR USE OF MOTEL GUESTS ONLY. SWIM AT YOUR OWN RISK. Finch came out with Iris, who was holding a camera, to survey the results. 'Nice work, Nat,' he said.

He stripped off his shirt and shoes, stood on the board in his bermudas, struck a weightlifter's pose, and told Iris to take his picture, which she did. Then he dove in and she snapped several more shots of him paddling around. The hair on his body was as white and near as thick as that on his head and with his compact torso he made Banyon think of a big walrus frolicking in the water. Finch wanted Iris to come in, but she had on her work clothes and said she didn't feel like changing into her swimsuit. Finch splashed water at her. She snapped, 'Cut it out!'

'What if I don't?' said Finch.

'You'll find out,' she sternly told him, putting the camera on the table.

'All right, you old stick in the mud,' Finch said, swimming to the ladder nearest her, 'give me a hand out.'

She reached down to him and Finch grasped her hand in one of his hands and the ladder's rail in the other one and started climbing from the pool. Halfway to the deck he suddenly let go of the rail and fell back into the water, pulling Iris with him. She came up sputtering, yelling, 'Goddamn it, Herman!' but she didn't sound as if she was all that angry. Finch splashed her again and she splashed him back, laughing harshly. Her skirt billowed out around her thighs, her under- wear was visible, her shirt was plastered to her chest, her long hair was in her eyes and all over the place, and she was more wildly beautiful than any creature on God's green earth to Banyon, who, if he'd known how to swim, might have jumped into the pool and torn her away from Finch, who now grasped her tightly around the waist so that she couldn't get away. 'Throw me one them big donuts, Nat,' he hollered, nodding at the plastic, circular lifesavers he'd lined up along the fence.

Banyon mechanically picked up and tossed a donut to him. Finch hoisted Iris, who put up only token resistance, into the donut and began spinning her in circles. 'Wait'll I get my hands on you,' she squealed.

'Watch out for the killer shark!' yelled Finch, before diving. A moment later he broke the surface chanting the JAWS theme song and knocked her out of the donut. They wrestled each other in mock earnestness. Banyon was torn up with jealousy watching them. He felt they'd forgotten he was even there. He speculated that his fear of and ineptness in the water was obvious to them and that Finch, foreshadowing this opportunity to show him up before Iris, might even have sensed it way back when he'd ask Banyon to fix the filter. He felt self-conscious, like a third wheel gawking at them. They'd stopped paying attention to him, so he left.

He walked across the parking lot to the Newport, which looked even more like a patchwork to him than it had the day before. Creases and bubbles he hadn't noticed were suddenly visible to him beneath its bad paint job. The trunk door appeared to be off-center, leading him to recall he'd never opened it. He inserted and turned the Chrysler's key in the trunk, then lifted on it. It wouldn't budge. He angrily kicked it. Both it and the left rear door popped open. A couple of oily old rags, a jack, a nearly bald spare tire lay on the trunk floor, which was riddled with three or four bullet-sized holes. For the life of him, Banyon couldn't recollect what had led him to buy the car; he began to feel like a fool for having done so. Raucous laughter and splashing sounded in the pool. 'Here comes Orcá!' shouted Finch.

Banyon shut the trunk and passenger door, got behind the wheel, started the Newport, and pressed down on the accelerator, making the big V-8 roar as if it were an ornery old lion he'd shot a dart into. He backed the car out of its space. Driving it toward the road, he was stopped by Finch, madly flapping his hands and yelling at him from the donut. Iris, treading water to Finch's rear, gazed at the Chrysler with an expression Banyon couldn't read. Finch called out, 'You'll turn some heads with her – count on it, young man!'

Banyon revved the engine with the clutch in. The Newport made a strident backfire. Finch hollered, 'Stop shooting. I surrender!'

'It never done like that yesterday,' Banyon barked out his open window.

'A hot one like her'll let one go just out of excitement now and again, Nat.' Finch waved as if rude noises were to be expected from the car. 'You headed any particular direction?'

'Out for a ride's all.'

'That case whyn't you drive into town, pick up the primer and paint you'll be needing at Felix's Hardware on Main Street? I already ordered and paid for it.'

Banyon nodded.

'Then check and see at the Sears outlet a few doors down if a couple items I sent for come in yet.'

Smiling, Finch flicked his head toward Iris. 'And no need to report in moment you get back, Nat, 'ccount I might be otherwise occupied.'

Banyon burned a long patch of rubber as he left. He hit the highway and goosed the Newport. Its steering wheel had even more play in it than he remembered and on his way to town, he derived some pleasure from periodically lifting his hands from it, allowing the car, which was as wild as ever, to wander precariously close to the shoulder before he would once more grab the wheel and crank it, righting his course in the nick of time. He soon recalled what had sold him on the car, the thrill he got from driving it, a sensation that on this trip blinded him to the Chrysler's deficiencies right up until he turned it off in front of Felix's, when, if he'd thought about it, they would have become blatantly apparent to him again.

No one in the store offered to wait on him before he announced in the paint section that he'd come to pick up Herman Finch's order, at which point a trim, bespectacled male clerk in a Felix's red apron and visor snapped to attention, declaring, 'It'll be just one tiny minute while I shake it up for you. How is Mr. Finch?'

'Seemed pretty good when I left him,' said Banyon.

The man acted fidgety. 'What's he got ya doing for him mostly?'

Banyon nodded at the paint cans. 'This here and a few other little things.'

'Work on and around the premises, you mean?'

'Where else would I be doing it for him?'

This response seemed to relax the man some.

'Generous man, Mr. Finch.'

Banyon wasn't in a mood to agree with him, so he let the declaration dangle.

After he'd mixed the paint, the man handed Banyon half a dozen brushes of various sizes and told him to make sure Mr. Finch knew that Tim Boyer hadn't charged him for them. Then he helped Banyon carry the paint out to the Newport and load it in the trunk. Afterward, he awkwardly seized and shook Banyon's hand. 'Tell Mr. Finch Tim Boyer said "Hi", that he's working his tail off to get square, is putting aside every free penny he makes, and hasn't been anywhere near a craps table, slot machine, or card game in, oh, just ages. Would you do that?'

'If I remember to,' said Banyon.

'I appreciate it, sir,' said Tim Boyer, returning with his swishing gait to the store, 'and you have a good day.'

He ordered a hamburger and lemonade in the Main Street Pub next door to Felix's, but was told they didn't serve food or fancy drinks, so he had a Coke instead. He stared from his bar stool into a narrow, grease-smeared mirror in which his blurred face looked pretty much like the four or five others reflected in it on either side of his. He turned from the mirror and gazed directly at the faces, discovering they belonged to people at least forty years older than him. One was a sag-bellied woman with a glass eye. Another was a dwarf with the shakes. Banyon got the impression they were all angry at him for being young, handsome, and full of energy, and he didn't blame them. The dark, smoke-laden room didn't have a pool table, jukebox, or even a television. The only thing to do in it was to drink and watch your image or someone else's in the worst possible light. Banyon imagined that everyone in the place but him was already dead and hadn't come around to knowing it yet. He wouldn't take near as long to know it about himself, he decided. And he'd never spend a single sunny day, or any day he was breathing, sitting in a bar, waiting to know it. He thought of Iris's wet, sun-drenched body spinning in a life preserver, her harsh laughter, her soaked panties.

Then he thought of Tim Boyer's nervousness and wondered if Boyer owed Finch money. He recalled Finch describing Earl as a 'likable weasel' who'd been deeply in debt when he disappeared. And Pam's rumor about a card dealer being in the lake for crossing or being in the way of his landlord. Remembering his own obligation to the same landlord, Banyon got an aggrieved feeling. He told himself that of the loan sharks he'd encountered, Finch didn't bring to his mind any. On the other hand, no one he'd ever run across brought to his mind Finch or, for that matter – and even more so – Iris. He'd take her away from Finch, Banyon promised himself, standing up to go, and having her would be worth, whatever it cost him.

The huge, sweaty clerk at Sears handed Banyon two packages, one light and rectangular, as if it might contain clothing, the other deeper, squarer, and slightly heavier, remarking, 'Don't let's let nobody get hurt out there, now.'

'From what?' inquired Banyon, mystified by the comment.

The clerk, though, only nodded and smiled oddly at the bigger box.

Banyon stopped the Newport a few minutes later on the

edge of a field of mowed timothy being raked into ribbon-candy-shaped coils by the efforts of a bikini-clad girl in a straw hat operating a Fifties era Case tractor. A redtail hawk scoped for prey from the field's sole tree, an expansive weeping willow that the farm's owner must have judged to be too beautiful to chop down. The scene evoked in Banyon both pure elation and sheer dread. He had an urge to inhale the most potent air he'd ever smelled, to make himself utterly high, to reach the limits of euphoria, at the same time he wanted to turn and run from that place as fast as he could. He understood at that moment that he knew as little about motives – Finch's, Iris's, his own as the hawk knew about why it flew in certain patterns or returned day after day, as Banyon felt certain it did, to that same tree.

He picked up a handful of grass, put it next to his nose, breathed deeply. Its wild, natural scent formed in his mind a picture of Iris, naked as all animals. He imagined their date that evening, the things they would do to one another, the way she would make him feel complete inside instead of half-empty: a painted picture instead of a sketch. His penis got hard as he thought of her. He flung the grass in the air. The tractor driver tipped her hat and yelled something to him over the noise of her machine. Banyon waved and screamed back to her – no words, just a primal shout – but it didn't matter. They were communicating on a more basic level. Banyon hopped into the Newport and, staying erect the whole way, drove fast and reckless to the Deepwater.

He left Finch's packages next to the door separating the residence from the unmanned office, then showered in his cottage, dressed in his only clean dungarees and his one button-down shirt, and sat on his stoop watching the descending sun turn the lake red. At eight, he walked to the near-empty diner, noticing that, with ten or so vehicles parked by newly arrived guests, Finch's Caddy and Indian occupied the lot, though Iris had told him Finch always departed for the casino by that hour on Saturday nights.

The on-duty waitress was a hare lipped girl named Lily, who didn't return his smile, fucked up his order, spilled water on him, and made no apologies. Banyon, though, felt sorry for her because of her lip, which marred an otherwise pretty face, and tipped her big anyway before he returned over the now darkened woods trail to the motel, before which, to his great consternation, Finch's car and motorcycle still sat.

What was the son of bitch waiting for? Why hadn't he gone yet?

Banyon pictured Finch and Iris, five hours after they'd been pawing each other in the pool, still at it, only now on dry sheets, with their clothes off. His belly hurt bad, as if he'd been punched in it. And he felt betrayed, by someone or something, he wasn't sure what – Iris maybe, or Finch, or his own optimism. He entered the office, found it yet unattended, the residence door closed as before, and Finch's packages gone.

Having no idea what he'd say to whoever responded, he banged the service button on the front desk, waited two or three long minutes, then, when no one appeared, rang again. The door's eye-level peephole slot squeaked open. It shut a moment later. The door pushed outward an inch. The room it concealed was darker than the office. Seconds passed. Banyon nervously swallowed. He inclined his head toward the narrow crack, ten feet away. A voice hissed, 'Go through my bedroom window.'

Banyon didn't a hundred percent trust it.

'Make sure no one sees you.'

Then he was sure. 'Where's Herman?' he whispered.

'Where I said he'd be. Walnut gave him a ride.'

The door shut.

Banyon did as he'd been told. Five minutes later he found her waiting for him on a big queen-sized bed in just the tiniest pair of crotchless bikini briefs and all his negative thoughts of her, himself, and other various aspects of the world vanished.

'You smell right.'

'Even down there I do?'

'Especially down here. I'd live happy forever smelling this smell – me and the other wild animals.' He inhaled her. 'I'd follow it anywhere, even if I couldn't see what was giving it off, if I just picked it up in the air somewhere.'

'Like how bees do, you mean?'

'Right into the honey, I would.' He touched her with his tongue. A tremor passed out of her body, into his. 'I'd follow it to hell if it took me there and spend eternity wondering how it could of.'

She moaned. 'God, that feels good, Nat.'

'I'm doing it to.'

'Quit saying why you are and only do it.'

In the woods beyond the window, a whippoorwill repeated its name. Voiceless music played softly on the headboard cassette deck. An overhead fan's rotating blades made a soft thumping noise. All these sounds were as indistinguishable to Banyon as one wave from the next would be if they were breaking over him.

'Watching you two in the pool today 'bout killed me, or made me want to do it to somebody else.'

'You ruin everything, Nat, when you say things like that.'

'I won't say 'em no more, but I don't have to like it.'

'I don't like it either.'

'Then why do you do it?'

'Do what?'

'Act with him that way?'

'I don't ask you why you drive so goddamn fast, do I?'

'I don't get what you mean.'

'Was you who told me we're just the same, Nat.'

Banyon looked off, out the darkened window, toward a slight rustling in the trees. With a sudden shiver, he wondered if the rottweiler might be out there, even while telling himself it couldn't be. 'I think he knows.'

'About us?'

'Not that exactly.'

'Exactly what then?'

'Something. Something about me he does.'

'Past stealing the car?'

'I can't put my finger on what.'

'He knows plenty, I got no idea what all. But he's got a long arm, just ask the people around here beholden to him.'

'Like me, Iris?'

She scowled, not angrily, at him. 'Why did you, Nat?'

'I don't know why, or what made me buy the Newport even. That's the truth.'

She nodded, seeming unsurprised.

'You mad that I did?'

She shook her head. 'He did that way to me too.'

'Did how?'

'Got hold of me, without me even knowing it. He can do that better than anybody.'

'That why you married him?'

She frowned self-consciously. 'I didn't add up to much back then, Nat.'

'Back then don't matter to me, just now.'

'And the guy I was traveling with come to even less.'

What had seemed like disparate data intersected in Banyon's thoughts. 'Did he deal cards?'

'He did till those Onondagans found out two days after they hired him he wasn't even a little bit Indian like he claimed to be, after which they let us hang around the tables till we'd crapped out.'

'How'd it lead you here?'

'Robbie had met Herman at the casino. We came looking to bum a room for the night and Herman offered to hire us both on until we could put together enough cash to get moving again, only Robbie must of got tired before then of flipping burgers or of me or of both and disappeared one night with all I owned, which wasn't much, plus, according to Herman, what was in the office cash register.' She stared past the screen, into the blackness issuing its mystifying sounds. 'Left me without a penny to my name, no clothes, no car, and nobody to turn to but Herman, who'd been coming on to me before then, and, after, came on a lot stronger and looked to me a lot better.'

'A rumor I heard,' Banyon said, 'puts Robbie in the lake.'

Gazing up from his groin, meeting his open mouthed stare, dark blue eyes, reflecting the room's scant light, urged something from him – a declaration, a promise – he wasn't sure what.

'Don't stop, Iris, please!' Her mouth full, head bobbing, eyes never leaving his, wanting what? Maybe just to watch, to recognize in him the same animalism he had brought out in her, to see the power she held over him, to confirm to herself that a moment existed when he was capable of doing or agreeing to anything. His hands gripping the back of her neck. Pressing against her ears. Begging. Railing. Demanding. His gasp. 'I'm going to – Iris! – okay?'

Her only reply to keep doing what she was until, her eyes still locked with his, she made the question moot. Had that meant she'd wanted to? Not minded? Not understood?

Her head bob, as she swallowed.

Rolling over, they were hardly aware of changing positions. Their coupling on the ceiling in shadows, impossible for them to see. Her hands choking the bed rails, her knees denting the mattress, her face wetting the pillow, her muffled voice urging – commanding – him, on all fours over her, to put it higher up – Not there! Here! In this! – to push harder into that tight place, go deeper, move faster, to do with her what he'd not done with anyone before because doing that with a woman struck him as trusting her with a veiled piece of himself. But she made his fear of confiding in her go away. She made whole parts of him go away, parts that told him to shut up, be careful, protect your ass and your innermost secrets from the world. She told him of all the ways Herman had made or tried to make it with her, she'd never allowed him to make it that way.

'You want to look at it, Nat?'

'I'll look at it if you want to show it to me.'

She toweled off his back, after their shower. 'I only want to show it to you if you want to look at it.'

'Where is it?'

'Upstairs.'

'There's only one reason to look at it, right?'

She wrapped the towel around his waist. 'Never mind. We don't have to look at it.'

She walked naked out of the bathroom in front of him and down the hall. Banyon followed her. 'There's something else I'd rather do.'

'I'm too sore right now to do any more of what you'd

rather do.' She sat down on the edge of the bed, picked up her underpants, pulled them on. 'I think you didn't get enough love when you were a kid, Nat. Am I right?'

'I don't know what is enough. I guess I never had it at all.'

She widened her eyes at him, stood up, walked to the closet, and got a robe. 'You want to watch television?'

'Nope.'

'We could play a card game.'

'When do you expect Herman'll come back?'

'Not till nearly daylight.'

'I want to finish the job he hired me for and I don't want to leave here owing him nothing.'

'You don't want to owe him nothing?'

'Terms of what he and I agreed to, I mean.'

She laughed shortly. 'That's funny.'

'What's funny about it?'

'I think he'll look at it as you owing him plenty.'

Banyon shrugged. 'That's different.'

'Different in what way?'

'I gave him my word on painting the place. He ain't given me a reason to break it.'

She made the hollow laugh again, then walked over and tenderly kissed him on the cheek. 'How 'bout Parcheesi, Nat? You want to play a game of Parcheesi?'

'Take me up to look at it.'

'I don't want to talk you into anything, Nat. We can just enjoy what we got while we got it' – she squeezed his arm – 'take everything we can from it until . . .'

'I'm not going to do that.'

'If you really mean that, Nat, I'm the luckiest woman alive.'

'He owes you, you said.'

'I'd say he owes me. I'd say he owes me plenty.'

'I ought to see the setup at least.'

'Put your pants on then, and I'll show you.'

A big wooden desk, a swivel chair, an eight-foot pool table, a puffy three-cushioned couch positioned beneath a suspended wall rack holding three rifles and a tube-shaped camera lens sat on a thick rug amid the pleasing smell of unsmoked tobacco. Framed photographs of landscapes, water, people decorated the walls. Banyon nodded at a shot of a fit, muscular boxer, around his age, in the classic fighter's stance. 'That him?'

Iris nodded.

Finch looked more than capable of taking care of himself. Banyon had the sensation of staring backward at him through a small, one-dimensional window. It struck him that Iris would be quite taken with this Finch. He wondered if Finch, in his mind's eye, saw himself as he had been then, and if he believed the rest of the world did as well. On a shelf above the desk, two cigars of the sort Finch sucked on but never lit were broken into pieces, as if to make their smell more prominent. A military decoration of some kind lay in an open box next to them. 'He saved some people,' said Iris, 'in a war.'

Banyon looked at her.

'I'm not exactly sure how. Or when.' She nodded at a photo of Finch in an Army infantryman's uniform, one arm encircling a tall, black-haired woman in a bridal dress. 'I'm his number four.'

'Where's one, two, and three?'

She shrugged. 'He loves me the most, he says.'

'I love you the most, Iris.'

Her expression at him, which was neither overly warm nor overly cold, he couldn't interpret. 'He used to bring me dancing some.'

Banyon pulled at a couple of the desk drawers and found them locked.

'He still does take us to dinner Sunday nights at a place in town.'

'He's a nice man.'

'I've decided that's maybe the scariest thing about him.'

Banyon pointed to a closed door left of them. 'In there, right?'

She nodded. 'I've been in here maybe six times, the last when I came up to tell him something – I don't remember what – and didn't wait for him to answer my knock. He was crouched over it – I could see some big wads with rubber bands around them – and he shut it and told me, not mean or anything but there was no mistaking he meant it, never to walk in on him again that way and, then, real quiet like, not to forget I was his wife.'

'Not to forget you were his wife?'

She flicked at her hair. 'I took it he meant keep my mouth shut.'

Banyon strode to the door and opened it on a deep closet; a locked filing cabinet, supporting two upright fishing rods, faced him at arm's length; a fighter's heavy bag slouched against the wall right of it; on the clothes bar hung rubber waders, a hunting vest, worn leather boxing gloves, a speed bag. 'He work out still?'

'Until lately he hasn't.'

Banyon stepped into the closet.

'Now I hear him up here every night.'

Banyon glanced over his shoulder at her.

'He says you've rejuvenated him.'

Banyon couldn't register what that meant, though Finch had told him nearly the same thing. It made him feel almost embarrassed for Finch. The two boxes he'd picked up at Sears were stacked on the floor left of him; a .45 Magnum dangled in its holster from a hook above them. 'He doesn't make me work for him, Nat.'

'What?'

'He'd just as soon hire someone to clean the rooms and tend the gift shop. I won't let him, though, because I don't want to feel beholden to him.'

Banyon heard her step to the desk side nearest him.

'Even so, I can't get away from knowing that I am.'

'I am to a whole slew of people,' Banyon heard himself say. He kneeled down on the floor, ran his hand over the rug, searched for a crease. 'I got rotated around from family to family. Most of 'em were pretty nice, but I can't hardly remember which ones now.' He found it, put his fingers beneath it, pulled upward. The rug came away, revealing a wood piece fit into the rest of the floor. 'A few years I was in a group home with a lot of others in the same way. They were pretty nice to me there too. Sometimes I wish I could remember a few of 'em better. Usually, though, I pray not to.'

Iris, facing him, half-sat on the desk edge, pressing her butt into the wood. 'Nat's an orphan?'

Banyon yanked up the wedge, revealing the safe. 'Till he got here he was.'

Blinking rapidly, as if against a bright light, Iris's deep-set eyes recalled to Banyon hibernating animals, of a species foreign to him, prodded from sleep. 'This might blow your mind.'

'What might?'

'Me and him – we are too.'

'You and Herman?'

She nodded.

Banyon couldn't put into words how the knowledge affected him. He pointed at the safe, a heavy-duty Sentry with a combination lock. 'What else do I need to know?'

'I don't have any idea what its combination is or where he's got it writ down.'

Banyon stared at her.

Iris didn't respond to him and didn't turn away from him either.

Banyon kept looking at her.

'I love you, Nat.'

'Are you still sore?'

'Not so bad.'

Struck by the reality of what they were contemplating, Banyon told her, 'Let's close this up now and go back downstairs.'

Nine

Pam told him a nighthawk had knocked itself out colliding with her apartment window that dawn and had just laid there on the building's terrace until, in a few minutes, it raised its head and peered around every which way as if it was scared and maybe had amnesia, so she'd picked it up, placed it in her lap, softly rubbed its back with a finger, and whispered to it things she'd figured would be most important to it. 'You know about building a good home above a nice country field and learning to glide high enough off the ground to pick out mice or rabbits or whatever else to eat and to steer clear of assholes with guns and to find a mate better than a worthless buzzard.'

'A hawk wouldn't take up with a buzzard no how.'

'It might if it's brain was scrambled, stud.'

'What did it do when you were talking at it?'

'It listened, by God – unlike any other creature with a cock and balls I've ever met – and when it heard all it needed or cared to, it flew off.'

'Coffee black and a honeybun, Pam,' Finch growled, entering the diner, dangling the larger of the two Sears boxes in one hand. He sat down opposite Banyon, laying the package on the floor beneath their booth. His eyes looked shot. He hadn't shaved in a while. The cigar in his shirt pocket was mashed as if maybe he'd slept on it. He asked when Pam and Banyon had last seen Dog. Pam didn't have a clear recollection of the time. Banyon said he didn't either. Finch said, 'It's been gone three nights now.'

Overnight guests fueling up to hit the road, a booth full of Indians, a mini-crew of Mexican laborers, a pair of Ma and Pa Kettle types at the counter between two lone male coffee drinkers comprised the midmorning crowd. 'Likely off chasing something,' said Pam.

Finch watched her pour coffee into his cup. 'It ain't never for more'n a day before.'

Banyon couldn't believe now he'd kidnapped Dog, or even remember why he had, if he'd ever known. He said, 'Maybe it got an itch to move on.'

Finch just looked at him.

Picturing the Rottweiler's teeth ripping into the porterhouse, then it tearing down the road after him, Banyon was some angry at Finch for missing the dog so much; on the other hand, seeing Finch sitting there as if he'd lost a piece of himself, he felt a little sorry for him. He shrugged. 'It being a stray, how you said.'

'What I said is that nobody I knew of owned it 'fore me.'

'Better watch out he ain't too nice to you, stud' – Pam picked up Banyon's empty juice glass – 'or he'll come to thinking he owns you too for taking you in and treating you decent.'

Finch's face turned a dark shade Banyon had never seen it before. 'I can't remember what it was made me hire you, Pam. Go 'head – remind me.'

To Banyon's surprise Pam lowered her gaze and didn't reply.

From a booth near the rest rooms someone hollered for

a refill. Finch's cheeks slowly lost their flush. 'Hop to it, girl.'

Pam quickstepped it toward the coffeepots in the alcove right of the counter. The gift shop door opened; a pregnant lady in a purple sack dress carrying under one arm a little painted Indian drum walked out. Banyon pictured Iris behind the shop's register in the same nice blouse and cream-colored skirt he'd first seen her in, responding to questions about the gifts – if they were handmade, by who, and from what. He visualized how her hair was fixed, the smell of her perfume, the color of her underwear, the still tender place beneath it. 'It wouldn't just light out on me, Nat. Not's good as I treat it.'

Banyon faced Finch again, concerned that Finch had noticed him eyeing the shop entrance. 'I gave Dog a home and nobody can tell me, goddamn it, Dog didn't think highly of Herman Finch.'

'Maybe it liked you and the Deepwater just fine, Herman, till it happened onto something it liked better.'

Finch cocked his head at Banyon, as if examining him for the first time from a whole different angle. 'Maybe it what?'

Banyon spun a finger around the rim of his cup. 'I've heard anyway – a wandering nature is bred in the bone.'

Finch slapped a hand on the table, making the dishes jump. 'That's a damn depressing view of animal nature, young man!'

'A bear maybe killed it,' Pam suggested, putting Banyon's pancake order down in front of him.

Finch picked up Banyon's plate and made a big show of looking under it. 'I don't see my honeybun. Where could it be?'

Pam told him, 'A fresh batch'll be out the oven in five minutes.'

'Ain't an animal with fur around here bad enough could

murder Dog.' Finch shoved his cup at her. 'Something's fishy' – he sniffed the air – 'that's Herman Finch's conclusion.'

Pam gave them more coffee. 'How 'bout you get the cops out here to drag the lake, Herman, case it drowned swimming in it.'

'Go get my goddamned honeybun, Pam.' Finch glowered at her. 'I don't care if it's cooked or a lump of raw dough – and bring it to me in a takeout bag. I haven't got all day to sit here waiting on it.' He reached beneath the table and picked up the box as she departed. 'I hate a wiseass, Nat, male or female.'

He shoved the package at Banyon.

Banyon stared at it, picturing the Sears clerk saying, 'Let's not let nobody get hurt out there now.'

'For you,' declared Finch.

Banyon looked at him.

Finch made a sly smile.

'What?' asked Banyon.

'You'll find out,' answered Finch.

Banyon suddenly felt everyone in the restaurant was watching him. Sweat formed on his brow; it slowly rolled down his cheeks as he deliberately pierced the brown wrapping with a fingernail. He pulled his finger toward him, removed the paper from the box. He heard Finch giggle. He saw himself throwing down the package and running from the diner. Instead he quickly opened it. Inside lay a pair of Everlast leather boxing gloves. 'Extra large,' Finch told him.

Unable to recall ever having received such an expensive gift before, Banyon was suspicious about why he'd been given this one. He took the gloves from the box, held them up to the light. One of the Mexicans whistled admiringly. With a hand motion Finch encouraged Banyon to try them on. Banyon did. They fit perfectly. 'Those are regulation sixteen-ounce gloves, young man.'

'It's mighty generous of you, Herman. I'm grateful.'

Finch waved dismissively.

'This is the first I've even wore any.' Banyon wiggled his fingers in the gloves. 'I just always got it on with my bare hands.'

'Real fighters do it with gloves, Nat' – Finch nodded gravely – 'by an agreed upon set of rules.'

'Like no biting, kicking, or head butting?'

'Or hitting below the belt.' Finch threw a couple of air-bombs across the table. 'Think you'd like to get it on with me?'

'With you?'

'Go at it the way I just said. In a ring.'

'I don't think I'd feel right about it, Herman.'

'Why wouldn't you?'

Banyon smiled uncomfortably. 'I'm quite a bit younger than you, for one thing.'

'You're telling me you are.' Finch dipped a shoulder, feinted at Banyon, bobbed his head a few times. 'Your reach is longer too, you're in a hell of a lot better shape, you're faster, and, from what I've seen, your hands might even be quicker.'

Banyon didn't respond, hoping Finch's words would end the discussion.

Finch, though, kept looking at him. Banyon wasn't sure if he'd been asked to spar or if he'd actually been challenged to a fight. He wondered if Finch, who wore a bemused expression, had somehow learned of Banyon's duplicity, if maybe he'd whiffed Banyon in the house somewhere or on Iris, and this was his response. Within the big gloves, his hands began to perspire. He was aware of the gift shop door opening a little behind him and to his right, but he didn't dare look at it. Not taking his eyes from Banyon's, Finch waved to the person who'd opened the door or to someone who'd come out of the room. 'Hand me your water, would you, Nat?'

Banyon glanced at his water glass, then back at Finch.

'I want to show you something.'

Banyon reached for the glass and, remembering too late he was wearing the gloves, knocked it down, splashing water on the table and sending the glass skittering off its edge; Finch left-handedly snatched the glass like a fly out of the air. A cluster of nearby patrons applauded the catch. Female laughter Banyon suspected might be Iris's sounded to his rear. His look at Finch reflected his pissed-off feeling at being made a fool of. 'On the other hand, Nat' – Finch placed the glass upright between them – 'I've got an experience edge on you.'

Banyon heard the gift shop door close. He glanced at it, but didn't see Iris or whoever had opened it. He looked at Finch again. 'We'll make it a festive event, Nat. Maybe roast a pig around the pool 'forehand.'

'What?'

'And I'll get a few people I know to put a purse together – give the winner a decent pay day.' He smiled at Banyon.

'I don't want to fight you, Herman.'

'You'd be doing this old man a favor if you would, Nat, more than you already have just by being the good-looking, strong-as-a-bull, cocksure son of a bitch that you are, and I say that with gratitude.' He reached over and clapped Banyon's shoulder. 'I look at you and see me thirty years ago and get juiced up wondering if my older, smarter self can whup my own youthful ass.'

Again forgetting about the gloves, Banyon put a hand to his brow to wipe it and conked himself in the head.

'You better take those off, Nat, 'fore you KO yourself.'

Pam arrived and handed Finch his honeybun in a grease-

soaked paper bag, as Banyon wrestled to remove the gloves.
'You going skiing, stud?'

Banyon ignored her.

'Me and Nat are going to rumble.' Finch put a napkin in
the bag. 'That is if Nat'll agree to it.'

Banyon got off the gloves and tossed them back in the box,
viewing Finch's proposed fight as a no-win situation for him,
one that could result only in his being accused of pummeling
an old man or, in the unlikely event the bout went Finch's
way, laughed at for getting beaten up by someone old enough
to be his grandfather. And what would Iris think? He said, 'I
ain't mad enough at you to do it, Herman. I ain't even mad at
you at all.'

'What's that got to do with the price of eggs? I'm talking
about a gentleman's competition, Nat, and a shot at some
good money.'

'How much money?'

'I can only tell you at the moment it wouldn't be peanuts, by
which I'm referring to just the purse – never mind side bets.'

Pam walked away shaking her head.

Finch stood up. 'Whatever you decide, Nat, the gloves are
yours.' He started for the door, then abruptly stopped, turned
back to Banyon, reached into his pocket, and pulled out a
thick wad of bills. 'I almost forgot – payday.'

He peeled off two fifties, four tens, and five ones, then
handed them to Banyon, who, with his overtime, figured he'd
earned another hundred, which Finch had deducted as a
payment toward the Newport. 'Just twenty more weeks as
full as this one, young man' – Finch put away his remaining
wad – 'and that hot rod'll be all yours.'

Banyon tossed rocks in the lake, wishing he knew how to
swim. He'd of settled for having a boat or even a fishing pole.

If he had church clothes, he could at least go to church, he thought, and listen to some music. When he got bored or lonely as a kid he would find a tree to perch in, but he was too old for that now. He went up to the pool and sat next to an old black guy with a wood leg who claimed his biggest regret in life was that he hadn't told his boss at the factory where he'd bottled pickles for thirty years to fuck himself about five days into the job. A humungous woman Banyon had never seen before wheeled the maid's cart along the corridor outside the rooms.

Two kids in life jackets paddled circles around their pale-bodied parents, who drank canned beer from Styrofoam floaties. Bumblebees noisily pollinated purple columbine and clover at the road's edge. Finch and Iris, both nicely dressed, came out and got in the Caddy. 'I got to live with the fact I kissed a man's ass for three decades,' the retired pickle worker told Banyon while twisting the top from a schnapps pint in his lap, 'for a little peace on a job didn't even pay me a pension.'

He put the bottle to his lips. As he drank his mouth made gulping, bait-snatching movements. His hand choked the bottle and shook. From the departing Caddy Finch hollered to Banyon they were going to a picnic and wouldn't be back until evening. Iris's hair blew out the passenger window. The radio was playing loud Spanish music. Banyon had an abstract vision of a long line of people leaving, walking away, abandoning him. An empty feeling in his stomach formed from an empty feeling in his head. He was certain that if he screamed at that moment no one would hear him. Offering him the pint, the retired pickle worker said, 'My whole life could have been different. That's what gnaws at me.'

Banyon took the bottle. 'Don't talk to me no more about pickles.'

'If you think this is about pickles,' the man retorted, 'you're in brine up to your ears.'

Banyon snatched the bottle's top from the table between them, recapped the pint, and returned it to the man. 'Don't talk to me no more about what you shoulda done.'

'I'm just saying what happened to the balls I was born with.'

'One more word on it and I'll throw you in the pool.'

The man shut up.

'You can talk to me about something else if you want to,' Banyon told him, but either the man didn't want to or couldn't think of something else. He closed his eyes and lay his head back against his lounger. In a few minutes, he started to snore. Banyon got up and went over to the office, where a snaggletoothed stringbean, reading *People* behind the desk, introduced himself as Hugh Muskrat, register fill-in whenever Finch needed him and the boyfriend of the week-end maid, Carol Small Eagle, whom Muskrat urged Banyon to rate, looks-wise, from one to ten. Banyon declined on the grounds he'd glimpsed her for only a few seconds, from a distance. 'Sugarcoat it, why don't ya,' Muskrat mumbled dejectedly, putting his head back in his magazine.

Banyon left and walked around behind the motel. He hiked west through the woods, which got thicker and thicker until, after not very many minutes, he could hardly move in them. Twenty feet from a hognose snake warming itself on a moss-shrouded rock, he took a quarter from his pocket and began to flip, catch, then slap it onto the back of his opposite hand. A pileated woodpecker hammered on a rotten tree above him. A canopy of dense pine boughs filtered the sun's glare, permitting in only narrow light-bands. A hundred times he flipped the quarter, making it come up heads exactly as often as tails. He tried to see beyond the treetops, to where he conjectured forever to be. The knowledge that he didn't know much, which made other people – Finch, for example – seem to know a lot struck him. He put the coin away, retraced his steps to the rear of the motel, and stood before Iris and Finch's bedroom window, through the screen of which a light breeze riffled the closed curtain. He put his fingers on the screen, checked to make sure no one was watching, and, remembering how Iris had snapped it out by pulling on it, pushed lightly. Nothing happened. He pushed harder. The screen fell into the room. Hoisting himself over the ledge, Banyon quickly followed it.

He had no idea what he was after: knowledge maybe, information that would put him on a more even footing with everyone else at the Deepwater who impressed him with knowing more than him, one thing, maybe, that would make everything else – Iris's behavior, Finch's, even his own, especially his own – more sensible to him. On Iris's side of the bed, which retained a faint odor of her, he lay down, gazing up at the ceiling, as he imagined she did each night as she lay next to Finch, trying to think what she would think, but he soon realized he didn't have a clue, that as much as Finch hid a cache of money, she kept a cache of private thoughts.

An aspirin bottle, a Kleenex box, a water-stained paperback, on its cover a picture of a half-naked man and woman galloping on a lathered-up horse, lay on her headboard. From between the book's pages protruded a torn strip of manila paper, adorned by several completed games of tic-tac-toe; the X's were in blue, the O's in red, suggesting to Banyon that Iris had played the games with Finch or, pretending to be two people, had done so alone; his mind drew contrasting pictures – the first of a couple being casually intimate in bed, the second of a husband and wife miles apart on the same mattress – and he didn't know which to believe. Alternate versions of

reality faced him as they had from his first day at the Deepwater. Great or atrocious luck had befallen him. Either he was
in sweet clover or deep shit.

In the cupboard above Iris's pillow were three books with
covers similar to the first one; a prescription bottle of a
medicine he couldn't pronounce; an encased diaphragm;
spermicide; a snapshot of a seaside beach house; a book of
poetry; a sheaf of pencils; a miniature drawing pad containing
several sketches given one-word names – LIE, smooth, dark
water like that backing the motel; FACT, one boxer pummeling another one; HOME, a beach house similar to the one in
the photograph; LOVE, two sets of bodiless eyes locked with
each other; HATE, nearly the same sketch as LOVE; MAN,
stacks of cash piled high on a table; WOMAN, a few scattered
bills on a dirt floor; BOO, a huge dog, maybe the Rottweiler,
staring outward; HEAVEN, a hand waving goodbye; TRUTH, a
blank page.

Banyon didn't even know she could draw.

A summer nightie lay beneath her pillow. He put it to his
face and smelled her. A moment later, feeling ashamed, he
stood up from the bed and rearranged the coverlet.

The thought occurred to him that something at the Deepwater – the air around it, or the buildings themselves – had
transformed him into a person he hadn't been a week before,
someone he was waiting to meet or who had been waiting to
meet him. In the mirror above the bureau, he studied his face,
but detected in it no obvious differences. He couldn't dismiss
the possibility, however, that an alteration of himself might
include his own inability to recognize it. He began looking in
the bureau drawers, which were in two parallel columns.
Those to his right, which he opened first, contained clothes
clearly belonging to Iris. A few items of sexy lingerie, among
them the crotchless panties Banyon had made love to her

through, or a similar pair, occupied the bottom drawer with her underthings, sleeping attire, and a battery operated dildo.

At that moment Banyon remembered glancing into the open door of a room in which two people – they must have been a set of foster parents – were humping each other and the feeling that he'd not seen enough and, at the same time, had seen too much. He quickly shut the drawers. The odd, dizzying thought entered his mind that he could have done a lot worse than to have had Finch as his father. He recalled then what he and Iris were contemplating doing to Finch. 'There's more than one side to it,' he told his reflected self.

Not caring to study on all the possible sides to it, he opened the top drawer in the bureau's left column.

A compartmentalized tray serving as a depository for cuff links, a jackknife, an old-fashioned pocket watch, a nail file, loose change had been placed in half the drawer. Socks and underwear took up the remaining space. A mostly hidden paper object stuck out from beneath one side of the clothes; Banyon reached under them and extracted the object, which turned out to be two envelopes from a developing lab. He carefully removed the four-inch-by-four-inch color photographs they contained and, one at a time, lay them atop the coverlet.

The first grouping showed Iris, naked or near to it, a dozen different ways. She posed coyly, sweetly, seductively. Then more graphically. She was captured while blowing Finch, whose face was marred by the white flash his camera made as it snapped at their mirrored image. A microscopic look at her ass and pudendum, under a harsh light, filled an entire frame. Banyon had an urge to blot out what Finch had exposed of her. At the same time, seeing her frozen in certain postures made him hot.

Now, in the second bunch, she was at work behind the

desk, now emerging from the woods trail, now watering the shrubbery surrounding the pool. Here was the same stretch of highway before the motel at three different hours; guests walking to the pool, to their vehicles, to the ice machine; a long view of the woods-obscured lake, during sunset, in moonlight, being pelted by rain; Banyon trudging through the forest toward his cottage; a small piece of the cottage through the trees; the Rottweiler chewing a large bone; the LeMans parked in the lot, then Banyon behind its wheel; the Rottweiler staring at two strangers going into a room, at Banyon, at Iris; the one-armed-bandit junkie unlocking her Dart; kids playing catch in the outdoor corridor; the Newport alone, then Banyon getting out of it; Iris biting into a sandwich; Banyon, scraping paint, sitting on the portico stoop, downing a lemonade, eyeing Iris passing him with her maid's cart. Banyon realized with a jolt that each shot had been taken not just of, around, or at the Deepwater, but from inside the main building; in every case it appeared that the photographer had been in either the office or in the room adjoining it in Finch's residence.

At the bottom of the second stack, a black-and-white close-up of Finch, which looked around the same vintage as the boxing photo on his office wall, showed him climbing from the driver seat of a white muscle car. The scene was familiar to Banyon, who couldn't put a finger on why, until he looked back at the photo of himself stepping from the Newport. He did a double-take. The two pictures depicted not only remarkably similar occurrences, but striking physical resemblances, he thought, between himself and the young Finch. He peered more closely at the two identically shaped sedans they were exiting. He felt his heart skip a beat. Finch's muscle car, concluded Banyon, was his own Newport, thirty-odd years and an untold number of paint jobs ago.

An object whirred past his head. At first he imagined it had sliced right through him. Then it was all around the room. A bird of some kind. Banyon swung at and behind it, trying to head it back out the window it had entered by, but it wouldn't go. It dive-bombed at him, then, as he ducked, veered left, exited through the hallway door, and winged off toward the guts of the house. Banyon cursed. Chasing it didn't cross his mind; only getting the hell gone from there did. After putting everything back as near as he remembered to how he'd found it, he picked up off the floor a blue feather, evidently dropped by the bird, crawled outside, replaced the screen, then cleared out.

Ten

Above the lake, a meteorite shower occurred; silent traces, like God's finger slashes, sliced through the sky. In a gentle breeze the tops of the trees lining the shore swayed in rhythm with the water's hypnotic lapping. Fish snatched flies out of the air, then returned to eat them in the dark silence they had leapt from. Banyon tried to remember Finch ever asking him to pose for a picture or even having seen him with a camera, and couldn't. He wondered if certain lives repeated themselves through the ages and in what life Finch had first met him. Had he a home or a family somewhere he might've left and returned to it or them; but where he was at, and the people there with him, were as much as he knew of home or family, and his memories of the world behind him were less a refuge to him than they were a hell.

A poster offering two Finch-funded rewards – of five hundred dollars for information leading to the Rottweiler's return and of seven complimentary Deepwater dinners for a verifiable account of how a bluejay had found its way into his kitchen the previous evening – took up half the diner's bulletin board. 'He thinks he's the target of a conspiracy,' Pam told Banyon.

Banyon ordered a breakfast of pancakes and sausage.

'Course I never know when he's serious,' she said.

'I get the feeling more and more he never ain't.'

She wrote down his order.

Banyon sipped his water. 'Why's he want to fight me, Pam?'

Pam shrugged. 'Don't ask me why men ever want to.' She peered coyly at him. 'What reason did he tell you?'

'Something about wanting to see if he can beat himself at my age up.'

'You think he can?'

'I don't know if he can himself, but I'd wager he can't me.'

'Guess you can put as much money on yourself as you want to you take him up on it.'

'Which of us'd get yours?'

'Since my last marriage bottomed out, stud, don't nobody get it but me.'

Though the temperature remained high, the humidity lessened. Banyon put in ten-, sometimes twelve-hour days all week and was thankful to be able to. He got the motel prepped and a coat of primer on it. Working, he tried not to think, but he felt as if a thought valve had been turned on in his mind that opened wider and wider the more he attempted to close it. He did his best to hate Finch, but only half-succeeded at it. His orphaned self maybe even liked – loved? – Finch more than ever after learning Finch cared enough about him to take and save snapshots of Banyon as Banyon imagined his own father, if he'd had one, might have. Iris's lover, on the other hand, couldn't forget the pornography of her and the pictures of the Newport and of Finch and of himself looking like young Finch's twin and how Finch – or someone – had been secretly photographing him for God or the devil knew what purpose, memories that made his insides go all cold, as if a frigid hand had reached up out of a grave and grabbed them.

He woke up in a lightning storm, dreaming that Finch was waiting to photograph his corpse and that Iris was sketching him dying.

'Help!' he hollered.

The dead who'd walked before him shook the cabin with their thunderous laughter. They pissed on his roof. Eternity's giant cameras flashed at him.

'The lighting in here, it's not so good. It makes everything darker.'

'That's part of it probably, but not all of it.'

'Well, I trimmed my hair yesterday.' He pointed to where. 'Just a little off the back. I like it close, against my neck.'

She shook her head. 'Maybe it's not that you look different at all. But that you're looking at me different.'

'I don't think so. No.'

'Do I look different to you?'

'Now you're saying it's you, not me, that does?'

'I'm saying if I do to you, then maybe that makes you look at me different and makes me think you're the one does when it's really me.'

Banyon wanted to ask her about them, Finch's photographs – and about her drawings – but he was afraid of how the knowledge that he'd searched her bedroom would sit with her; a tiny flicker in her right eye suggested to him not well. 'I can't follow it no more.'

She got up from the laundry room floor, on which they'd risked a twenty-minute quickie while Finch ate lunch, and pulled her pants on. 'You were supposed to say, "You look as beautiful to me as ever, Iris, and I love you." '

'You do, Iris. And I do.'

'He's getting ready for you.'

Banyon looked at her.

'Every night he is. Boom. Boom. Boom.'

'I ain't even told him I'd do it yet.'

'You'll do it.'

'What makes you so sure?'

'You came after me, didn't you.'

Like all aspects of his life, the fighting he had done to that point had been instinctual. Or emotional. A physical response to the pushing of buttons attached in his brain to fear, anger, perceived threats, etc. Sometimes the person who'd pushed them got hurt, but never Banyon. No one trounced him. Not since he'd been on his own.

The endeavor itself – throwing punches and avoiding them – was to him as spraying stink was to a skunk. He didn't do it out of enjoyment. Or even from choice. Never had he planned a battle; he'd either found himself in one or about to be. Making something, such as the Deepwater or its swimming pool, look or function better than before he'd worked on it gave him a certain amount of pride, but not pummeling someone; from that he derived no thrill, only a sense that he had successfully maintained the small space God had apportioned him. If he had to think about doing it, actually plan out a thrashing, he wasn't sure he could bring it off, at least not very well, especially of an old pops he wished around half the time was his father.

Finch hadn't directly pressed him to commit to the fight, though he seemed to be readying himself for one. He nearly scared Banyon into falling off the stepladder he was on by sneaking up behind him and loudly slapping his own bare gut, flattened and hardened some by his evening workouts, declaring, 'Ten flabby pounds of me is history.'

112

Banyon eyed him up and down, nodded with what he hoped would pass for admiration.

Finch flexed his biceps. 'I feel capable, young man, of tearing out a bear's asshole. What do you think of that?'

'You look good, Herman.'

Finch did a Tarzan fist-pound on his chest. 'My tits are all but gone, Nat — did you notice?'

Banyon nodded. 'I don't see much of 'em.'

'How old am I, Nat?'

'I don't know,' answered Banyon.

'Guess.'

Banyon shrugged. 'Fifty?'

'Wrong.' Finch palm-banged his belly again. 'I'm not going to say the number out loud, because from the one you're at it you couldn't take it in.' The look he gave Banyon froze him internally and made him recall the separate photos of Finch and of him in which they looked nearly identical while climbing from, some three decades apart and in almost the exact manner, what Banyon felt certain was the same car. 'Only you can believe I've lived your life twice over and so have seen where you're coming from and' — Finch made a circular motion with one arm — 'where you're headed.'

'When?'

'What?'

'When did you see them places?'

'You're at it again, Nat' — Finch made a sneaky expression — 'coming at me with all that mystical stuff.'

Banyon had the disturbing sensation that whatever he could or might say at that moment, Finch would be anticipating, that, at one time or another, Finch had felt, and maybe even spoken, every conscious and subconscious thought in Banyon's mind. So he said nothing. Turning back to the motel, he resumed working. He sensed Finch, still behind the ladder, watching him. 'You one a them that sees in your head what she'll look like when you get done with her, Nat, or the kind that can't see past each part of the getting there?'

Banyon glanced over his shoulder, whereupon Finch made a smooth, up-and-down brushing motion with one hand. Banyon felt almost as he had once in the Rottweiler's presence. 'I try to make each of 'em while I'm on her,' he told Finch, 'feel near to right as I can.'

'Strokes, you mean?'

'What?'

Finch did the movement with his hand again.

'Yeah. If it's painting I'm doing.'

Finch studied him with acute interest. In fact, Banyon prided himself on trying to make every stroke perfect by applying, first, just enough paint or primer to his brush-head, then just enough pressure to its handle to cover completely the swathe without losing even a drop. 'What about what she'll be when you finish with her?'

'If I do every part of her that way she'll come out way you want her to.'

Finch stepped back and appraised the work Banyon had done so far with an estimable nod. 'You tried out your gloves yet?'

'Who'm I gone try 'em out on?'

'I got a heavy bag I ain't using you can haul down your cottage you want to.'

Banyon shook his head. 'I can't see no reason to it, though I thank you, Herman.'

'I'd be surprised I couldn't put together enough of a purse for you to pay off your car you win it.'

'I wouldn't feel good 'bout how I done it.'

Finch slowly shook his head, as if to indicate Banyon had misperceived his offer. 'What I'm proposing, Nat, it may be illegal if the law cared about it, which it don't, but it ain't a bad thing or a dishonest thing. It's about the most honest thing, in fact, two men can do.'

Banyon laid his brush carefully atop the primer can on the ladder's highest rung. 'Maybe, Herman – if you want – we could spar some.'

'Together?'

'See where we're at, you know – before agreeing on a big shebang.'

'Strikes me as bad tactics for both sides, Nat – like sending the enemy your flight plan 'fore you bomb 'em.'

A covey of spandex-clad bikers, their ride's tires clicking uniformly, whizzed by on the road. 'There's lots of people would fight you, Herman.'

'I expect so, Nat.'

Banyon waited several seconds for Finch to add to his response, but he didn't. He stood on the lawn, watching with Banyon dozens of grackles, like wind-borne ashes, fly over the motel before putting down in a heavily foliated red maple behind it, whereupon they instantly became imperceptible but for their loud rasping. Finch reached into his back pocket, pulled out his wallet, removed from it a photograph frayed at its edges and slightly wrinkled from having been sat on. He handed it to Banyon.

Banyon tried not to change his expression as he looked at the shot, or one similar to it, of the seaside beach house he had found in Iris's headboard, the same one she'd sketched a picture of and called HOME. 'You got any dreams, Nat?'

'Dreams?'

'Places like that' – Finch nodded at the picture – 'you'd like to end up being at one day or things you'd like to become.'

Banyon thought about it for a minute. He couldn't come

up with anything. 'If I have a good day,' he said, 'I dream the next one'll be just like it.'

Finch nodded. 'Nothing, though, you know' – he waved toward the road and beyond – 'out there?'

Banyon wasn't sure what he meant. 'In which direction?'

'In any direction.'

Banyon felt self-conscious and slightly stupid. He passed the photo back to Finch. 'You own that place, Herman?'

Finch shook his head.

'Who does?'

Finch slipped the photo back in his wallet. 'Nobody does. It's just somebody's dream.'

He replaced his wallet in his pocket. 'We're having another card game tomorrow night, Nat. Think you can join us?'

Banyon shrugged.

'A few of us – including me – 'd be obliged for the chance to win back some of what you took from us.'

'I'll try to make it.'

'We'll save ya a seat then,' said Finch, walking away.

He took the gloves from their box, held them in his hands, marveled at their lightness and new, leathery smell, and realized he'd been less than truthful in telling Finch he'd never worn any before. A man whose house he'd lived at a few months had lent him a pair to use in basement bouts with the man's son, who'd been three or four years older and much bigger than Banyon. The man stopped the contests only if Banyon said 'Uncle', which he never did, or was knocked down, which he refused to be, or the boy drew blood from him, and throughout them the boy's father loudly urged – coaching, the man called it – his son to do more damage to Banyon. Around the perimeter of the homemade ring, which was made of wrestling mats, empty rock salt barrels, and baling twine, the boy's siblings and neighborhood friends cheered and yelled, and two large German shepherds, which scared Banyon even more than his opponent did, barked, growled, and bared their teeth at the combatants.

Lacking sufficient reach or bulk to get at the boy, Banyon spent most of each bout ducking and bobbing away from his punches, but, sooner or later, one would connect pretty good and stun him just long enough to allow the boy to tag him again, however many times it took to make him bleed. Banyon couldn't imagine giving up, but was also petrified of going down for fear of being torn to pieces by the German shepherds. 'Stay up! Stay up!' he repeated to himself over and over, through several fights and repeated head and body blows. To keep standing was his only plan. Everything else was improvisation. When the boy, in their last encounter, fired a sloppy roundhouse right, Banyon instinctively ducked under it, hopped forward in a squat, and came up throwing, with all his weight, an uppercut, which squarely hit and shattered the boy's jaw, resulting in Banyon being transferred the next day to a reformatory.

He feinted, bobbed, jabbed at his glove-wearing self in the bureau mirror. He felt clumsy, as he had when he'd worn them in the diner, and foolish, battling with his own reflection. He took off the gloves, unleashed a few bare-fisted volleys. With or without gloves, he felt the same. He threw them back in the box and went outside.

No light shone from above. Looking out from the lake's shore, he saw only a dark, static body. Rustling movements sounded in the trees. Croaks and whistles shattered the still air. In showing him the beach house picture had Finch been telling him, wondered Banyon, that fighting him was his dream? Or had he been referring to a dream of Iris's? Or of

Banyon's? Or had he been saying something about the photograph itself or about the place it depicted? He dozed off, sitting, and came to experiencing himself again as two people, one of whom was drowning in the night-shrouded water and the other of whom reclined comfortably on shore, refusing to lift a finger to help. As he had every night for over a week, he heard floating through the woods from the motel, 'Are you out there, Dog?'

Eleven

He woke up convinced he was following a trail to a place that would eclipse everywhere he'd been and the person he was before he got there. When he finished priming the building that afternoon he was at once both anxious to begin painting it and reluctant to from an unsettling feeling that every stroke of his brush would bring him closer to the uncertain destination at the job's end.

He left his brushes soaking in turpentine and drove north. Ten miles out, he sensed, more than felt or heard, the Newport laboring. At a restaurant – service station bordering the reservation he stopped and raised her hood. Hot and trembly, she made a little tick, as he imagined a bum heart might, deep inside of her. The attendant likened her to his ninety-two-year-old grandmother. 'She does that way too' – he frowned at her gently hissing engine – 'just for being pissed off at having to live still with all that ails her.'

Banyon, who'd not asked for any help, slammed shut the hood. An electric socket wrench groaned from the open bay behind him. In the oily, bug-filled air, an orderly geese flock crossed the overcast sky. The attendant made a gear-shifting motion in the space next to him. 'She fights going into them high ones, don't she?'

Banyon's scowl said that she did.

'And kicks like a mule even if you ain't hardly touched a toe to her?'

'Like she's possessed by a mean old sumbitch,' confirmed Banyon.

The attendant nodded. 'Her transmission's addled top a everything else. Cost more'n you'd likely pay for me to tear her apart and find out how bad.'

'I'm guessing she's overheated's all. I'll just let her sit some.'

'Could be you're right to. Them coffee-grinding sounds been coming out of her a long while now and you ain't killed her yet.'

Banyon stared hard at him. 'How do you know how long anything's been coming out of her?'

'I got good ears, friend.'

Banyon kept staring at him.

'Think I ain't heared her growlin' and bitchin' all the times you've zoomed by here same way you just was?'

Banyon reared his head back as if he'd been slapped. 'I ain't never zoomed her by here till today. I ain't owned her but a week.'

'Musta been her without you in her them other times.'

'Any idea who else mighta been?'

'For all I know nobody was' – the attendant spit – 'or it's been you forever and now you're pulling my dick.'

Banyon went into the restaurant and ate lunch. When he came out a half hour later, the attendant sat drinking a soda in a lawn chair under the pump awning. Banyon added water and coolant to the Newport, hopped in her, and left. The attendant appeared never to look at him.

Banyon sped the Newport deep into the reservation, then slammed on the brakes, spun her around on the dirt shoulder, and headed her full-throttle back to the Deepwater. She ran

like a frisky, unbroken colt, as if she weren't the same car she'd
been an hour earlier.

He covered the front wall of the room nearest the road with
the dark-blue paint Finch had picked out to match the
Deepwater's name. Then he stood back and looked at it.
The wall suggested to him a bottomless lake. He imagined his
eyes as fish swimming through it. This made him remember
sinking like a stone to the floor of a farm pond; not being able
to breathe; the near-silence of his bubbly shouts; the pond
slithering into his lungs and refusing to leave them; his limbs,
his entire body, unable to help him. The sensations of
drowning were as real to him as the smell of the paint he
was using.

He sat, gasping, onto his stepladder's lowest rung.

A car stopped across the road, a hundred feet past him. The
driver got out, walked a short ways into the field adjacent to
the shoulder, and began pissing. He looked back at Banyon
and right through him as if Banyon were a clear glass pane.
Something about the driver, whom he couldn't see clearly, or
the car, a fire-red sedan with a black racing stripe – or both –
struck Banyon as familiar. He wasn't sure what. A lone hawk
glided well above the deep undergrowth the man stood in.
Pale light oozed through the clouds. A sharp whistle came
from the field. The man diverted his gaze toward the sound. A
tractor-trailer roared by, blowing the grass around him. The
man zipped his fly. Then he walked back to his car, leaned in
through the passenger door, pulled out a rifle, and returned to
where he'd been. He kneeled down, put the gun to his
shoulder, and aimed into the field at something Banyon
couldn't see.

A loud bang.

Cowbirds flew up from three places in the thick brush

beyond the man. Smoke trickled out the end of his gun. He levered out a shell, caught it in his hand, shoved it into his pants pocket. He strode to his car and tossed the gun into the backseat. He glanced at Banyon, then waved. Banyon didn't acknowledge the gesture. The man climbed into the sedan. A moment later, he drove off. A slight breeze carried the smell of gunpowder across the highway. Banyon watched the sedan until it disappeared. He looked at his watch. Four-fifteen. He looked back at the dark blue wall; amid all that white, it made him dizzy. Though it was an hour before he normally quit, he washed out his brushes. Driven by a compulsion to verify why he was at the Deepwater at all, he walked over to the gift shop and told Iris, 'I want to buy something to remind me of here' – he circled his hand in the air to indicate the overall area – 'when I'm in a different place later.'

Iris pursed her lips in a way he couldn't fathom. She hid the expression from her other customer, a long, bald drink of water wearing a safari suit and studying on, at mid store, a rotating case full of costume jewelry. 'I guess you mean a keepsake.'

Banyon smiled at her, but she didn't smile back. 'Exactly right, Iris.' He nodded pointedly at her nametag as if he'd just read it. 'A special thing I can keep forever.'

'That's about everything we have.'

'What's the most special thing you got?'

She answered him as if he were just another customer in off the street. ' 'Bout any of the crafts made by one of our local artists.'

'Who of 'em's the most local?'

She only scowled at him.

'I mean, Iris, which of 'em's families have been around here the longest?'

Her lips moved slightly up at the corners but that's as far as she let them go. 'Any of the Indians, I guess.'

'An Indian keepsake, Iris, is what I want.'

Iris showed him a shelf full of small, wooden animals hand-carved by a blind Onondaga chieftain who'd created them entirely from his wife's descriptions. Banyon was impressed with the detail of the pieces and with how much they resembled their intended subjects, which the artist had never laid eyes on. 'I'll take me one them weasels,' he told her.

Iris got a weasel out for him and placed it on the counter. 'What else?'

Turning his back to the bald man, Banyon winked at her. Iris acted as if the wink hadn't occurred. 'I'll browse,' said Banyon.

Iris pushed at her hair, in the tightest bun atop her head he'd seen it in yet. The shop smelled of incense and her perfume. Various shaped straw baskets dangled from the ceiling. Banyon picked up from the counter and examined a small birch bark teepee in which two figures, each about half the size of a human thumbnail, sat. He wanted to ask Iris a million questions and at the same time didn't want to know a thing more about her than he did. His lack of knowledge about her somehow heightened his want of her. She dampened her lips with her tongue. He heard her swallow. He looked at her again. She blinked firmly, then lowered her eyes. Banyon turned the teepee over in his hands. The bald man brought a bag of wampumpeag and a bear tooth necklace to the counter. Iris rang up the items on the cash register, put them in a paper bag, and handed them to the man. The man paid her and left. Banyon laid the teepee next to the weasel, followed the man to the door, then locked it. He walked back to the cash register. 'What do you think you're doing, Nat?'

Banyon unzipped his pants. 'Ain't nobody but Pam and the cook out there.'

'What if one of 'em comes in?'

'We got a right to be in love.'

'Like we got a right to jump out of a plane without parachutes.'

He seized her by the waist and kissed her. Her mouth was hot and wet. She tasted like peppermints. 'It's our right anyway.'

She bit his lip, drawing blood. 'Herman wouldn't see it that way.'

He spun her in a half-circle, making her face the counter. 'I know Herman and I think he might.'

He pushed roughly against the back of her shoulders. She bent over, grabbed the shelf near her knees. Her words came in pants. 'You don't know him, Nat, like I know him.'

He yanked up her dress, tugged aside her briefs, pulled open her cheeks. 'I know him as if we was twins born thirty years apart.'

She shuddered. 'What's that mean?'

'I don't know what it means.' He drew his penis out through his fly and placed its tip into her. She moaned and backed against him. 'I ain't known for sure anything since I got here, Iris, except this right here' – he leaned slowly into her, millimeters at a time – 'is the rightest thing either of us 'll ever do.'

They harshly exhaled together until no space divided them. Then Banyon pulled himself all the way out of her and, grunting, plunged back into her hard. Stifling a shriek, she gasped and told Banyon to shut her up. Banyon clapped a hand over her lips; to keep from screaming, she took two of his fingers into her mouth and sucked them. Reaching back with one hand, she dug her fingernails into his leg. Five minutes later Banyon paid for his weasel and teepee, kissed her once more, and walked back to his cottage; on his way, he glanced up and saw several vultures circling above the brush-shrouded field into which he'd earlier seen a man fire a gun.

Jabbering creatures from the pond, the field, the motel between them, enlivened the humid, mist-filled night three hours later. The doors to a few occupied rooms stood open. A radio played top fifty tunes. An unseen man and woman argued in Spanish somewhere near the portico, on which a bent-up old couple silently smoked cigarettes. Four parking spaces from the office, between Finch's Caddy and Walnut's Eighty Eight, sat the shooter's red-and-black sedan. On his way to Finch's card game, Banyon abruptly stopped walking. In the lot's overhead lights, he could now clearly see the car, which had in-state tags, though a part of him wished he didn't.

He peered into its front passenger window. The wood on the dash had been stained dark brown; black cloth upholstery concealed or had taken the place of the white vinyl seat covers; no lettering marred the glove box; even the floor rugs, bloodred now instead of tan, had been changed to match the car's new paint job. Banyon would have bet that even its serial numbers had been altered. The [modifications would fool most of the world, maybe even the sedan's rightful owner, but they didn't fool Banyon. He cautioned himself not to think too hard, not to try to figure things out, a task, at any rate, that struck him as impossible.

He told himself just half of him was standing there and that the other half, the only half capable of being hurt by mankind, was safely asleep somewhere. That made him feel better.

He turned back toward the office and saw or imagined someone moving away from the window. A moment later when he entered the room, no one was in it. He called out, 'Hello?', but got no answer.

125

Instead of ringing the bell, he walked behind the desk, toward the residence door; on his way to it, his eye caught a slight movement, at waist level, below the desk. He turned that way; swinging by its strap from a hook beneath the phone, as if it had been hung there just seconds earlier, was a camera with a long lens. Banyon's limited knowledge of cameras told him only that, with its many dials and gadgets, this was a fancy, expensive camera and not some cheap Brownie or Polaroid. He recalled the photographs he had unearthed in Finch's bedroom, every one of which could have been taken from within this room or the attached residence. His heart beat against his chest as if it wanted to escape his body. He pictured Finch – or someone – snapping his picture from the office window not two minutes ago as Banyon stared at and into the very same car he had sold for next to nothing to Finch's unnamed friend two weeks before. The residence door opened and Finch said, 'See you discovered one my secrets, young man.'

Male and female voices came from behind him. He was wearing a loud, button-down shirt over pressed bermudas. At that moment Banyon realized not only how much trimmer, but younger, Finch now looked compared to when they'd met, as if he was shedding years as well as fat on his new regime. Responding to Banyon's perplexed look, he nodded at the camera. 'Everything happening in the big old world out there' – he moved his arms in a wide arc – 'happens in the little old world out here.' He pointed his unlit cigar at the window past Banyon. 'On a smaller scale, course.'

'What?'

'Even more curious to me, Nat, than the situations folks find or get themselves in is how they react to them.'

'I can't make no sense of that, Herman.'

'I like to catch people unawares, Nat, and freeze 'em that

way.' Finch indicated the camera again. 'They make for more interesting subjects when they're unawares.'

'More interestin' than what?'

'Than when they know what's coming.'

'You like to take sneaky pictures of folks?'

'I think they'll make a good book someday.'

Thinking of the pictures of Iris posing naked, Banyon said, 'You ever take 'em of anybody who knows what's coming?'

Finch giggled. 'Never. But sometimes I take 'em of people who think they know what's coming – 'cause they see me with my camera and whatnot – but when they see the result they usually find out they didn't.'

'There's some weird shit going down here, Herman.'

Finch giggled again. 'You're telling me! I see it all right out my window!' He turned and headed back through the door. Heeding a feeling that he would drown only if he fought the world's natural flow, Banyon followed him into the front room. Walnut and Petersen filled two of five seats at the card table. The female voices came from farther down the corridor, possibly in the kitchen. Making no reference to them, Finch sat down in a chair facing the interior of the residence, leaving Banyon a choice of two seats with their backs to it. 'Hope you brought all the money you won from us last time,' said Walnut.

Banyon didn't say if he had. He didn't sit down either.

'You got to take a seat to play,' Petersen told him.

Banyon did, directly opposite Finch. 'We got a surprise for ya later, Nat,' said Finch. 'Anyway, I do.'

Banyon looked at him. Finch, throwing his ante into the center of the table, shook his head playfully at him. 'You're just gonna have to wait on it, young man.'

'Let's get started,' said Petersen, tossing in his quarter.

Walnut shoved him the cards. 'You deal it Petersen.'

Petersen picked up the deck and shuffled it. Banyon closely watched him, a broad-shouldered, lankly built man with pale-blue eyes in a moderately tanned, nondescript face, who, perceived Banyon, a person might spend a few hours with one night and barely recognize later, especially from a distance. What betrayed him, his most distinctive trait, which also suggested he might be more physically dangerous than he appeared, were his precise, coordinated movements – while handling the cards, walking, taking a drink, aiming and firing a rifle. 'I seen you earlier today,' Banyon told him.

Petersen, holding the deck in his left hand, silently raised and waved his right one at Banyon as he had from the side of the road that afternoon.

'I couldn't place you then.'

Petersen tapped the deck. 'Glad you ain't just rude.'

'What's the game?' asked Walnut.

'Straight up,' said Petersen. 'No wild men.'

Finch said, 'You was by here today, Pete?'

'I pissed in the field 'cross the way' – Petersen nodded toward the highway – 'and shot at one them woolly varmints threatenin' to run your place over, Herman.' He dealt the cards. 'Then I finished driving out to the reservation and bought me a month's supply of that sweet-eating buffalo meat they sell by the pound.'

Finch said, 'Did ya hit it?'

'Hit what?'

'What you was shooting at, for Christ sake.' Petersen nodded.

Walnut laughed. 'Now, Herman, you only got a hundred ninety-nine them varmints burrowin' under the road toward ya.'

Banyon said, 'Wasn't just you, Petersen, I couldn't place before tonight.'

Petersen met his gaze. Banyon flipped his quarter into the ante, never taking his eyes from Petersen's. He picked up his cards, looked at them, then looked back at Petersen. 'You was driving my old car,' he said.

Petersen frowned. 'Doing which with what?'

'It's sitting out front right now.'

'My red Lemans?'

Banyon nodded.

'When'd you own it?'

'If you come here in what I guess you must have, Pete' – Finch laid a five-dollar bill onto the quarters – 'Nat had one a lot like her, only a different color, up to a couple weeks ago.'

'No. That ain't right,' said Banyon, not knowing which of them – Petersen or Finch – to look at or who of the two, if either, had done him wrong. 'I had her exactly, only she's been painted and a few other things since I did.'

Petersen stroked his chin. 'Well, what did you do with her – whichever the fuck one it was that you did have?'

'I sold her.'

'To who?'

'To a confidential friend of mine,' said Finch.

Petersen nodded as if he was thinking that over. Then he said. 'I'm taking mine downstate first thing tomorrow. Fella down there's gon' give me four thousand five-hundred cash dollars for her.' He smiled at Banyon. 'That about what you got for yours, Nat?'

Banyon didn't answer.

Walnut, laughing harshly, tossed in his hand. 'Five dollars to you,' he said to Banyon.

Banyon looked down at his cards, but he couldn't differentiate between them. The faces and numbers all blurred together in his mind. He automatically slid a fiver into the pot. He asked Petersen, 'What did she cost you?'

Petersen smiled. 'Nothing terms of money.'

Banyon upped the bet two dollars.

Petersen dropped seven ones onto the pot and called. 'A good friend of mine give her to me a week so ago for a big favor I done 'im. What ya lay out for yours?'

'Not dime one way I heard it,' interjected Walnut. 'His brother lent it to him.'

Finch said, 'That was sort of a fib made up by me 'ccount the real story is more complicated than that.' He gave Banyon a familiar pat on the shoulder. 'Is it all right I said that, Nat, considerin' a poker game in this house is like a confessional and everybody at it priests?'

A shriek of laughter came from the kitchen. Banyon was pretty sure he'd heard Iris's voice out there more than once. He wished they were alone someplace, fenced off from the rest of the world. He looked at Finch, wondering if just him, no unnamed friend, had paid Banyon peanuts for the Lemans, had it modified at a chop shop – maybe even in Walnut's garage – obtained new papers for it – and what? – signed it over for a large profit to Petersen, who would resell it? Or were all of them – Finch, Walnut, and Petersen – in on fleecing him together. 'I'm not an idiot, Herman' was all he could think to say.

'I'd mess up the son of a bitch said you were, Nat.' Finch unleashed a few air bombs over the pot. Then he took from his hand three cards and threw them face down on the table. 'Give 'em to me big and red,' he told Petersen.

Petersen dealt him three cards.

Finch peeked at them. 'These are small and black,' he said.

Petersen shrugged. He looked at Banyon. Banyon held up two fingers, then eliminated from his hand the four of diamonds and eight of clubs. He got back the six of spades and nine of hearts, leaving him jack shit. His instincts told him a bluff wouldn't go. He folded even before another bet was made. No sooner had he dropped out then Petersen did, giving the hand to Finch. It struck Banyon that once he'd thrown in, all the drama had left the game, that the other players had only been waiting on his play. Finch dealt a game of stud, won by Petersen, then poured a round of whiskey shots. He lifted his glass toward the empty chair. 'Better days, Earl,' he said, 'at wherever you're at.'

'Atop a hell of a lot better luck,' added Walnut.

'And a new slew of born-yesterday suckers to cadge off of,' concluded Petersen.

They got back to cards. Banyon's uneasy feeling increased. He had the sense they were playing for stakes beyond money, the exact nature of which only he, among the four of them, was in the dark about. His inner radar was out of whack, causing him to stay in games he shouldn't have and to quit too early on some. While his modest stake – he'd brought only thirty dollars – dwindled, he mostly listened as the others discussed the mixed blessings of the tourist trade and how only the Indians, with their casino, were making any real money off it anymore. Finch turned on the cabinet stereo, playing country ballads low enough not to hinder their conversation, but loud enough to snuff out completely the voices from down the corridor. Banyon began to wonder if he had heard women talking at all, as no one else at the table had as much as mentioned them. Then he worried that he had made up anyone not in that room, that he had imagined rather than remembered most of the people he thought he'd encountered before then, worst of all Iris. He tried to mentally reenact her voice, smell, touch, but he couldn't. His brain showed him only a series of snapshots – of Iris crossing the lot, entering a room, diddling herself, blowing Finch – posing, he suddenly realized, exactly as she had been in Finch's photographs of her.

Overcome by a want to see her with his own eyes, he abruptly stood up from the table, saying, 'Piss call.'

'Use the second-floor can, Nat,' Finch told him, offering no explanation for why. He watched Banyon go up the stairs directly outside the front room, then waved him to his right, past Finch's office. On the bathroom floor was a scale and, above it, a grid charting Finch's weight for the past three weeks. The grid indicated Finch had lost twelve pounds in the period. A photograph of him, in gym shorts, before he'd trimmed down, was taped to the bathroom wall. Banyon again was struck with how different Finch now looked. Thinner, yes, but also younger and more vibrant. Through the floor vent, the female voices once more reached him. He couldn't distinguish one from the other or what they were saying, but from their general tone he got the idea they were having a high old time of it. He pissed, washed his hands, and peered into the mirror. He looked more haggard, he thought, and weathered than he had. The disturbing thought occurred to him that as Finch was getting younger, he was getting older; time was taking them in opposite directions. The voices through the vent suddenly stopped. Not a living sound was evident. Banyon put his ear to the floor and heard only the flushed water running through the pipes. The overhead light blinked off. He jerked open the door on more darkness.

Stars shining through the dormer windows at the ends of the now unlit hallway gave it the feel of a dusky tunnel. Banyon anxiously moved along it, came to the stairs, then started down them; as he passed the level of the windows, the light grew dimmer; midstairs, it vanished completely. On the floor beneath him, which was several degrees blacker than the one above him, only a small red glow was evident. When he reached the first-story landing he could make out, around the front room card table, the outlines of not three, but four indistinct figures, one of which was smoking a cigarette. Half of him tried to bolt blindly from the residence; the other half pulled him back. The smoker's lips snapped as they sucked on the cigarette. The cigarette crackled as it burned. A chair creaked. Change jangled. In the hallway beyond the room, utter silence prevailed. Worse even than his overall fright was Banyon's fear that he'd lost Iris to the darkness. He stepped quietly toward the kitchen. Finch's voice called out, 'Find it all right, Nat?'

Mystified that anyone in the front room could see him standing in the blackness against the stairwell, Banyon briefly worried that the lights had gone out only to him. Flashbacks, lacking particulars, to occasions as a child when he'd imagined himself as a target in a house full of strangers in a world which had refused him a place to hide hit him. 'Yeah,' he said, entering the room.

'The lights on up there?'

'They was for a while, then they weren't.'

Standing before the table, he watched the silhouetted smoker – Petersen, he guessed, puffing on one of his filterless Camels – put his head back and blow out invisible smoke.

'You didn't miss much down here.' Finch's voice struck Banyon as being disembodied.

Walnut's voice added, 'Petersen took a pot littler'n his dick's all.'

'And Walnut's been playing with his and thinking we didn't know it ever since the power went,' Petersen said. He dragged on his cigarette, the red glow making a small piece of his nose and mouth visible. Their voices indicated to Banyon, who could distinguish them only as three faceless shapes, they were sitting exactly as he'd left them. The fourth figure, in Earl's old chair, didn't speak. And no one spoke to, or of, it. An odor sweeter than smoke tinged the air. Banyon couldn't place it, but was certain he'd smelled it before.

'It don't come back in a minute, I'll go turn on the generator,' said Finch.

Banyon had the unsettling feeling that the mysterious figure was dead or – though it was human-shaped – inanimate, as he hadn't seen it move.

He wondered if he was imagining it, if it would vanish if he sat down on the chair it appeared to be in. Then he identified the smell. Cherry blossoms. More precisely, their concentrated odor. A perfume he'd more than once smelled on Iris. An unseen foot kicked his chair, pushing it away from the table. Finch said, 'Have a seat, Nat. We'll get back to seeing soon.'

Banyon sat down. As he did, the mysterious figure stood up, her shape confirming her femaleness, and moved into the dark void behind Banyon. 'Who's that?' he asked.

Only Finch's chuckle answered him, the others quiet laughter, and what he guessed was a match-head scraping against emery paper. Then a small flame danced above the table and in it flickered three male faces older than Banyon thought any living faces could be. He gasped loudly. The match went out. The voice he'd been taking for Walnut's said, 'Strike another one, Petersen.'

Suddenly more petrified of sight than of blindness, Banyon shut his eyes. Steady breathing sounded behind him; Banyon pictured at his back a knockout succubus, exhaling a lethal, perfumed scent. Across the table, the smoker's lips snapped. More scratching. Then a voice said, 'That's better.'

Banyon looked because he knew he couldn't hide from them looking at him.

He saw Finch holding a small candle aloft in one hand and Petersen lighting it with a cardboard match. He thought it

134

odd that Finch had evidently been carrying the candle on his person, that guests at the motel weren't pounding on the door wondering what had happened to their electricity, and that, even for a few seconds in a shadowy light, he could have mistaken the faces of Finch, Walnut, and Petersen for the faces of three men too old not to be from another world or dead in this one. 'What's going on?' he asked.

'One them hairy varmits,' said Petersen, 'likely chewed through a downed power line.' He crunched his cigarette out in the ashtray left of him. 'Zzzzzzt!'

Walnut harrumphed.

Finch said, 'When Dog was around he used to kill 'bout one of 'em a week.' The near-darkness hid his expression. 'Now they're over there multiplying like lemmings.'

Banyon heard little scratchy noises behind him. He had the feeling more than one person, thing, or animal he couldn't see was in the room. He didn't dare turn around and look, though, and was nearly certain he wouldn't be able to see anything if he did. 'Fuck this, Herman,' he said. 'Go turn on the generator ya got one.'

Finch giggled. 'We could all close our eyes and wish for 'em to come back on.'

'Now you sound like Earl,' said Walnut. 'Wishing birdshit was money and him a park bench.'

'Suck the wishes and bullshit out of Earl' – Petersen knocked his Camel pack against the table – 'and he wouldn't be no heavier than a Deepwater crab.' He inclined his head at the pack, pulled a cigarette from it with his lips, leaned farther forward, and, talking at Banyon, lit the cigarette in the candle's flame. 'Bet you've probably come across some of old Earl's wishes and bullshit still floating around in that Newport, ain't ya?'

Banyon didn't say if he had. He wasn't sure he could speak

at all. Finch wedged the unlit candle-end into a whiskey bottle's open top and placed the bottle midtable. He said, 'You got a big mouth, Petersen.'

'Come on, Herman.' Petersen scowled. 'What's the god-awful secret?'

'That car is what it is, son,' Walnut said to Banyon. 'No matter who owned it.'

Banyon said, 'Who did?'

'I bought her first with money I made fighting three decades ago,' answered Finch. 'Four years later I drove her here from Missouri and sold her to Walnut for money to eat on.' He threw back a whiskey shot. 'Walnut's been selling her ever since.'

Walnut moved his chaw into his opposite cheek. 'She keeps coming back to me.'

'Walnut thinks she jinxes people, but I don't believe it and my not wanting you to either, Nat, is why I kept you in the dark on her.' Finch chased the whiskey with half a beer. 'Truth is a long string of sorry-asses bound no matter what for bad ends had her 'fore you and after me, the last being sorry-ass Earl, who run her, a timeless classic deserving of a hell of a lot better, ragged till Walnut grabbed her back 'ccount of Earl not paying on her.'

'Like he didn't pay on nothing.' Petersen yakked smoke at Banyon. ''Cept with somebody else's money. You don't believe me, ask his wife, poor thing.'

'I don't know his wife,' said Banyon.

The others all chuckled, as if he was making a joke. Banyon edged his chair back a few inches, then, cognizant of the breathing that way, moved it ahead again. Finch said, 'Coming back to the subject of wishes, Nat, I gave a good deal a thought to what one you might make.'

Banyon said, 'I ain't never much bothered to.'

'They're less trouble than praying, Nat.'

'I've never known either of 'em to bring about much that' – sadness, even greater than his immediate terror, suddenly overcame Banyon; his skin felt tight, as if it were holding in too much, as if a pinprick might burst him – 'wasn't already in the cards.'

Finch shrugged. 'You think I ain't aware what day it is, Nat?'

'I don't know what you're talking about, Herman.' Banyon reached for his beer glass and found it empty; a picture of the glass, with nothing in it, not a single drop, rooted in his mind. His mouth felt parched; he imagined his entire face that way, as dry and wrinkled as the three old faces he'd briefly seen in the matchlight. He was at once anxious and afraid to touch it.

'It's on the employment form you filled out your first afternoon here.'

Banyon put a hand up and stroked his cheek. Across the table Finch's features miraculously seemed to him to transform themselves into a face as smooth and youthful as the one beneath his own fingers. Finch answered his openmouthed stare across the table as if it were a question.

'Your birthdate, Nat.'

Banyon, who attached no more significance to exactly when he'd been born than had any of the people who'd raised him, made up and wrote down a new set of numbers at every job he took.

'What are you looking to do to me, Herman?'

A hand touched Banyon's shoulder from behind. He jumped. Then he froze. Something in the touch, which was soft and unthreatening, kept him from turning around. The familiar cherry blossom smell became more prominent; even as he tried not to let it arouse him, it did. Fingers explored his neck, moved beneath his collar-front, walked slowly down his chest to his belly. Banyon felt impotent, even as he grew hard. Every alienated, terrified feeling from his orphan past conspired to hijack his mind. He had no idea who, if anyone, he could trust; who he ought to run from, love, hate; if in a moment he would be dead or just irrelevant. He stared at Finch, staring at him with one of his unreadable expressions. Walnut, or maybe Petersen, whistled bawdily. The hand slid beneath his pant waist. More whistles. A catcall. The candle went out. A mouth smothered his lips; a darting tongue penetrated them. In the blackness, its owner breathed, 'Happy birthday, baby.'

The lights came up to reveal a tall, big-breasted redhead he didn't know, kissing him to laughter and small hand claps. From the dark void, half-heartedly singing 'Happy Birthday,' walked Walnut's huge wife, a whip-thin brunette looking as if she'd been ridden hard and put away wet too often, Pam, Iris. Placing a decorated cake with burning candles before him, Pam said, 'Blow hard, stud.'

A few guffaws.

Banyon mentally lit out for the orphan's netherlands; from his out-of-body refuge, the here and now became a minor discomfort to bear. Events occurred around him like a disturbing play in which he was a set piece. He blew out the candles. The redhead kissed him again. Finch introduced them: 'Nat, Carla. Carla, Nat.'

'I hope you don't think me too forward nor nothing.' Carla, moving away from him, acted a little embarrassed. 'Herman talked me into it.'

'My matchmaker side made me do it.' Finch handed Banyon a serrated knife for cutting the cake. ' 'Less you managed to behind my back, Nat, you ain't had a date since you been here. Have you?'

Banyon, too quickly shook his head, wondered exactly

who, or what, Finch was: a middle-aged man who occasionally looked either older or younger than his years; or an
ageless, chameleonic ghost who knew Banyon and all of his
sins and desires better than Banyon himself did. His arm now
around Iris's waist, Finch sat her down on his lap. She
wouldn't look at Banyon. Finch said, 'Carla ain't had any
worthwhile company of the opposite sex to speak of lately
either, Nat.' He started plucking the candles from the cake.
'Not since old Earl run out on her and her little ones.'

Banyon suddenly pictured the world as a small plane taking
him on closer and closer sweeps of the ground. He looked
hard at Finch. Finch kissed Iris's ear. Banyon turned to Carla.

'We hadn't been getting on much,' she said, tugging
distractedly at her dress hem, six inches below her crotch,
'for a good while 'fore Earl disappeared.' She smiled at
Banyon, but seemed nervous, as if she didn't want to be
there any more than he did.

The brunette, who'd attached herself to Petersen, said,
'Somebody'd have to have the patience of Job to get along
with Earl.'

Petersen dragged his Camel down to a nub. 'After 'while
everybody round here run plumb out of that.'

'I didn't come here to talk about Earl,' said Carla.

'That's right.' Finch nodded at her. 'You came here to
forget about him.'

'I can't make myself feel right 'bout it,' said Carla.

'Earl and you was estranged, honey,' Walnut's wife said.

'That ain't what I mean.' Carla looked at Banyon. Banyon
thought she might cry. 'You seem nice 'nough. I hope you
have a good birthday anyway.'

She ran out of the room. The other women all hustled after
her.

'My fault,' said Finch. 'My fucking fault for trying.' He

banged his glass onto the table. 'I just thought, you know, Nat, here's for all intents and purposes two unattached young people, both good folks, who . . .'

'What?' asked Banyon.

'That's a nice woman there, Nat, who deserves a lot more good times in her life than Earl gave her and, well, fuck it.' Finch threw his hands up. 'It was a bad idea.'

Petersen scrunched out his cigarette. 'She weren't ready for it, that's all.'

Walnut said to Banyon, 'Cut the cake. Somebody might's well eat it.'

'You do it,' said Banyon. He handed Walnut the knife, put what little money he hadn't gambled away back in his pocket, and left.

Twelve

He imagined his mind as a house in which the furniture had been rearranged while he slept; he inhabited the same space as always, but now it looked and felt different; he sensed nothing was missing from it; certain things were just in new places; a darker hue, as dark as the emerging face of the Deepwater, colored his thoughts. He found his switchblade under his pillow. 'I put it there last night,' he told himself.

'Right as rain, you did,' another self answered him.

Jumping rope from predawn until sunrise, he worked up a good sweat. Then he entered the shallow water, barely up to his knees, past the lake's craggy, rock-covered bank. A familiar fear instantly gripped him of being grabbed, overwhelmed, obliterated. His memory didn't tell him if he'd been thrown into a farm pond out of fun, from meanness or in the hope that it would teach him how to swim. He waded in up to his waist. His fear intensified. Every ripple of his wavery, distorted reflection showed him his own terror. He peered through and beyond his image, clear to the lake's soft bottom; terror-free eyes, eyes lacking life at all, stared up at him from a man's partially eaten face. Banyon screamed. A splash came from his left. He reactively wheeled and punched at it, hitting a ten-inch bass in midflight. The fish cartwheeled over the water to shore. Banyon stared back into the lake. Mud stirred up by his shifting feet made the water turbid. He envisioned disembodied limbs groping for him. During several anxious seconds he failed to relocate the dead face. He rushed, panting, from the lake. He picked up the flopping bass and put it back in the water. The fish just lay there, sideways on the surface, barely fluttering. Banyon pulled it out again and killed it with a stick. At breakfast he tried to give it to the Deepwater cook, who didn't want it. No one else in the diner did either. Banyon tossed it up on the restaurant's roof on his way to work.

Every dark-blue swathe he added to the motel left its imprint on his mind. His brush, even the paint, felt heavy. A fear that his labors were obscuring physical evidence of a crime he'd helped commit overcame him. He felt like a coconspirator. He wondered if he could trust his own eyes anymore or if they were in the grip of whatever strange power reigned at the Deepwater. At midafternoon a bone-white man dressed only in his underwear came out of a room four doors down from Banyon and complained the paint smell was making him dizzy. Banyon told him to join the crowd. The man went back inside and slammed the door. Finch left with Iris in the Cadillac shortly after. With every stroke he made Banyon imagined himself growing weaker and Finch getting stronger. He washed out his brushes and drove to town.

At a Main Street gin mill he ate dinner, drank more than he normally did, and accepted a late-thirtyish woman's invitation to dance with her on a raised platform before the jukebox. Afterward the woman bought them drinks and told Banyon she'd recently left her husband, who'd gambled away all their money plus a lot more he'd loaned from the wrong people, leaving her, after she'd worked hard her entire life, in Shitsville with him, a story similar to tales Banyon had heard from other women and which made him feel as bad for her as he had for each of them. He told her she was beautiful, though she wasn't exactly, and let her feel up his ass and rub against him while they danced. She asked if Banyon would take her home. Making a fist and touching her on the chin with it, Banyon replied he'd better not because he was a fighter in training.

The woman leaned forward and stuck her tongue in his ear.

Banyon said she reminded him of his mother.

The woman said she was up for anything. She bought them more drinks. Banyon began feeling misty-eyed and as if he wanted to apologize to the woman for her bad luck. He called her Mom and asked her at one point where she'd gone to without him. 'Just to the ladies' room,' she told him. They played a giggly game of Patty Cake, Patty Cake. The woman said it was hell for a woman getting old and that she was thinking of taking an aerobics class. She took a long piece of dental floss from her purse and showed him a cat's cradle. A man with one arm in a cast, two black eyes, and blood-stained wads of cotton up his nose hobbled through the front door, prompting the woman to breathe, 'Oh, Christ. It's him, Mr. Small-Time, my walking corpse of a husband.'

Looking harder at Mr. Small-Time, who was headed their way, Banyon recognized him as Tim Boyer, from Felix's.

'If he starts in crying or even whines a little bit,' whispered the woman, 'I'm hauling ass. Matter of fact, I'm hauling it anyway. You ought to come with me, Junior.'

She started to stand just as Boyer abruptly stopped ten feet before their table. He stared openmouthed at Banyon, evidently just recognizing him. Then, wearing a petrified look, he turned and quick-limped from the bar. The woman gave Banyon a puzzled frown. Banyon gave one right back to her.

'I didn't do nothing to that guy,' he said, 'but buy paint off'n 'im one time.'

The woman forlornly shook her head. 'That bunch he owes has packed it so tight up Mr. Small-Time's ass he's seeing them in his own customers now.'

She called Banyon Junior again and told him to give his mom another whirl. Banyon said he was tired. She either didn't care or didn't believe him. She reached down and squeezed his penis through his pants. Banyon told her he was in love with a younger woman. The woman asked, 'What in the world's that got to do with obeying your old mom?'

Banyon excused himself, went to the men's room, and from there right out the front door to the parking lot. Driving home he heard in the Newport's tortured growl the voices of those the vehicle had belonged to before it had belonged to him and after it had belonged to Finch and he wondered what bad end, in Finch's words, each of its previous owners had come to and why he'd been picked by Finch – and maybe Walnut – to own the car now. Then he mentally replayed his fish-killing jab, thrown as quick as lightning and purely from instinct and, in a flash, he knew he would fight Finch and why: for the same reason he'd clobbered the bass, not because of what it was, but because of what it might have been.

He taunted his shadow-boxing image, cast by the moon on the cottage's outer wall, ridiculed it for mimicking his every move, for not throwing a single creative punch, for not having flesh-and-blood balls and a heart.

Exhausted afterward – it was past midnight – he fell into bed and unconsciousness. Something soon woke him. Intent on knowing what, he made himself wide-awake again. Anything seemed possible in the world of mysterious noises he was lying amid – that he'd danced with his mother that night, that he'd lived his current life at least once before in Finch's body, that Finch's soul was looking for a home in Banyon's flesh, that all he believed to be real was a dream or that, perhaps worst of all, all he believed to be a dream was real. He grabbed his switchblade from beneath his pillow, turned on his reading lamp, and for several minutes carved a shapely woman from a small, pine stick. He thought that after he touched it up some he'd give it to Iris. His second self told him he was foolish for having her on his brain at all, that she wasn't what she seemed to be to his first self and that, just maybe, she wasn't even alive period.

He switched off the light and slept more. When he woke next her naked body was lowering itself in a squat onto his erect penis, which her right thumb and forefinger was inserting into the opening between her legs. Banyon closed his eyes and let it be an ecstatic dream. Each of his hands moved to her ass. His mouth bit blindly at her nipples. Her extended exhale of breath – or was it his own? – stopped only when she could sit down no farther. Then he heard her grunting and blowing air through her teeth, the wet squishing of her genitals pulling at his, her soft cursing at him – or herself – like a jockey urging a horse toward the finish line. And it felt so good. Banyon's mind centered on reining in his body, on letting her get off on it until she couldn't stand it anymore, at which point, with an animalistic yelp, he let everything go into her.

'I didn't have it ready for you yesterday.' She handed him a gift-wrapped box, the approximate size and shape of a paperback book. 'Anyway, there wasn't a chance to give it to you.'

Banyon felt like crying from an emotion he couldn't describe. 'It weren't really,' he told Iris.

'Weren't really what?'

'My birthday.' He couldn't remember when a person he cared about more than a little had given him a present. Finch's gesture two nights before didn't count to Banyon, not because he didn't care for Finch (even while he was trying not to), but because he didn't consider a date with Earl's wife to be a present. He wasn't sure what it had been. 'I just made them numbers up.'

'Why did you?'

'The real ones weren't known for sure by anybody around to say them when I was found, I guess or somehow they never got writ down.'

'Nowhere you were raised up at ever gave you a birthday party?'

'A few places did on some day them or the state decided on, but those never stuck in my mind much.'

'From now on' — she nodded matter-of-factly, as if she'd just reached back in time to re-create him — 'it'll be today.'

Banyon softly shook the package, from which no noise came.

'I'll write it down, Nat, so neither of us will forget.'

Banyon carefully took the wrapping off the box.

Iris picked up, folded, and placed the paper atop her clothes on the floor. 'If you don't like it, Nat, I want you to pretend you do anyway.'

Frowning at the box, Banyon turned it over in his hands. 'Is it something to wear?'

'It's something to dream on. A dream's what it came from too.'

Banyon opened and pulled from the box the drawing entitled HOME he'd last seen in Iris's sketch pad; now it filled a plastic frame, covered in glass: on a rough coastline of boulders and Scotch pines, the wooden, two-story beach house with a widow's watch, sat on a small, grassy knoll; wind whipped the trees and hurled gulls through the air over the whitecapped sea breaking onto the rocks and a narrow strip of sand before them; in sight of no other buildings, the house, much more so than any one Banyon had ever been in, gave him the impression of being both warm inside and sturdy outside, as if even a hurricane couldn't damage it. 'You drew this?'

Iris nodded.

'How did you?'

'It's just something I've always been able to do.'

Banyon lay a hand on her thigh, lacking words again to say how her giving it to him made him feel.

'I saw it way up north on the coast of Maine, where Herman took us before we were married. I made him get out and take a picture of it because I decided I'd been born there.'

Banyon just looked at her.

She put a hand over her breasts, almost as if she were suddenly embarrassed to be naked in front of him. 'My deciding where I was born is no different, Nat, than you deciding when you were born. We're both orphans, remember?'

'You can be born there if you want to be, Iris.'

'Well, I think now I was wrong about that. More likely I was born in some hovel or on the streets.'

'It don't matter where you were born.'

'I know it doesn't. It only matters where you get to later.'

Banyon held up the picture. 'You want to get to here, Iris?'

'I want us to together, Nat.'

Banyon laughed. 'What if it isn't for sale?'

'We don't have to own that exact one, Nat.' Now Iris laughed. 'It doesn't have to even be as nice as that one.'

'How nice does it have to be?'

'I don't want to joke about it anymore, Nat.' She quit laughing.

Then Banyon did. 'Herman showed me a photograph of what you drew, Iris. He said it was somebody's dream. He didn't say whose.'

'He thinks it's ours together, Nat – his and mine. What he's been putting in that safe since we were married is supposed to make it come true.'

'He told you that?'

Instead of answering him she said, 'I didn't used to mind him being in my dream, Nat. Anyway, I couldn't see how else to reach it. Then you came along.'

Out the window behind her, early dawn light filtered into the thin woods and onto the mostly dark lake past them; on the water, nothing moved, nothing anyway that Banyon could see. A tern's *keek* sounded. A mourning dove cooed intermittently. In Banyon's mind flashed a vision of the dead man's face he'd seen – or thought he had – beneath the outwardly calm water. He looked at Iris. 'How'd you get out without him hearing you?'

'He left a little before I did.' She pushed at her hair. 'He said he'd try to be back by lunch.'

Banyon looked at his watch. 'At three-thirty in the morning he left?'

'He got a call.'

'From who?'

She shrugged. 'About Earl.'

'What about Earl?'

'He's not lost anymore. That's about what I got from it.'

Banyon swallowed hard. 'He was lost?'

'You think that ain't the right word for it?'

'How would I know?'

Iris looked at him tenderly, as if he were a small child. 'What did you think, Nat – he just disappeared into thin air?'

Instead of telling her what he thought, Banyon said, 'I don't know him even, but as a bad card player.'

'Whatever you do know of him is all you ever will know of him. That's my guess.'

'What are you saying?'

'I'm not saying. I'm guessing's all. Which, if I know that bunch, is all the police or Earl's life insurance company'll be able to do either.'

Banyon remembered Earl's wife running from the room in tears. 'Is Earl dead?'

'I didn't hear that he was from the little I did hear.' Iris picked up from the windowsill and drank from the can of beer they were sharing. 'I didn't hear that he was alive either.' She handed the beer to Banyon. Banyon finished it off, crushed the can, and dropped it on the floor. Iris took his right hand and pressed it to her left breast, then put her free hand against the same place on him. They closed their eyes as one. Banyon pictured them traveling a hundred miles per hour away from the Deepwater. The pounding of Iris's heart coincided with his own. She moved Banyon's hand in a circle. Banyon rubbed her breast. Her heart rate quickened; her nipple grew hard. She made the same things happen in him. Iris wanted to know if he felt better from what she did to him or from he did to her. Banyon said he didn't know, that he felt best when he couldn't tell the one thing from the other. Whatever they took from and did to Finch, Iris told him, would be for a better reason than Finch took from and did things to them.

Thirteen

Returning to the parking lot after breakfast, Banyon met Finch on the wood's trail. Stopping before him, Finch nodded back at the motel. 'I hope all your hard work isn't going to keep people away, young man.'

Banyon eyed the building for a clue as to what Finch was talking about. Unable to find one, he indicated as much with a confused expression. 'That paint, Nat.' Finch frowned. 'It's going on darker than I figured on.'

Vaporous clouds, half-masking the sun, created above the structure a slick glaze, painful to look at. 'It matches the lake, Herman.' Banyon kicked at the leaves beneath his feet. 'Like you wanted.'

'But will it scare off the tourists, without 'em even knowing why?'

'Will it what?'

'You know, send out some kind of subconscious message about gloom and doom?'

Banyon pushed at his bandana. A dream he couldn't remember had left him feeling unbalanced, as if he were two people, one a few pounds heavier than the other, sitting opposite each other on a seesaw. 'I don't know nothing 'bout that.'

'Advertisers, Nat, think of it as giving off a good or bad stink.'

'You want I should switch to a lighter shade?'

Finch waved off the suggestion, then dropped the topic, as if it hadn't concerned him much to begin with. His red, swollen eyes, his stubbly cheeks, his wrinkled, sweat-stained khakis suggested he'd not slept, shaved or showered since returning from his middle-of-the-night departure. 'Two backpackers late yesterday, Nat, stumbled upon this over past the west side the reservation.' He pulled from his shirt pocket, then handed to Banyon a color photograph of a bloated, vaguely human-appearing cadaver that looked to have been hacked or chewed on.

Banyon gasped.

'Shape it was in Carla didn't want any part of trying to identify it, so she asked me to.'

Finch pressed an index finger between Banyon's shoulder blades. 'A little spider tattoo right here and his big buck teeth convinced me it was Earl. I'm sure his dental records'll confirm it.'

Finch took back the picture. 'Cops figure the night he left here he hiked the five-odd miles up the road to the field 'cross the river from his place, then, too tired or drunk – you 'member how lit he was, Nat – to walk three or so more to the bridge, he tried to wade home using the pull rope he's got over there, got swept away by the current, washed up thirty-five miles later in a pine forest the river cuts through, and, 'ccording the coroner' – Finch glanced down at the picture, shaking his head – 'got half-ate by a wolf or feral dog.'

A vision of the Rottweiler charging through the pine forest he'd turned it loose in on the west side of the Indian lands flashed before Banyon, who feared he might scream or howl from a tearing pain in his guts. 'At least Carla can get on with her life now, Nat, and quit wondering if he's going to just show up again someday.'

'What?'

'Earl, rest his soul, had dragged her down with him something awful.'

Banyon pictured the redhead he'd been offered as a birthday present in Shitsville with Tim Boyer's wife, each of them there for having a husband in debt to Finch. 'Old likable weasel Earl' – Finch softly tapped through his shirt pocket the photograph of Earl's remains – 'could, though, Nat, make you laugh like nobody.'

'I didn't even know him,' said Banyon, from a strong want to emphasize the point.

'You didn't miss much beyond the laughs, which didn't come all that often and, in truth, weren't all that big.' Naked terror suddenly joined all the other emotions Banyon felt for or about Finch. 'Most folks round here, Nat – including the law – 'll tell you that in dying, Earl, for the first time in his life, done right by the people he was most beholden to.'

Banyon said, 'I guess you mean his wife and kids.'

Finch didn't say what he meant. 'You two,' he told Banyon, evidently referring to Banyon and Earl's widow, 'walked right away from the get-together I arranged for you the other night. Weren't but Petersen, Walnut, and me left to eat the cake Pam baked for you.'

Banyon suddenly remembered being a small child backed against a wall and having to choose between getting pummeled fighting or getting pummeled standing still. He pictured Earl's mangled face, appearing hauntingly similar to the face he'd come eye-to-eye with in the lake. What had once struck him as random occurrences now struck him as parts in a single, unfolding event.

'I got a weakness, Nat, for liking certain people too much

and scaring 'em off or getting my ass burned for it.' Scratching his head, Finch glanced up at an acorn-eating squirrel dropping spent shells from the canopy. 'Comes from growing up an orphan I guess, and getting yanked away from anybody I ever got half close to.'

Banyon's thoughts moved circularly, like tired birds over a garbage scow a thousand miles from land. 'I've come around to wanting to fight you,' he told Finch.

Acting not at all surprised at Banyon's change of heart, Finch said as long as the motel was painted by two weeks from next Saturday they'd get it on that evening. Then he took off for the diner.

Wheeling her cart down the corridor at him, Iris wore short, tight cutoff jeans and a T-shirt. Her thick hair fell wild and unchecked to her shoulders. Banyon had never seen her work but in a neat shirt tucked into a skirt or pants, with her hair fettered in a bun behind her neck. Her untamed look signaled to him that, as close in thought as the two of them had been, they were now aligned in their goals like twin planets orbiting a common moon. 'Did he show you the picture?' she whispered at him.

Banyon breathed, 'I couldn't even make Earl out of it.'

'You could make a dead man out of it, couldn't you?'

Banyon nodded.

'Ask yourself who'd take a picture like that.'

'I took it the cops had.'

'Did you take it too that Earl drowned in the same water he was found next to?'

'I took it for Gospel I was shown a dead body. The rest, 'cluding it maybe being ate on by a wild dog, I took with a grain of salt.'

'A dog made hungry enough'll eat whatever it's fed.'

'I'd as soon leave the dog out of it. Anyway, it could have been a wolf.'

'He's showed that picture all round the diner.'

'Why did he?'

'Why else? So people'll know what can happen whenever he wants it to.' She vanished behind her cart into the white room next to the one he was making blue. A thick, gray cloud arrived from the east to blot out the sun. The wind picked up, carrying a death smell from the field across the road; twigs and loose dirt skittered through the lot; a lawn chair tumbled into the pool; birds flew with the gale's help or against it into the woods, away from what was coming. Thunder boomed. Rain drops fell – one, two, three of them – onto Banyon's face, reminding him of a clock's ticking; an uncertain interval had passed, he suddenly realized, while he'd been mentally away from the premises. He put down his brush, strode to the open window of the room Iris had entered, and said, 'I took him up on the fight he offered me, Iris.'

No word came back to him, no sound even indicating she was inside still. He strode to the door, turned the handle, and found the door locked. He looked up at the sky to see the clouds rapidly dissipating and the sun peeking through them. He experienced a familiar feeling of having had the wool pulled over his eyes, not a feeling tied to a specific event, but a general suspicion that had adhered since childhood to his brain. He went back to work, painting in a zone in which his physical movements were everything he was conscious of.

Excruciatingly aware of each occurring moment, he stared out his front window, through the thin woods, at a fog bank creeping slowly forward from the lake's center. Raindrops roughened the water. A pulpy stench, an owl's hoot, a flicker's *klee-yer* reached him. Moisture–laden pine boughs drooped and creaked, giving the impression of cowed prisoners. In the overcast dusk a pair of red foxes stopped and lapped at the water before trotting off into the trees.

An irritation in his throat urged him to clear it with a guttural sound from which it seemed a greater noise should follow. The bed he was sitting on squeaked. His stomach fluttered. A blue heron rose up from the lake to be consumed by the mist. He willed himself not to blink, even for the purpose of moistening his eyes; to experience every second and then move past it; not to remember it; to engage only the next second. Each tick of his bedside clock brought the fog closer; made the light dimmer.

His right haunch itched. He rubbed it against the bedpost. A raw steak smell tantalized him, though he had no meat on the premises. A branch or pinecone fell onto the roof. A feeling as if his back hairs were rising came over him. A low growl sounded somewhere in the room. His eyes told him he was alone. Harried panting took the place of his breathing. He gazed again at the fog. His mind fought to stay with him. A loon laughed. One of his legs unaccountably rose sideways from his hip. A moment later, he stood, urinating, over the toilet. Back at the window, he saw the fog at the woods edge; in no time it was halfway through them, toward the cottage; shortly before dark the dense cloud loomed alone before him; then it enveloped him.

The noise he'd failed to fully reach earlier was a howl. Now, charging through the thick pine forest after fresh game, he expelled it completely.

Fourteen

He performed stomach crunches in the dawn light holding a flat, forty-pound rock behind his neck; then he balanced the rock between his shoulder blades and ripped off three sets of fifty push-ups. On a tree limb he did pull-ups and, hanging by his feet, inverted toe touches. To practice his hand quickness, he tossed bunches of pinecones in the air and snatched as many as he could before they hit the ground. He had a long bout afterward with his shadow, which struck him as being faster and potentially more dangerous than in their last go-round; but his flesh-and-blood self struck him as being those things as well. A kid maybe ten years old wandered down from the motel while he was having at it. He stopped ten feet from Banyon.

Banyon, just for show, loosed a machine gun flurry of jabs, halting each one a half-inch from a pine trunk showing his own image.

The kid gave him a big, gap-toothed grin.

Banyon picked up his rope and started jumping it, every third skip crisscrossing it, every fourth one plunging into a crouch, every fifth one leaping a foot off the ground. Sweat marred his vision. A fuzzy halo surrounded the kid; behind him, a light mist over the lake refracted the sun in a band of colors; shiners flashed in the water, eyed by a low-flying kingfisher. Banyon began flinging the rope backward over his head, jumping it first on one foot, then on the other, in increasing intervals of ten. The kid clapped his hands and whistled. Banyon shut his eyes. He leapt faster and faster. The kid broke out laughing, as if he was at the circus. An obscured image of nonstop motion filled every cell in Banyon's brain. He went like a son of a bitch. He heard the kid chant, 'Go! Go! Go! Go!' He flung the rope ten feet in the air, caught it blind, and started right in jumping it again, not missing a beat. He opened his eyes. The kid wore an awed look, as if he'd seen magic. Banyon wanted to tell him he'd only seen Nat Banyon. At the same time he had an urge to hug him for believing he'd seen more than was there, but was afraid if he did the kid would think he was a pervert. Instead, he tossed him his rope – he had another one in his gym bag – and left him by the lakeshore, trying to jump it.

An unusual meat craving led him to order chicken-fried steak with his normal poached eggs and pancakes breakfast. The jukebox played a ballad about two cowpoke pals who'd outlived the world they'd been born to. Pam said it got to her heart like no other song she'd ever heard and that in her book a friendship like those old boys had beat love any day. She topped off Banyon's coffee, poured herself some, sat down opposite him in the near-to-empty diner, and asked if Banyon and her were friends. Banyon said they were to him. Pam dabbed at her eyes. Banyon wasn't sure if she'd been crying or was hung over. She reached across and put a hand atop one of his in a way that made him feel as if she was looking at and touching him while seeing and feeling an entirely different person or thing. She smiled toward him. Her face was flushed, and now Banyon could see actual tears on her cheeks and what a knockout she'd been fifteen, or even ten, maybe only five, years ago, and he imagined her being struck by that same thought a hundred times a day.

She quietly mouthed the words to the song.

A man in a Parcel Post uniform stood up from the counter, slid some bills under his empty plate, and walked past them toward the door, saying to Pam, 'Same time and place tomorrow, lover.' Pam didn't acknowledge him. Banyon watched the man go outside and get into his truck, leaving only him, Pam, and two counter customers inside. When the song ended Pam, looking a little embarrassed, took her hand back. She poured herself a cup of coffee. A moment later she pulled a loose cigarette and a pack of matches from her smock, put the cigarette between her lips, broke off a match to light it with, then changed her mind and put the whole business pack in her pocket. 'I bet we had us a time,' she said.

'What?'

'In another world' – she sighed – 'I bet we did, stud.'

'We might've,' said Banyon. He put his last piece of steak into his mouth. 'I don't remember.'

Pam laughed.

Suddenly Banyon pictured his teeth tearing into human flesh. His mouth filled with blood. He grabbed a napkin, spit what he'd been chewing into it, dropped the napkin onto his plate, pushed the plate away, and stood up, wanting only to be outside, back working in that zone where his mind would show him only what his eyes saw. He watched Pam looking at him curiously. 'I bit my tongue,' he said.

'Drink some of this,' she told him, handing him his water glass. Banyon swished some water around in his mouth and swallowed, envisioning thick, warm blood rolling down his throat into his stomach. Seconds later he left the restaurant and walked across the road, through the field of dense brush, tracking the dead smell that had been coming from it for two days. Briars and thorn apples tore at him; his feet sent dandelion pods flying and smashed clover, toothwort, and Indian pipe; half a second before he would have stepped on it a grouse flew from cover. The odor grew stronger as he advanced. It led him a hundred yards past midfield to a shot woodchuck, sprawled at the top of its hole. Petersen's bullet had nearly cut the animal in half. Banyon nudged the carcass into the hole with his foot, then stomped it several inches into the ground. He returned to the diner and asked Pam, 'When's Earl's funeral at?'

She shrugged. 'In a few days probably. It'll take 'em that long to do an autopsy if they're going to and make him look decent.'

'That girl Carla?'

'I can tell you where she lives at if you want.'

Banyon nodded.

Pam wrote down the directions on the back of an order slip and handed it to him.

'She had life insurance on him?'

'That's what I heard.'

'You think she'll get any of it?'

'I think she'll get all of it, but I don't think she'll keep much of any of it for long, poor girl.'

'Why don't you think she will?'

'For the same reason I don't think you've got a Chinaman's chance of beating Herman in a fight he's arranged unless he wants you to.'

'What?'

Pam, though, only pursed her lips and stared toward the motel.

He pictured Finch as the axle keeping a giant wheel from rolling any which way. He told himself that Finch, not a third party, had bought the LeMans; later Finch gave it to Petersen for doing him what Petersen called a favor. What favor, Banyon's second self wanted to know, was worth a forty-five-hundred-dollar car?

Did you watch Petersen?

Watch him how?

He nearly took that woodchuck's head clear off from a hundred yards.

He shoots good.

He kills good, you mean.

That still don't tell me what I asked you.

He left the card game early that night, get it?

Don't even take me there.

A half-hour or so after Earl went he did.

I don't want even to chew on that.

You need to understand like I do how it could happen – Finch pushes a button and we're dog meat.

Just shut up and fucking paint.

If you hadn't gone all loopy over a whiff of sweet air we wouldn't need to worry how many buttons he pushed. We'd do this here like we agreed to and hit the road.

Not without her are we hitting it. She's the only thing left makes any sense.

Ten to twelve motorcyclists on chopped Harleys roared into the lot, circled it twice doing fast wheelies, reentered the highway, and sped west. The silence in their wake recalled to Banyon the world underwater. The temperature shot up in the following hours, as if God had goosed the earth's furnace. The highway's asphalt surface softened, giving it a rubbery smell and causing it to crackle and pop beneath passing vehicles' tires. The rhododendrons turned limp and pathetic. Most birds shut up and quit flying. Banyon four times went to the portico and drank three lemonades in less than five minutes. At quitting time he was still parched. All he wanted was to drive, fast or slow, with the windows down, to force the still air into movement.

He pictured Earl traveling in front of him on this desolate, single lane road, only on foot and in the dark instead of at twilight; his Coke-bottle glasses fogged up by the night heat; his leisure shirt sweated through; mumbling about how the world kept putting it to him in the ass; fingering with mixed emotions the bills in his pocket from the big hand he'd won; keeping an eye out for nearing headlights; pissed, scared, woozy, pretty goddamned jumpy at where the day's end found him.

On the other hand, maybe on that warm night, under a bright moon, with the crickets chirping and peepers peeping, nothing but his surroundings felt real to him and about them he had no complaints. Maybe he was enjoying the hike, the sounds and smells from the marshy woods to his left and the gently hissing river making a zigzagging line between his right side and a few muck farms, apple orchards, and long stretches of government-owned forests into which it sometimes vanished, when the headlights came up behind him. Maybe his fear instincts told him nothing as the car pulled up next to him and he was offered a lift home, or maybe they spoke up, but they didn't say whatever they did very loud, and Earl was too drunk or tired to want to hear them anyway. He gave them the brush-off and climbed huffily into the front seat next to Petersen.

The abandoned building lot Pam had instructed him to watch for to his right loomed ahead like a giant scythe slash in the woods before the river. Banyon pulled over onto the shoulder.

Why you stopping?

Banyon glanced nervously around the Newport while halting it in front of the clearing of stumps and knee-high brush. Even as his eyes told him he was alone, his ears said that he wasn't.

So you can wade home, Earl.

Amid corpses of cars and appliances and a wheelless tractor, Earl's shitheap of a house sat a hundred yards up the far bank at the edge of a dirt road. The river was maybe eighty feet wide here; from Banyon's position, well back from it, he couldn't tell how deep or swift. A guide-rope Earl was said to have put up after his car had been repossessed to cut six miles off his walk to and from the highway when the river's depth permitted it spanned the river between two trees.

Fuck you. All the rain's made the water too high.

I'm pulling your pud, Earl.

Then let's get going.

Their voices were either coming out of the Newport, Banyon realized, or out of him.

I gotta take a piss. Get out with me, have a snort.

Banyon stepped from the Newport and stood on the shoulder, pissing into the high grass, eyeing near the river's far bank a dark channel that looked powerful enough to carry downstream any good-sized object that got into it. He lifted the beer can he'd gotten out with to his mouth and drank. He smacked his lips. The pinkish sky above the water was streaked gray. A dog barked someplace. He closed his eyes and felt himself sway gently on his feet.

That there's Polaris, Earl, the North Star, and it's setting right over your house.

Where?

Where I'm pointing. The last star in the handle of the little dipper, see it?

Oh, yeah.

You know what that means, it shining right into your place like that, Earl?

No. What's it mean?

A windfall's coming.

For who?

Your family if you stare straight at it and say so.

Here comes our windfall.

Here it comes, Earl.

Banyon tasted blood again. He opened his eyes and saw or imagined a body-shaped something bobbing past him in the dark channel. He glanced above the water just as, in the growing dusk, a fluorescent pole light blinked on outside of Earl's house. He climbed back in the Newport, drove three miles to the bridge over the river, crossed it, then drove the same distance up a dirt road to sagging, clapboard house he'd been watching minutes earlier.

In the junk-strewn yard a small covey of pullets squawked and sissy-stepped from the open cavity of a stripped refrigerator; a filthy goat and a one-horned milk cow tethered to a gutted car body grazed on a patch of weeds; a boy and girl, maybe six and five, swung on a creaking swing set strangling in ivy beneath a giant white oak tree. Banyon stopped before them, smiling. They kept on swinging as if he weren't there, one corner of the set regularly lifting out of the hole it had been placed in and loudly slamming back into it, their bodies casting arcing shadows in the growing dark. Banyon remembered a voice telling him he'd be okay wherever he got sent to live next and for however long, if the place just had a swing and at least one big tree to climb. 'That was my daddy's car,' said the boy.

Banyon looked over his shoulder at the Newport, then back at the little boy.

'It brung him bad luck and made him drown in the river.'

'That ain't what made him drown,' said the little girl. 'The water did.'

'Nope.'

'Yup.'

'Because he had to walk everywhere, you little brat, even 'cross the river, after somebody took it back from him is why he did.' The little boy, at the top of his swing, kicked his legs out toward Banyon. 'Was it you?'

'Me?'

'Who took it back from him?'

Banyon shook his head. He peeked up at the sky; the moon was now a crescent-shaped bone; the clouds wisps of gray-black smoke; the shapes of two circling vultures ashes from a burning incinerator loosed into the dying day.

'It ain't no good,' said the little boy, 'you ought to get rid of it.'

Banyon stepped over to the oak, grabbed a fat limb just above his head, swung himself up into the tree, and sat down near the trunk, dangling his feet toward the ground.

'It broke down all the time,' said the boy, acting not one bit surprised at Banyon's behavior.

'It went really fast,' said the little girl. 'That's all he cared about, how fast it went.'

'Shut up,' said the little boy. 'You don't know nothing.'

The little girl said, 'That's what Mommy said.'

The little boy peered up at Banyon. 'She don't know nothing.'

Banyon winked at him.

The little boy said, 'Were you friends with my daddy?'

'I played cards with him,' said Banyon. Now he couldn't remember what thought, or series of them, had brought him here, to the home Earl had failed to reach the last night of his life. From his vantage point the entire lot laid out before him, from the road's edge, to the rear of the house, down a sloping field to the river. Small inconsistencies stuck out to him in the place's overall trashy appearance – potted tulips on the windowsills; a welcome sign on the front door; a small circle of mowed lawn around two willow trees holding up a hammock; a neat, fenced-in vegetable garden out back; Earl's widow weaving her way toward him through the front-yard junk in a pressed, white cotton shift, her dark red hair falling in a smooth, thick wave down the right side of her face. 'What are you doing up in that tree?' she called out.

Banyon didn't have an answer for her. He swung down out of the oak, allowing her to see all of him. When she did her cheeks flushed slightly. 'Oh, it's you,' she said.

'He's got Daddy's old car,' said the little boy.

She looked over at the Newport. The warm air, already rich with pollen, was further sweetened by her perfume, not the same brand she'd had on the night she'd kissed Banyon and put her hand down his pants. She turned back to Banyon. 'Guess it's your turn now.'

Banyon wasn't sure he'd heard her correctly. 'What?'

'Hope you own it outright' was her only answer.

Banyon didn't say if he did.

Black eyeliner highlighted her pale-blue eyes. She shifted uncomfortably from foot to foot. Amid the dump she lived in, she, along with her kids, suggested a rare find, a worthwhile article thrown out by mistake. She should've been beautiful, thought Banyon, who couldn't figure out why she wasn't quite. 'My condolences to you and your young ones,' he said.

She nodded to him.

'That's what I come to say.'

'Our daddy's up in Heaven,' said the little girl.

'He ain't yet,' said the little boy.

'Is too.'

166

'Not till we bury him and say prayers over him will he be.'

'Ain't he up there now, Mommy?'

They both looked at her.

'If he's not now, he will be real soon,' she said. She turned her back to them, walked fifteen or so feet, faced the swing set again, and leaned against the car body to which the grazing animals were tied. She pulled a cigarette from her shift pocket and lit it. Banyon walked over and leaned next to her. They watched the kids swing, as the set creaked and banged. Cicadas, as if on cue, began a deafening buzz in the fields to both sides of them. Carla said, 'You're going to fight him.'

Banyon's expression said their minds were on the same subject.

'How'd he make you agree to it?'

'He didn't make me agree to nothing.' Banyon yanked a spindly piece of grass from the ground, stuck an end of it between his lips, studied on the oak he'd climbed, imagined the darkness into which it was slowly receding as an ocean devouring a sinking ship. 'It was my idea.'

She half-smiled. 'He always makes it seem that way, don't he?'

'Is that how it was for you?'

She raised her eyes to him; in them Banyon read her answer as yes. He didn't know what difference, if any, it made to him. The goat suddenly lowered its head and ran at them; Carla stopped it dead in its tracks by flicking her cigarette at it. 'Earl weren't much good, even for them.' She nodded toward her kids. 'No matter how much they think they miss him now, we'll be better off without him. And not just because of the money.'

She walked over to the cigarette and scrunched it out with her foot. Seeing her coming the goat trotted to the end of its tether; it warily watched her return to the car. 'I'm real sorry for ruining your birthday party that night.'

167

'Why'd he throw us together that way?'

'Guess he thought I was lonely. Or you were. Or one or both of us ought to be.'

'You think he's a bad man?'

Bats sliced through the air above Carla's head. She flicked her hand upward as if she might hit one. 'I think my family's worse and better off for him at the same time.'

Banyon pushed away from the car. 'I don't even know sometimes if he might be my father.'

Carla gave him a strange look.

Banyon shrugged. 'How much of the insurance money won't you have to give him?'

'Are you a cop?'

'No.'

'Then don't ask cop questions.'

Night had completely arrived. The only proof of two children being in the yard with them was the creak of the swing set and their arcing shapes in the moonlight. Banyon waved toward them, even as he guessed they wouldn't see him doing so. He missed who they'd touched in him worse than ever. He asked Carla if she was an orphan. He couldn't tell for sure if her head was nodding or shaking from side-to-side as she walked away from him in the darkness.

A voice on the Newport's radio said that the medical ex-aminer had confirmed that the deceased man found two days ago in a pine forest near the Coppin River was drowned on Herman Finch's say-so for being a welcher and a bad father and husband and that he was already dead when a huge, black, half-Rottweiler, half-human beast dragged him into the trees and ate him.

Banyon jerked his eyes to the dash. 'What?' he gasped.

The announcer told about a brush fire in the southern part

of the country, a line dance to benefit the police department, more devilishly hot weather on the way.

Coming out of whatever world his mind had taken him to, Banyon peered back out through the windshield at humanoid fog-spirals standing in the road like star-gazing pneumas. He glanced at his watch. Two past nine. The Newport vibrated above its engine like a pot about to boil over. A deer crossed the pavement near the limit of his vision, before plunging into the blackness beyond it. He sensed a presence with him in the car, an invisible entity tracing his body like a magnet searching for a common pole; he visualized Finch in his study, mentally steering the thing.

Just ahead of pulling the station's plug for the night the DJ invited everybody to tune in again at five A.M. Back at the Deepwater Banyon took out of its frame his birthday present from Iris, taped it to the ceiling above his bed, and lay down to sleep with the lights on, gazing up at HOME.

Fifteen

At midafternoon Finch ambled over and silently stood behind Banyon while he worked. Banyon imagined him reaching out with his mind to muddle up Banyon's concentration, to put doubts into his head. Banyon began to notice maddening imperfections in the job – small streaks and air bubbles – barely detectable to the naked eye. He dribbled white paint onto the blue wall beneath the window he was trimming. Acutely aware of Finch watching him he carefully lay down his brush, picked up a rag, wiped off the drops. His uncustomary sloppiness made him suspect Finch was willing him into it.

Finch began talking about his time in the war, as if he was aware that Banyon knew he'd been in one. He said that during those days of pants-pissing fear and killing and maiming while trying not to be killed or maimed he'd learned what things in life were most important (he didn't list the things) and had taken out on the enemy he'd been hired to kill much of his rage at the parents who'd abandoned him and at all the other faceless people who'd never loved him. He seemed not to care that Banyon didn't respond or even turn around and acknowledge him. Banyon swore to himself that Finch would never see him make another blunder. Finch interrupted his own description of his first time taking a human life to say, 'A good soldier goes about his work the same way you do yours, Nat, as if he's alone in a vacuum and nothing or no one can touch him as long as he don't kick a hole in it.'

Steeling himself against the remark, Banyon kept painting.

'I get the feeling, Nat, you're afraid one missed stroke might blow you to kingdom come.'

'I ain't but putting paint on a building, Herman.'

'And you ain't going to kick a hole in it from wherever you're doing it at.'

'I'm doing it right here. I ain't gone nowhere.'

Finch laughed. 'You ain't gonna go down easy, are you, Nat?'

'I ain't gonna go down at all.'

Finch's shadow shifted some on the wall next to Banyon. 'I hope you've stepped up your training some.'

By way of an answer Banyon said, 'I'd take that heavy bag, you're still offering it.'

'Pick it up tonight you want to.'

Banyon nodded.

'Walnut's agreed to host us in his big garage.' Banyon heard Finch chewing wetly on his cigar. 'Looks as if we'll draw a fair crowd, Nat, and a decent purse.'

'I can't figure why, Herman, since nobody round's seen either of us fight.'

'People love a betting event. Don't matter if they're putting money down blind, Nat. 'Specially when blood might flow.'

Banyon turned from the wall. 'How they gonna set odds on us?'

'Feelings, vibes' – Finch threw his fingers into the air – 'whatever.'

Banyon dipped his brush into the paint can at his feet.

'We ought to have our own wager, don't you think, Nat?'

Banyon wiped most of the paint on his brush back into the can. 'I ain't got but around a hundred bucks.'

'How 'bout something 'sides money? Anything I'd want?'

Banyon shrugged.

'You think on it, Nat' – Finch ran a hand back through his thick mane of snow-white hair – 'see what you come up with.'

Banyon went back to painting.

Finch started in again on the war, on how in its flip-flopping between horror and elation it had foreshadowed all of his marriages, except his present one. A wasp began circling Banyon's head, as if it were contemplating an attack. Banyon swatted it out of the air and stomped on it; two others immediately fixated on him in the same way. Finch yanked an aerosol can from his rear pocket and rushed at Banyon, spraying him with the can. Banyon spit and frenetically waved at the pungent mist. Then he sprinted away from Finch. Rather than chasing him, Finch kept spraying the window he'd been painting around. 'There's a nest of 'em just beneath that sill,' he said.

'Christ almighty!' Banyon, standing a few yards away, swiped at his eyes. A pair of middle-aged, loose-skinned sissy types, dressed only in matching bikini bottoms, tee-heed at him from an umbrella-topped table near the pool. Chickadees pecked at breadcrumbs near their feet. The sun ricocheted off the water, knifing into the field across the road. Heat waves danced above the pavement. Finch turned away from the window.

'Been a bad summer for stinging pests, Nat.'

'You sprayed poison in my face, Herman!'

Finch re-capped the can. He glanced at the two sissies. They put their eyes back in their paperbacks. 'I didn't either.'

Banyon hawked and spit again.

'There's nothing lethal in this here, Nat.'

'What?'

Finch returned the can to his pocket. 'You could eat it far's that goes.'

'I don't want to eat it.'

'Course you don't. If you did, though, it wouldn't hurt you none.'

A decelerating car chirping its tires on the highway drew their attention. They watched a late-model Camaro, its driver waving out its open sunroof, enter the lot. 'That'll be Petersen' – Finch raised his hand and made a downward, whistle-pulling motion toward the car – 'back from the city in his new wheels.'

Petersen blasted out a series of short, rhythmic honks on the Camaro's horn. Banyon snapped, 'Bought with what he made off of selling my old ones.'

Finch distractedly snatched a dandelion from the lawn. 'You think we ought to call the cops then, Nat, tell 'em Petersen's maybe dealt in stolen property?'

'I ain't asking if he knew the Impala was hot, Herman.'

'What are you asking?'

'How he come by it in the first place.'

'You was sitting across from me, Nat, when he said how.'

'That mean the feller he got it from was the same feller I sold it to?'

'What I wonder is what the feller you stole it from's asking?'

Banyon didn't hazard a guess. The Camaro halted before the office.

'You think somebody you trusted's wronged you, Nat?'

'Part of me don't. The rest of me ain't for sure.'

'Good answer' – Finch held up the dandelion and blew at it, filling the air between them with flying white pods – 'and here it comes right back at ya.'

Banyon spat once more, but still couldn't get rid of the taste of bug spray. Finch handed him a dollar bill from his wallet. 'Get ya a lemonade, Nat.'

Finch suddenly appeared to Banyon as a physical combination of two people, one as young and fit as himself, the other past any hope of having a future beyond his next breath. 'Which war was it, Herman, you was in?'

Finch tilted his head and looked crookedly at him. 'Just how old, young man, do you figure me for?'

Banyon suppressed a sudden urge to fall to his knees before Finch, to tell him he'd fucked his wife, burglarized his house, stolen his dog, but that he wasn't as bad as all that made him sound and to ask Finch not to kill him or to stop seeing the good in him. 'I can't at all.'

Finch slapped his own stomach. 'Well, I don't look as old as a number you can't count to, do I?'

Banyon shrugged.

Finch playfully feinted at him. 'Leave it, young man, that you weren't around for the last war I fought.'

He took off for the office, saying over his shoulder, 'My mind's made up not to trouble no more on the color thing, Nat – the darkness, I mean – and to just let the Deepwater, you know, be the Deepwater.'

He dragged the heavy bag down through the trees and hung it before the lake on a pine limb. Minutes later, in the torpid air, he rapped it once with his bare hand, making it swing; its seesawing seemed to him to heighten the chirping and chattering in the woods at his back and the croaking and buzzing of the frogs and dragonflies among the pickerelweed and mud plantain in the shallows he faced. He imagined the contrary worlds of earth and water forming a circle around him, then closing in inch by inch. He pulled on his gloves, tightened them as best he could with his teeth. He jabbed at the bag; then popped it good. From atop a deeper, darker part of the lake two wood ducks watched him under the inflamed eye of sunset.

Banyon spit and slammed his hands together. He backed up, then rushed forward, gloves up, head bobbing behind them.

Conscious only of the impact his fists made with the stuffed canvas, he tore into it, pounding hard and steady at its center as if it didn't have a top or bottom, sending out over the water a tattoo suggesting the combined heartbeats of the creatures it held. A voice in his head repeated, 'Sap him! Sap him!' Instead of a bag Banyon saw the midsection of a faceless man who would kill him if he could. For ten minutes he ignored everything but the man's guts, relentlessly pummeling them, until he imagined the man, in his agony, briefly dropping his fists toward them. Quick as a flash of godly inspiration Banyon went upstairs with a vicious hook – *crack!*

The sound of that big kid's jawbone loudly shattering returned to him, along with a feeling as if another person inside of Banyon was walking out of quicksand on the heads of those who'd put him there.

Dropping his hands back down, he bore into the injured man, turning his belly to sauce. Only when his hands were raw, his arms numb, his lungs burning, and the man dead on his feet became a bag again did Banyon take a blow to watch in the growing dark a flock of Canadian geese set down near the far shore; he identified them from their honks and thick shapes. The sight, accompanied by much splashing, brought him back to himself. He took off his gloves, sat down on the bank, and watched a box turtle ten feet in front of him ascend a half-submerged boulder to within inches of its top, lose its grip, and tumble back into the lake. Pinkish clouds and the crescent moon's transparent shape accented the gray horizon. Banyon recalled a hopeful feeling he'd experienced the first few times he was sent somewhere new to live, before he'd started hoping only to go somewhere with a few good climbing trees. The turtle started back up the rock; near where it had fallen the first time it did again. Moisture stung Banyon's eyes. Not too far away a whippoorwill sang. A branch loudly cracked in the pines behind him. He wheeled around. Up the bank from him a ways, standing between two narrowly spaced trees, a gangly girl, just beginning to sprout breasts, gasped and backed up a step. Banyon told her, 'I'm hoping this turtle I been watching'll make it to the top of the rock it's trying to climb.'

The girl, not responding, put a hand to her face. Big printed daisies and brown-eyed Susans decorated her short yellow dress. Her red hair lay in a little kid's ponytail between her shoulders. Bats whipped through the air above her. 'No telling why it wants to get there.'

The girl seemed to be regarding Banyon's face with horror.

He reached up and touched himself where she was touching herself. He felt blood running from his nose, down his face; then he smelled and tasted it, wondering why he hadn't earlier. He swiped at it with the back of his hand. He smiled sheepishly at the girl. Then he nodded to the bag, saying, 'I must have head-butted it.'

The girl dropped her hands and lit out toward the motel. Banyon watched her until he could no longer see her or hear her breaking twigs and crashing into branches. He faced the water again, searching for the turtle, but it must have quit on itself because he couldn't find it. He picked up a flat stone and skipped it out across the lake. He had the sad feeling that whatever monster the girl had taken him for in the dusk would come back to haunt her in a recurrent nightmare. He touched his toes to the surface. Sunfish rose up to nibble at them. Banyon jerked back his feet; looking more closely at the swarming fish, he saw staring up through them the same blank eyes in the same decimated face he'd encountered in the lake a few days before. He leapt up, experiencing what he imagined the girl had experienced looking at him. He threw a rock at the face and eyes; they vanished; as the ripples he'd caused slowly faded, they came back again. Now Banyon understood that he'd been mistaken; the dead man was gazing up not from the lake's bottom but from its surface and he couldn't in fact be dead, no matter how much he looked to be, because his lips were forming words.

You pop the old man just right you could kill him in a heartbeat and make it look legal to boot.

I wouldn't never. Him nor nobody.

Or he could do the same to you.

Not in a ring armed with just his fists he won't. Not's long as I'm using mine.

Or Petersen might, with a flick of his finger.

Why would he?

Why wouldn't he plug the sorry bastard fucking his boss's wife? You ought to off 'em all, 'fore they do you and put you in here with me.

Banyon flung several more rocks at the water. This time the face stayed gone. After dinner he made himself go back and look for it again. In the moon's light, he saw, to his great relief, only the reflection of his own handsome self. He ran a hand back through his hair, adjusted his collar, went inside again, lay on his bed, and turned on the radio. For two hours past when Finch on that day normally left for the casino he listened to a call-in show for hunters, trappers, and fishermen. Then he kept his date with Iris.

★　★　★

Fighting every instinct he'd been born with, he halted deep inside of her just as he was about to rear back for his climactic thrust into her. 'What are you doing, Nat?'

'Making it last.'

He'd been aiming since birth, he realized, to be in this exact spot, where even if the world blew up he wouldn't hear it. Buried in her, he was aware of nothing outside of her. They might have been two halves of a single person and the appendage joining them could as easily have been extending out of her and into him.

'Makes me all breathless, Nat' – she panted – 'like how I hear mountain climbers get!'

He imagined their corresponding nerve endings crackling and sparking and his penis as an electric current he could hardly hold onto. At the depth of his penetration, invisible muscles held him in a viselike grip. He pictured the night sky and the two of them as the only stars in it, a billion miles from where their combined light hit. He asked Iris if she could see them up there too, shining down. She laughed (Banyon could feel it vibrating in his genitals) and said she could. They lay entwined and unmoving. They might've been dead, only they were both loudly mouth-breathing, and dead people didn't give off the heat they were giving off. Where his erection was making little twinges inside of her Iris tugged at him. 'What's that do?'

'Starts me up all over again.'

'Here's another one.'

He groaned.

'This time when I run with you up to the edge of that cliff, Nat' – she tugged at him again – 'you'll beg me to take you over it.'

Scarcely five minutes later Banyon did exactly as she'd predicted he'd do.

★   ★   ★

She picked up his hands and folded them into fists. 'How good are you with these, Nat?'

Banyon shrugged.

'I mean, are you better than he is with his, do you think?'

'I ain't never seen his in action.'

'You're both going in blind against each other?'

'That's how he wanted it.'

'What will you get out of beating him if you do?'

'Money enough to pay off the Newport maybe and to start us down the road.'

'What will he get out of beating you if he does?'

'Same thing, I guess – money, I mean – plus something else – I don't know what.' He looked closer at her, but couldn't read what was in her eyes. 'What do you think?'

'I think he's looking to become you.'

Banyon felt his heart beat accelerate.

'Or at least to take from you all he had at your age, which is what he sees you as having now.'

'What have I got he'd want?'

' 'Bout everything he'd like to have where he's at in life, but money. And he's got plenty of that already.'

'You mean, Iris, I got you?'

'Whether or not he's for sure onto us, Nat, he knows I don't love him.' She pressed his fists into her breasts. 'My guess is you look to him like all the reasons why I don't and that he's got it in his head to pound all the youth and sass and good looks right out of you, hoping it'll bring him back to feeling how he did when he was all full up on them same things.'

'Maybe he's just coming back around again.'

'Back around from where?'

'He ever tell ya his age?'

She shook her head. 'He's old though.'

'He ever look to you like he ain't?'

'What do you mean?'

'Or like he's so old he ought to be dead?'

She looked at him with mild alarm.

'Ya ever had the feeling, Iris, you knew him long before your memory says you met him?'

'That's just how he gets into people's heads, Nat, and gets them to trust him.' She squeezed his hands, placed them firmly beneath hers in his lap.

'How?'

'By making himself seem familiar to them.'

'I don't get you.'

'Like saying he's an orphan.'

'He ain't?'

'Maybe he is, maybe he ain't – who knows with him – but him telling me he was when I first met him made me feel, I don't know, on the same wavelength with him.'

'I don't know, Iris, if maybe he could be my father sometimes.'

She gave him a tender look. 'Or at least that, if he wasn't really, he might've been a good one?'

'Something like that.'

'He had me thinking that way early on too, Nat.'

Unclothed still, she made them an omelet. As she gently shook the pan over a burner's low heat, her bottom, firm and smooth and cloven so perfectly as to suggest God might have split it with a fine chisel, scarcely undulated; facing it from a chair at the kitchen table, Banyon inclined forward and kissed it. Not interrupting her cooking, Iris opened her legs for him. Banyon reached down and slid his middle finger up between them. The popping sound of the eggs sizzling in grease, wordless piano music playing on a portable tape deck above the refrigerator, the succulent slap of his finger moving in and

out of her became more noticeable in the absence of conversation between them.

He pulled his finger out of her and wiped it where he'd
been kissing her. Iris, sighing and releasing air from between
her legs, spread her feet wider apart on the linoleum floor.
Banyon put the finger he'd pulled out of her back into her,
along with another one, and kissed some more. Iris reached
back with the hand she wasn't cooking with and forcefully
pushed his head down lower. Her inner thighs were sopping
wet and slick, with a strong musky scent. The tape deck
clicked off. A temperate breeze carried the now faintly
discernible calls of the lake's loudest inhabitants through
the open screened window at their backs. Banyon pictured
the lake. He slipped his tongue into Iris. She tasted salty and
irresistible in a mysterious way, a flavor he didn't so much love
as feel he couldn't get enough of. Odd, he thought, that, as
petrified as he was of being in the water, he was so drawn to
staring out at its beautiful face and to gazing down into it,
toward its dark center. Iris moaned.

'He comes home last night and says not to think he wouldn't
be watching over this place and me after he was dead.'

'What did he mean?'

She waved her hand at the kitchen smoke. 'The morning
after Earl was found he went to his lawyer's, he said' – She
reached up and switched on the oven fan – 'and had the
lawyer make out a will for him for the first time in his life.' She
half-turned from the stove on which an omelet to replace the
one she'd burned cooked. 'He compared it to taking out flight
insurance.'

'What's he insuring against?'

'Dying from your punches.' She turned back to the stove,
away from Banyon's stunned look. 'He did it, he told me, to

protect his loved ones, what with him being so old and whatnot for what he was getting into and you being so young.'

In an interior room imprisoning Banyon's worst impulses a voice raged, Let the son of a bitch bring it on then, that's what he wants! 'What about if he does from something else?'

'Does what?'

'Dies.'

'Whatever he dies from.' Iris switched off the burner, severed the omelet, forked the pieces onto two plates, and carried the plates over to the table. 'It's just the fight, he said, is what led him to it.'

'Why?'

'Seems, Nat, you been on his mind.' She placed one of the plates in front of Banyon and sat down across from him, before the second one. 'He gave it back to his lawyer after he'd showed it to me. Otherwise you could see it.'

'I don't need to see it.'

'You might not believe it if you don't.'

'I'll believe it if you tell it to me.'

'One thing it says is that the combination to his office safe's in a security box at a bank in town and that the people at the bank are only allowed to give the key for the box to him and, after he's dead, me and you.'

Banyon stopped a forkful of omelet halfway to his mouth.

'If it comes to that we should open the safe alone, he told me, without letting the IRS or nobody else in on it.'

Banyon laid his fork down. 'Me and you?'

'I said you might not believe it.'

Banyon picked up his fork, then put it down again. 'I'm in his will?'

'You're a beneficiary.'

'A who?'

'An heir.' Iris wiped smudged lipstick from the corner of her lips. 'For punching him to death you'd get half of what's in his safe.'

Banyon locked eyes with her.

'Trying to figure it out from studying on it, Nat, is like sniffing through a dump to find the worst stink in it.'

'What would you get?'

'Everything you don't.'

'That don't make sense.'

'It's gotta make more of it to him than it does to us.'

'He knows,' said Banyon.

'About me and you?'

Banyon nodded.

'He don't make gifts to people who get in his way, Nat. He makes them have accidents – like he did to Earl – or disappear – like I'd bet anything he did to Robbie before telling me that poor boy had lit out with the till money.'

'He showed you the will to tell us he knows.'

'Leaving all he's got to us if you kill him and making sure we know about it is a strange reaction to it if he does.'

Banyon imagined he'd been severed in two; his mind's eye showed him a picture of the halves walking slowly away from each other like gunslingers in a shootout. He tore into his omelet and was dismayed to find it not only cold, but undercooked and filled with black remnants of the one Iris had burned and not completely scrubbed from the pan before she'd laid in the next one.

'Some kids dream to go to Disney World and they tell their parents about it and one day their parents take them,' said Iris. 'At least that's what I've heard. Did you ever dream 'bout going there, Nat? To Disney World?'

'I never heard much of it,' Banyon told her, 'till I got older and seen ads for it on TV when it just looked to me like a bunch of big freaks running around in cartoon getups.' The clump of loose eggs, half-cooked cheese, and charcoal slid like wet concrete down his throat.

'I never did neither. All I ever dreamed of as a kid was to hook up with somebody who cared enough to even know I had dreams.' Iris stood up from the table. Their sweat and carnal juices had dried on her, giving her skin a pasty sheen; like Banyon, she reeked of sex. 'But it wasn't till I met you, Nat, that I figured out what I really wanted was to have the same person I loved love me and then for us to make our dreams come true together.'

'Maybe he's writ the combination down, Iris, and put it somewhere in the house.'

Iris looked at him. 'It's in that safe deposit box, Nat, and it's in his head. It ain't no place else.'

She asked if he'd liked the omelet. Banyon told her it was the best he'd ever had. Iris said she was glad to hear it because she'd been hoping to prove to him that she was good not just at loving but at cooking and would make him fat and happy in their dream house if they ever got there. After showering, they toweled off, lay on the bed again, and looked up at the slowly rotating ceiling fan until Banyon, around two, got up, dressed, and headed for the window. Before exiting through it he said, 'If you're right and he don't know, Iris, that would mean he's telling the truth about all of it.'

'What all of it?'

'That we're his loved ones.'

Iris switched off the headboard light, putting herself and the room into darkness. 'Bad luck for him, then.'

★   ★   ★

Shadows of wind-bounced pine boughs on the lake's surface suggested a falling man's flailing limbs; farther out, a pair of stiffly bobbing coots or ducks might have been decoys of themselves.

If he ain't onto what's up, why wouldn't he tell you about the will himself?

If he is onto it, why would he make a crazy will like that in the first place?

Maybe it ain't even legit.

She's seen it, she said.

Did you see it?

I didn't need to see it. She told me about it!

For the fourth or fifth time, an owl's hoot invaded the mostly quiet woods.

Even if she did see it, it don't mean it's any good if he signed and gave his lawyer another one after it.

Why would he?

Maybe he suspects what's up but ain't sure, and he showed her a phony will to see if she'll tell you about it and is counting on you being so curious you won't be able to keep from asking him about it, and then he'll know.

An interval of absolute silence begged the question, Where are the crickets? The peepers? The frogs?

Or maybe it ain't phony and he's still testing you.

Or maybe it ain't phony — Banyon peppered the water with a handful of twigs, drawing not even a glance from the floating birds — and he ain't testing us.

That'd mean he loves you like a son?

Why's that something to smirk about?

He's upstairs every night practicing to kill you.

Comes to that he don't see me anymore than I do him.

Comes to that you're all he sees.

He's just looking not to go down, to stay on his feet. Like every fighter.

Like her?
What?
Could be she . . .
No.

Sixteen

By the week's end he'd finished painting the L's long side. Working, he tried not to think; he might as well have tried to stop a flood by not looking at it; his thoughts loosed other thoughts; periodically one of them would take root and bloom in his consciousness. He pictured Finch secretly photographing him from the office, pasting the developed pictures into an album spanning several lifetimes, then, late at night, going through and removing from the album selected shots – of Banyon, Iris, Dog, the Newport, Earl – and, with sewing needles, pinning them onto his study wall in different combinations. He woke one night to his own scream, a piercing pain between his shoulder blades, and a vision of Finch shoving a needle into that exact spot in a snapshot of him.

He stumbled, naked, with no clear recollection of how or when he'd gotten that way, into a warm, black night marred by fog patches. He sat bare-assed on his stoop, drinking a beer, watching bats wing like tossed rocks in and out of the vaporous, white clumps. A whippoorwill, suggesting some amnesiac victim, kept repeating its name. Two opossums waddled past the step. A porcupine, or maybe a muskrat, chewed on a nearby tree. Love and hate appeared in Banyon's mind as two of the creatures he could hear but not see moving in the dark spaces around him; identical-looking snakes, one deadly poisonous, the other with a venom containing a euphoric drug, they lived under the same bush and took turns biting whatever reached beneath it. Countless nightmares from which he'd woken alone, in buildings filled with people, to no one's soothing hand, to no one's comforting voice came back to him on an owl's screech. A door slammed at the motel. Banyon knew what was coming next. He covered his ears with his hands, but couldn't stop from hearing the shout that sounded at once as it was a thousand miles away and was being screamed inside of his own head: 'Dog! Dog? Are you out there, Dog?'

He bobbed up toward the world like a corpse suddenly dislodged from the lake's bottom; then he broke into the dawn, gasping. No delving into the ordeal, no reflecting on his wet cheeks, his depleted lungs, his burning eyes; no looking back at the night, no looking back period. No coffee. No food yet. In the bathroom mirror he saw a pretty good approximation of what he'd hope to see: a man damn handsome; a man damn strong; a man as alive as anyone could be. He put on his sweats. He told himself he'd been born that moment. He tried to make the moment become him. He went outside.

He imagined God having sewn together the previous evening's fog clusters into a solid, white blanket, then thrown it over the world to halfway up the trees. Croaks, quacks, occasional splashing sounds offered the only evidence of the lake's existence. Unseen birds sang in the dense canopy above where Banyon, unconscious to even his own grunts and exercised breathing, jumped rope, did his calisthenics, and punched the bag until each impact hurt his hands and vibrated up to his shoulders. Only after stopping did he realize it was raining. The trees, himself, the ground, were drenched. He couldn't hear the birds, the frogs, the ducks; like pebbles hurled from Heaven, the drops pelting the water muted all other sound. The noise never tapered off; it never faded into a dull pitter-patter; after fifteen minutes or so, it just quit.

A few minutes later the fog lifted, the sun broke through the clouds, the lake's surface was glassy smooth. The birds started singing again. Far off somewhere a dog began to bay; its high-pitched howl activated in Banyon memories or hallucinations (he wasn't sure which) of the rottweiler: running through the pines; trying to find its way home; tearing out Earl's throat. He ran up to the cabin. The dog's eyes placidly followed him. They watched him shower; watched him dress; watched him slip his wallet and switchblade into his rear pocket. They trailed him to work. They refused to leave him. In the middle of the afternoon the dog's harsh, meaty scent moved in directly behind him. Banyon wheeled around; seeing the Rottweiler there in the flesh, he nearly fell backward through the window he was painting next to. Then he realized he was seeing only Iris; or what had just now changed into Iris.

'Can you do it, Nat?' she asked.

'Do what?'

'You know. Don't make me say it.'

'I don't know if I can do it. I ain't never before.'

'You think I have, for Christ sake? I ain't.'

'I know you ain't. I might not be able to do it trying to.'

'What do you mean?'

'Just punches might not do it. Even good ones.'

'If I put something in his food. Something that would slow him down . . .'

'No.'

'What's the matter?'

Banyon glanced to both sides of himself, then back at her. He whispered, 'I stole his dog.'

'You did what?'

'The Rottweiler. I took it.'

Iris didn't say anything.

'I offered it a ride in the LeMans is all and it hopped in. Every night I hear him hollering for it.'

'Why are we talking about you taking his dog?'

'I shouldn't have. He didn't do nothing to me to make me do it.'

'Well, okay, that answers it.'

'What?'

'You can't do it.'

'I didn't say that.'

Iris walked away. She glanced back at him only once before she disappeared into the office.

He drove west, following the route he'd blazed on his final ride in the LeMans. Scattered raindrops hit the Newport's windshield; they quit when he finally turned on the wipers; soon the late-afternoon sun became visible again, radiating a pinkish halo through the steel-gray clouds. Between moments of what felt to Banyon like absolute calm being shattered by his own motion, gusts of wind shook the car. At a gas-and-food mart just past the reservation border he bought beer, ice, and two six-pound steaks. He came back out into a day that felt at once too crackly and too still, as if it was about to explode. He put the ice, meat, and beer into the cooler. Nothing moved in the air. A picture above the cash register of two kids holding hands with the woman who'd sold him his groceries flashed before him. He imagined a gathering storm focusing on him. He walked back into the store and stood facing the counter.

'You forget something?' inquired the woman.

Now the air began to undulate; Banyon could feel it shifting and rearranging itself around him; and the cashier – this plumpish mother – stood outside the developing turbulence, sending out to him vibes he couldn't decipher. 'What's it like?' he asked.

'I ain't following you, mister.'

'Being where you're at?'

The woman eyed him warily.

'I ain't asking, Ma'am, to be disrespectful.'

The woman seemed to accept that he wasn't. 'It's all right most the time.'

'You ever think you ain't where you're s'posed to be?'

'If I ever do I cure it real quick by thinking 'bout where I am.'

Banyon squinted at her because he couldn't find her exactly; she seemed to be shimmering, giving off light patterns like he sometimes saw while he was having what somebody had once told him were migraine headaches. 'I might be a part of what you are,' he told her.

'A part of what I am?'

'Part Indian.'

'I'm an Onondagan.'

'People would just guess part Indian when I was a kid, 'cause my dark features. They didn't guess what kind.' Banyon pinched his nose beneath his eyes to try to make them focus better. 'You think I might be?'

'There's lots of kinds of Indians.'

'Maybe I'm your kind.'

'I don't think so.'

'Why not?'

'Most of us live right near by and know one another.' The woman glanced around, as if searching for a third person, but she and Banyon were alone. A ring of fox and beaver pelts circled the dark, dingy room just beneath its ceiling. 'Besides, I don't see it in you.'

Banyon felt his hand come out of his pocket. 'What kind could I be if I'm not your kind?'

'I'm no expert, mister. What kind do you want to be?'

'I don't care what kind I am really or even if I am one at all.' He brought his hand up to his waist and saw that it was holding his switchblade. The woman flinched. 'I'd just like to be some kind of something – that's all – and know what it is.'

'I wish I could help you, mister.' Banyon pushed a button on the side of the knife, snapping it open. The woman swallowed loudly. 'But I don't know what you are. And that's the truth.'

'Did you hear 'bout that guy got ate by something just north of here?'

The woman only sucked in her breath.

'Feller s'posedly drowned first?'

Backing up a step, the woman nodded.

'What do you think ate him?'

The woman made a funny little noise down in her throat. 'Same thing I s'pose that's been killing and eating buffalo calves and deer roundabouts the last few weeks.'

Banyon picked up from the counter; an apple; he started slowly carving off its skin. Doing so felt to him like the most rational act in the world, and the fruit smooth and supple as flesh. He wanted to peel it, as he wanted to paint the Deepwater, perfectly. 'What would you do to it if you got hold of it?'

'What?'

'The thing that's out there.'

The woman made the strange noise in her throat again. 'I don't know. I don't guess I'd want to at all.'

Banyon got the last of the peel off. He placed the apple on the counter, sliced it in half, and pushed one half toward the woman. 'When was you born, Ma'am?'

'January 8.'

'What year?'

' '55.'

'You know when I was?'

'No. When?'

'I'm asking you to tell me.'

Backing up farther, the woman collided with the rear wall. 'How would I know?'

'I hoped you might is all.' Banyon held the knife out to her by its handle, as if offering it to her. The woman looked as if she was about to lunge for it, then changed her mind. 'Would you kill it or would you try to get it back to someplace it mighta once belonged?'

'What?'

'That poor blood-thirsty thing out there nobody can find or name.'

The woman darted quickly out from behind the counter, as if expecting Banyon to grab for her. When he didn't, she stopped halfway down an aisle and looked back at him. Banyon had the sensation of having just woken from a dream. He looked down and saw the open knife in his hand. He folded it and returned it to his pocket. He smiled sheepishly at the woman and wondered how he'd ever mistaken her for someone who might have been his mother. Now she appeared less frightened of him than perplexed by him. 'Are you past it now?' she asked.

Banyon said, 'You know Herman Finch, Mam?'

The woman cautiously nodded. 'I don't owe him nothing. And my husband don't no more neither.'

'I was just wondering if you thought I looked like him.'

The woman cocked her head to the other side of her body.
'Would you feel better, young man, if you did?'

Banyon didn't say if he would.

'I could maybe see him in you,' said the woman. 'Sure.' She
placed the thumb of one hand on her top lip and its middle
finger, between her eyebrows. ' 'Specially from here to here.'

Banyon asked her for a box of wooden matches. The
woman got one from a shelf next to her, walked back to the
cash register, put the matches in a bag, and rung them up.
Then she picked up and dropped both halves of the apple in
with them and rung it up too. Banyon paid her. He picked
up the bag. He felt a need to apologize to her for something
but wasn't sure what. He just thanked her instead. Then he
left.

The clouds, darker now and thicker, moved just ahead of and
above him as he climbed; he drew closer and closer to where
they blanketed the top of the mountain, until, finally, he was
in them. The temperature plummeted. Air condensed into
fog on the Newport's windshield. After clearing it he still
couldn't see much past the hood. Even his headlights failed to
penetrate the mass. The entire bank swirled around him like
some gigantic predatory bird. The altitude caused his ears to
plug. When his open mouthed swallowing finally popped
them the whiteness struck him as being too quiet, as if
something at its center was holding its breath, or gathering
itself to attack. And the Newport, in first gear and going barely
twenty miles per hour through that soup, was making a high-
pitched, humanlike whine. A voice demanded, Can you hear
them?

Hear who?

The dead ones wailing.

Which what?

Every one of 'em, but you, that's owned it after Finch is riding in here for eternity.

You don't know that! You don't know even that they're dead!

I got ears, don't I?

Jerking forward, Banyon turned on the radio. Instead of hearing static as he'd expected, he heard a woman's unaccompanied voice, as clearly as if she was sitting next to him, sing, 'Down in the valley, the valley so low, hang your head over, Nat Banyon, hear the wind blow . . .'

'It's "dear," ' hollered Banyon. 'Hang your head over, dear!'

The singing stopped. Fuzz filled the speakers. Banyon switched off the radio. He pictured the houses he'd seen wedged into the hillside on his first trip over that road and their occupants with x-ray vision seeing out through the clouds, into the Newport, and directly into his mind. The whiteness suddenly felt to him like a contained room without exits. He flashbacked to when he was at the bottom of a farm pond, unable to breathe. No break appeared in the clouds, no visible hint of a world beyond the one he was trapped in. Only the car's motion told him when he'd passed the summit and begun to descend. He followed the pavement's yellow caution line into a sharp curve; partway through it he suddenly was confronted by a huge, man-shaped figure looming immediately before him. Banyon started to swerve, then, remembering the sheer drop to his right and the rock embankment to his left, slammed on the brakes instead.

The thing came running out of the fog at him. Around Banyon's height, it was much thicker than him and coal black. Halfway to him, it dropped down onto four feet and started loping. Then it began to walk. Banyon honked his horn. The figure acted deaf to it. Banyon put the car in park, opened his window, stuck his head through it, and hollered, 'Get out the road!'

He heard his voice go out and come back to him, like the memories of his childhood, fainter and fainter until it didn't return at all. The bear paid it no mind period. Banyon pounded his hand on the wheel. Bastard'll give me no choice, he thought. The bear stopped a little forward of the Newport, reared up on its hind legs, and placed its front paws on the car's hood. Banyon jerked on the emergency brake. He opened his door, stepped out into the road. The bear rolled its mammoth head toward him. Banyon raised his fists at it.

The bear didn't move except to scrape its claws across the Newport's paint job. Banyon felt his pulse rapping against his temples. Adrenaline flushed his brain. He saw only a sheer-white wall marred by a giant black spot. He stepped out from behind the door. The idling Newport made a boiling sound right of him. A hawk shrieked beyond it, in the void out over the valley. Banyon envisioned his child-self forever tiptoeing past the closed rooms of napping monsters. He beckoned with both hands to the bear to come at him.

The bear, eyeing him closely, backed away from the hood.

Banyon started dancing and firing punches its way. He danced to within five feet of the bear. His breathing was a staccato of sharp grunts. He jabbed toward the bear's belly. The bear turned and faced him straight on. It made a sort of bleating noise. For a moment it seemed to contemplate its options. Then it dropped down again onto all fours and ambled off into the fog hiding the ascent. Still dancing and throwing punches, Banyon for a few seconds heard it crashing around on the acclivity. 'If you run into his big ol' Rottweiler,' he hollered, 'tell it I'm coming after it.'

★　　★　　★

He came out of the clouds five minutes later into sunset. Jagged hills appeared as dark, squiggly lines on the dull pink horizon, which was branded by twin lines of jet exhaust. Long shadows lay on the scrub pines where the road leveled out beneath him; by the time he'd entered them and pulled off into the trees early evening had become twilight. He parked the Newport in the same clearing he'd parked the LeMans in. As he stepped out into the near-silence caused by his appearance in those woods a single bluejay squawked; as if cued by it, birds all around and above him instantly erupted into sound.

From the cooler in the backseat he took two beers and three peanut butter and jelly sandwiches he'd made at the cottage. He sat drinking the beer and eating the food on the Newport's hood, his back against the windshield, his feet surrounding the scratch marks left by the bear, peering up through the treetops at the cloud bank inching after him as if it were the manifestation of every hurt and slight he'd ever had. Parts of one sandwich he fed to a chipmunk; the chipmunk edged nearer and nearer to where his fingers dangled, then dropped the bread chunks from the side of the car until it finally reached for a piece still in them; barely conscious of doing so, Banyon suddenly jerked open his hand and snatched the rodent. He brought it up to within an inch of his face and told it, 'You oughtn't to have trusted somethin' seemed so easy.'

The chipmunk squealed and tried to bite him. Banyon's grip, though, paralyzed it from the neck down. With his other hand he held a small crumb to its mouth. The chipmunk stopped trying to escape or bite him long enough to eat the crumb. Then it went back to trying to escape or bite him. Half of Banyon wanted to cry for a creature so pathetic; his other half wanted to squeeze it dead for being so stupid. He put it down and watched it run off. A minute later it was back looking for more. 'There ain't no help for ya,' said Banyon. He tossed the remains of his last sandwich to it. Then he jumped off the hood, got from the cooler a steak and two more beers, put them in his knapsack, strapped on the knapsack, and headed east through the woods, toward where he intuited the water would be. He couldn't see it out there and he couldn't hear it; he could smell it, though. And he could feel it, sure as he could feel the chipmunk's imprint on his palm, the bear's warm breath on his cheek, the Rottweiler's eyes all over him.

In a few hundred yards red maples, oaks, and ash started appearing in with the pines; the needle floor gave way to nettles and brush, up to his hips in places. His tramping scared from the undergrowth half a dozen rabbits and a fox family. In the gathering dark his shadow, outsizing him by half, clung to him like one of his nightmares come to life. A pheasant flushed from a patch of fever bush at his feet; his heart was still pounding from the shock it gave him when he stumbled into an indentation concealed by brambles and, trying not to fall, blindly put his right hand down onto a coiled rat snake as fat as his forearm. Once through the indentation he pulled a beer from his pack and, leaning against a stinking buckeye tree, downed it in less than thirty seconds; minutes later, with the light nearly gone, he stopped and pissed it out.

He put his dick away and thought he could hear the river; then he cupped a hand behind one ear and was sure of it. He'd not gone far at the sound before the trees and ground cover started thinning out. Then the woods went back into pines, bigger and more widely spaced than those in which he'd left the car. In the near-dark he could make out not far ahead the shape of the moving water. Looking at it, he took a few steps toward it, tripped over something, and fell. Crashing noises suggestive of a large animal charging through the brush erupted to his right. He wheeled in that direction while still on his knees; he couldn't spot any movement nor much else that way but the outlines of trees and bushes. The crashing stopped. Banyon jumped up, pulled off his pack, got out his flashlight, and switched it on; playing it over the area, he could see only a thick cluster of juneberry bushes and the trees more clearly. He turned, directed the light down at where he'd tripped, and saw the carcass of a large male deer. Banyon squatted down and studied on it. A head, with six-point antlers, and patches of flesh were all that hadn't been eaten from the buck's bones. He guessed it had been dead at least a week.

Scanning the light beam back and forth over the ground in front of him, he resumed walking, slowly, toward the water. Rustling, as if from the footsteps of an animal moving parallel to him in the brush, came from near where he'd heard the crashing. He shot the beam at it. The rustling immediately quit. Again Banyon saw nothing to explain it. The disturbing thought struck him that, under the growing cover of darkness, something out there was watching – maybe even stalking – him. At that moment he realized the birds had stopped singing. In the entire forest could be heard only the river hissing softly in its channel and a faint rumble of thunder from the approaching cloudbank. He aimed his light back at the river. On the near side of it, not far from him, it branched off into a tributary that barely moved. He pictured the current spitting Earl out into that still water and up onto its mud banks. He took his switchblade from his left rear pocket and slid it into his right front one.

He moved out again. Ten feet from the tributary he came upon another dead deer in the weeds, this one a spring fawn, not much larger than a goat; its throat was torn out and its insides half-eaten; what looked to be nearly every ounce of its blood soaked the area around and beneath it, giving evidence that it had been killed recently, maybe within the hour. Banyon experienced a flashback of climbing seventy-five feet up a tree behind some foster home and refusing to come down because of something he'd seen or experienced on the ground – he couldn't remember what, or anything else about the incident – which had given him the same sad, helpless feeling as he had now, staring into the disbelieving eyes of this child-deer.

He made his way to the tributary's edge. Its shore was covered with the tracks of animals: deer, rabbits, raccoons, bear, a thick, muscular, midnight-black, ferocious dog. Banyon's mind's eye showed him the fawn, like the buck before it – and how many others? – coming here to drink and being set upon and murdered by the same creature now eyeing him from the brush. A few drops of rain fell onto the water. Then he felt them on his face. He remembered Finch asking what besides money Banyon had to wager on their fight that would be of interest to Finch. He turned away from the water. He saw a large shadow moving slowly between two trees several feet to his left; an upright, two-legged shadow. Banyon's legs began to quiver. His heart felt like a small carnivore trying to claw its way out of his chest. He pointed his light at the shadow, but it disappeared behind the second tree.

He backed slowly away from the tributary. The loudest sound to him in that darkness was his own breathing. A flash of lightning briefly illuminated the night and a human figure stepping out from behind the tree Banyon was staring at. 'Herman?' said Banyon.

The figure didn't answer him.

'Is it me, then?' asked Banyon.

Only silence from the figure, which moved closer to him. Banyon spun toward the woods, started to run, stumbled over the dead fawn, and went down into its pool of blood. His light flew out of his hand into the blackness. He screamed. The baby deer's blood was warm as bath water. He rolled out of it and pushed himself to his knees. He looked back at the shadow and didn't see it. Then he did see it, only it had changed forms. Now it was the four-legged thing he had feared it was all along. Banyon ripped off his pack, pulled out the T-bone, and threw it as far away from him, toward the shadow, as he could. He heard the thing growl.

He turned and ran.

On the heels of a harsh thunderclap a bolt of lightning seemed to split open the cloudbank from which rain began to pour. Banyon collided with a tree, went down, got back to his feet, started blindly sprinting again. He heard the thing breaking branches at his back. 'Stay up! Stay up!' Banyon cautioned himself. He ran headlong into a thornapple thicket and came out the far side torn and bleeding, only seconds ahead of it. A minute later it was so close its loud, wet panting filled his ears like his own breathing. Then it was just to his left, but still out of sight, an invisible body of muscle, sinew, and bone moving step for step with him through the hardwoods. He couldn't say for how long. Or why it didn't attack him before he reached the Newport, jumped inside, and slammed the door.

Seventeen

Whoever had thrown him into this crud-filled pond was watching him drown.

He came out of sleep, gasping.

Beyond the window the morning sky was black and ready to storm again. He sat up on the edge of his bed. He waited. First it came in drops; then sheets; then in a solid wall, as if from a burst damn. He stared out at it through the glass, feeling marooned in a shrinking air bubble.

He wondered for the first time, no matter what sort of shape he was in or how strong he made himself, if he could beat Finch.

A man like that.

If he's a man.

Whatever he is that was him out in them woods.

Or it was his dog.

Or they're the same thing.

He went outside in his gym shorts and ran three miles up the road and three back, seeing only his feet splashing down in front of him; everything behind and around him washed away; his entire world became the space he fit into. Passing cars sprayed him with their tires. Drivers honked. People yelled out their windows at him. Banyon stopped hearing them and everything else not a part of him, even the rain. He fired punches at a bodiless threat in the air. I'll beat him, he assured his other self. I'll beat him if he's a man, a spirit, a ghost, or even that goddamn killer dog long's he'll stand toe-to-toe with me so's I can get a bead on him.

After he'd showered, he lay on his bed waiting for the rain to stop. He gazed up at Iris's birthday present to him. He said it aloud several times: HOME, a simple word, like his name, like *punch, jab, hit, work;* like *love;* like *hate.* A word, he found, that took only half as many movements of his mouth to say as Herman, Iris; or Mother. And a third as many as Deepwater; or rottweiler. He spoke each one, the single-syllable, two-syllable, and three-syllable words. Then he repeated them, in reverse order.

He took out his switchblade. He started flicking it open, then closing it again. He pictured the shadowy person who'd stepped out from behind that tree; how, almost before his eyes, the person had become a four-legged beast that had chased him through the woods and nearly caught him; how he'd sat in the Newport for close to an hour, imprisoned by the storm, as it imprisoned him now, feeling, but never seeing, the thing circling him in that deluge; how the deluge had followed him from the forest, over the mountain, and, ten hours later, found him here. He shivered. The cottage refrigerator loudly kicked on. Banyon rolled toward the wall. He carved his name into the wall's rough pine planking; it looked to him like three letters that could mean anything. Or nothing. He carved LOVES IRIS beneath it, then a heart around the whole thing. Now NAT looked like something; he wasn't sure what, but something more than random letters. He closed his eyes. He saw his body, his hopes, his desires attach to his name. He saw his face appear on his body. He saw his eyes open. He saw his lips part on his teeth. He saw his hands reach out. He saw . . .

A dog's bark found him through the storm.

He woke, facing the wall still. The rain had stopped, leaving in its wake a near-silence that struck him as being a living thing hiding somewhere in the cottage. Someone had carved DAD and MOM on opposites sides of his heart. Banyon eyed the room; it told him nothing. He looked down at his side. His hand still gripped the open knife. He closed the knife; he put it in his pocket. The quietness just sat there, out of sight, watching him. Banyon suddenly had a vision of Finch standing over him while he'd slept. He leapt up from the bed. He made his way to the window. He peered through it at the lake; beneath a clinging mist, the water's surface appeared as smooth and empty as an erased blackboard. Not even a duck floated on it.

He slid open the window. A crow's cawing, a squirrel's chattering, a wet, pulpy smell reached him. As clearly as his eyes saw the water Banyon's mind saw the murdered fawn, its throat and insides torn out; it saw Earl's corpse; it saw the half-eaten face (now it struck Banyon as more sad than frightening) in the lake; it saw an Indian woman throwing a small child into a farm pond; it saw Finch standing ambiguously on the shore of the pond; it saw Iris cradling a dead infant in her arms; it saw the Newport when it was still shiny and new flying headlong off a mountainside cliff; it saw the car, with Banyon in it, landing and bursting into flames; it saw things, which, even if they could be true, would be impossible for Banyon to know.

He turned back to the room. He walked to the corner where his gym bag sat. He picked up the bag, carried it to his bed, emptied it onto the mattress. He picked out all of his knick-knacks (except for the teepee and the Indian carving he'd bought from Iris), the only pieces of physical evidence he had of his life before he'd come to the Deepwater. He brought them to the trash basket and dropped them into it. He returned his remaining belongings to the bag. He dressed for work. He told himself to get ready. He grit his teeth and opened the door.

'What happens after?'

Banyon raised his eyes to Pam, wondering from her question how much, if anything, she knew about him and Iris.

'Have you thought about it?'

'Only that I won't owe him nothing no more.'

'That's if you win.'

'Right.'

'If you lose you'll still owe him on the Newport and you'll still be his hired man?'

Banyon didn't say, just poked with his fork at his pancakes, which he'd hardly touched.

'How's it gonna be between the two of you?'

'How's what gonna be?'

'One of you being a winner.' Pam slid in across from him in the booth. They were alone, except for Joe Littlefeet, chain-smoking at one end of the counter. 'The other being a loser?'

'I ain't gonna lose.'

'He ain't gonna either he says.'

'It's why people make bets.'

'In front of 'bout everybody at Earl's funeral the other day he said he'd sooner go back into the ground – he said it as if he'd been in it and come out of it once already – than to look up at you from his ass.'

A chill touched the back of Banyon's neck as if a freezer door had been opened behind him; then, ten years before to his knowledge he'd been born, he was watching Finch, looking hauntingly like himself thirty-odd years later, step into the Newport, start it up, take it out onto the highway . . .

'Whatever this is all about between you two, stud, feels a whole lot bigger than your few weeks knowing each other could muster up.'

He came back to his body (that's how it felt to him) to see Pam pouring herself coffee from a pot she'd placed on the table. Now he wasn't sure if he'd actually traveled back in time, if he'd been vividly remembering a scene he'd witnessed, or if he'd only been fixating on his memory of the photograph he'd found in Finch's drawer. His voice came out as a pant. 'How long you known him?'

'Couple years 'fore he hired me. Four and a half altogether.'

'Who around knows him from out in Missouri?'

'Missouri?'

'Ain't that where he's from?'

'I don't know where he's from.'

'Don't no relatives come visit him?'

'He says he ain't got none.'

'How 'bout old Army buddies?'

'If you know he was in the Army you know something 'bout him I don't.' Pam shook her head. 'But then you two got that in common.'

'What do we?'

'For all anybody round here knows he didn't exist till we laid eyes on him neither.'

Banyon pushed his uneaten food away. He experienced again the vision he'd had earlier of the Newport, only now with someone in it he couldn't see clearly, sailing off a cliff and exploding at its bottom. A second later he was picturing himself as an infant foundling in the arms of Pam. 'He's made sure you're a ten-to-one favorite, stud. Did you know that?'

'Tell me another happy-funny story,' said Banyon.

'It ain't no story. He's got it around that you're quicker than greased lightning at the same time he's telling the world he's gonna whup ya.'

Banyon blinked at her, clearing his head.

'Maybe he wants to put every dollar he can find on him and you to fall down when he breathes on ya. Pay off what ya owe him that way.'

'I couldn't do it to myself.' Banyon stood up. 'Myself'd get pissed.'

'If you ain't all the fighter you think you are, stud, and then some' – Pam went up on her tiptoes and kissed him on the cheek – 'please, dear sweet Jesus, hitchhike the hell outta here 'fore somethin' happens to make me cry.'

His job contained him like a dimly lit cell steadily darkening through his own narrowing vision. Under a sky the color of month-old meat he worked through the lunch hour and half the afternoon, not stopping to piss, to drink, for a blow even until the ladder he was painting the top of the laundry room wall from was walked headlong into by a pink-eyed, ghost-white man whose age Banyon couldn't even guess at. Instead of apologizing, the albino started complaining to Banyon that he'd been cheated by some casino blackjack dealers who'd wised up to how his bad peepers handicapped him.

Staring blankly at the man, Banyon pointed dumbly to his own ears and mouth.

Ignoring the act – or not seeing it – the albino griped to him that he'd been made the butt of jokes, fucked over, and fooled his entire life because he couldn't see good. He'd think he was almost on top of something, reach out for it, and find nothing there; or vice-versa, as when he'd collided with Banyon's ladder. 'I can't hear you,' Banyon mouthed to him. 'And I can't talk neither.'

The albino asked him if on top of being a liar he was one of those thievin' casino Indians.

Banyon grabbed his brush and readdressed the wall. He tried to return to the rhythm he'd been interrupted in, but kept wondering why the albino had suspected he might be an Indian. He wheeled back around to ask why, but the albino was gone.

The sun later snaked partway through the clouds, half-drying the grass and parking lot, creating spirals of spectral-looking steam. Two doors from Banyon, Finch stepped out of the office, hesitated, approached him, and said, 'You oughtn't have gone over to Carla's place adding to her grief.' Snatching off his Stetson, he ran a hand back through his matted hair. Past him, on the road's near shoulder, a graying hippie couple in matching hightop sneakers and denim overalls perched on a sailor's bag, thumbs extended to the sparse traffic. 'Even to impress her little ones as a tree-climbing monkey.'

Banyon faced him from the ladder's lowest rung. 'I didn't, Herman, but offer her my condolences.'

'And ask her 'bout the dough she's going to be coming into.'

Before Banyon could reply Finch loosed toward him a volley of air punches. 'I'm going to be all over you time comes, Nat, like last night's rain. This time there won't be no car, no tree, no bush, no bed for you to hide in.'

'What?'

'I'm just telling you, get ready.'

Banyon hopped down to the ground. He sensed Finch trying to crawl through his eyes into his head. Finch told him about Earl's funeral, how from the moment the preacher had started the service off by complimenting Carla on looking better than she had since her single days it had become more of a celebration, with Earl's widow and kids and the handful of mourners laughing and chasing butterflies through the cemetery as Earl, attended only by the preacher and two grave diggers, was laid to rest. Later, at Carla's house, the drinks had flowed. Earl got dropped early on as a topic of conversation. Everybody raised their glasses to a debt-free future. Then they played a game of touch football. 'If you can beat me Saturday and I ain't dead after, Nat,' said Finch, as if Earl's burial related directly to their upcoming fight, 'I'll shake your hand and leave you to it.'

Banyon stared hard at him, divulging nothing from Finch's gaze, fearing his own was betraying too much of himself.

'Leave me to what, Herman?'

'Free and clear. Ain't that what you want?'

'You mean I won't owe ya on the Newport?'

'You won't owe me on nothing. My time'll be up and yours'll just be beginning.'

'What?'

'I'll just be an old, lonely man in your rearview mirror that's what you want.'

At that moment Banyon was certain that wherever in the world he'd come from, Finch had come from first; that whoever had abandoned him had earlier abandoned Finch; that all he'd longed for Finch had longed for before him; that every awful thing he'd done Finch had done ahead of him; that every emotion and thought he'd experienced – from to-die-for love to killing anger – Finch had experienced; that if all those things weren't true, Banyon by now would be as dead as Earl.

'And what do you want from me, Herman?'

'What?'

'If I lose?'

'You won't be worth a good shit if you lose, Nat – to nobody here – ever again.'

Banyon didn't say anything. Finch pulled on his hat. 'So just walk away if you do.'

'Away from what?'

Finch waved his hand in a circle, meaning to encompass everything in sight.

'What about what I owe you on the car?'

'That car'd only kill anyone kept it after losing.'

'Huh?'

'You lose, Nat, you walk away – alone – with nothing but that gym bag full of stuff you come with.'

Banyon nodded. Part of him wanted to turn and run; another part of him longed to wrap Finch up in a bear hug and cry like a baby on his shoulder; the part that won out hoped to pound Finch to a pulp come Saturday.

'You dream much, Nat?'

'Some, I do.'

'I hadn't for years. But since you got here I begun to again.'

'What about?'

'Some bad memories from long ago I thought I'd put behind me. Others – and these'd be more of the sort a dream of that beachhouse I showed you a picture of – I'd quit lusting after till you showed up.' He raised his eyes to Banyon as if Banyon knew exactly what dreams he was talking about. Then he told about a dream he'd had the night before in which a small child had been drowning. He clamped his fingers around his neck to show how the child hadn't been able to breathe. Twice as thick as Banyon's and slightly sunburned, his forearms, tensing in his sleeveless undershirt as his hands squeezed his flesh, suggested slabs of raw meat. Banyon suddenly realized that Finch's dream was his own dream of drowning in a farm pond, only from a bystander's point of view.

'Do you know the one I'm talking about, Nat?'

Banyon couldn't form an answer.

'Probably not all that uncommon you think about it.'

'What ain't?'

'Dreams about drowning' – Finch shrugged – ' 'specially among us orphans, who grew up feeling blessed just to be able to breathe the air the rest of the world does.'

Banyon turned back to the wall. A straight line from the roof to the ground separated where he'd painted from where he hadn't; Banyon imagined a similar line inside his head; he saw it, against his own efforts, moving deeper into darkness; he felt as powerless to stop it as he did to stop loving Iris. He heard Finch say, 'You're selling yourself short, young man.'

'For what?'

'What you done here. Or almost have.'

Banyon wasn't sure what he meant. 'I'm jus' doing what you hired me to do, Herman.'

Finch waved as if he was being too modest. 'Good hired help as hard to find as it is these days, that's no small task.'

'Rain or shine, Herman,' said Banyon. 'I'll have her done – and looking brand-new – for ya by Saturday.'

Finch nodded and walked away.

He found himself kneeling over a patch of freshly turned dirt in a sliver of moonlight before Iris and Finch's bedroom window, with no memory of how he'd arrived at the spot, feeling as if he'd been carried to it by a strong gust of wind. His switchblade, marred by soil, was open in one hand; the female figure he'd half-carved for Iris several days before lay next to him; his left palm was bleeding; his accelerated heart rate suggested he'd been working out, running, or having a nightmare; he was perspiring heavily in just his boxer shorts. I hadda been sleepwalking, he told himself.

And I'm the king of fucking England.

He backed out of the moonbeam, wiped off his knife, closed it, sat down with his back to a pine tree, twenty feet from the darkened window. He dropped the switchblade next to the carving, dabbed at the blood on his hand with his underpants, which were speckled with it already, and tried to remember whether he'd been into Iris's bedroom and back out of it or if he'd come here straight from the cottage. He could recall only that he'd had no plans to enter the room – and every reason not to – as Iris had told him earlier that Finch would be home all evening.

Thinking about it made Banyon sweat more and his heart to beat more rapidly. He looked down at his injured palm; a small slice mark appeared just beneath his two middle fingers. He pressed the wound into his right kneecap. Not a sound came from the window. He took his hand from his knee. The bleeding had stopped.

He picked up the carving, then his knife. He brought out the blade once more. He started in absently whittling on the female figure, the blade making a gentle *thwack, thwack, thwack,* the fine chips landing and sticking to his sweat and blood-damp thighs, the yellow curtain moving in a warm breeze over the screen before him. Well-worn, but mysterious ruts were activated in his mind. His hands gently caressed the wood; his fingers nimbly manipulated the blade; the figure began taking on a specific shape without him consciously giving it one. An owl's screech recalled to him the countless, now nearly indistinguishable voices of the people who'd presided over his childhood – voices not of strangers, but not of friends either – moving around, over, through him; and more familiar voices going back in time further than he could see or hear; but, until he'd come to the Deepwater, not a single voice, outside his own head, had touched him.

He scanned the canopy for the owl. Gazing up he had the

sensation that the treetops and stars had moved farther away from him since last he'd looked; at the same time the peeps, chirps, howls, croaks from the woods and water seemed to him to abruptly rise in pitch, as if a chorus that had been singing in one key had, en masse, begun singing in an octave higher; or as if the forest's inhabitants and the lake's inhabitants were trying to drown each other out in an intensifying argument. Banyon suddenly recalled Finch saying that when the time came he'd be all over him like last night's rain, as if he'd seen Banyon out in that storm; that come Saturday Banyon would have no car, no tree, no bush, no bed to hide in. And he remembered Finch's version of Banyon's own dream, in which Finch had been not the drowning child, but someone watching it drown.

Take a peek inside, why don't ya.

I got no reason to.

You're out here wondering's all the reason you need.

It'll be dark as Hades other side that window.

Just listen at it then. See what floats out to ya. Could be nothing will.

Nothing of what?

Not a living breath.

I sliced my own self whittling in my sleep's what happened!

Or you sliced too deep on what you was whittling on.

Banyon brought his injured hand, which still held the woodcarving, up to his face. A seam of coagulating blood mostly closed the half-inch-long cut. A small amount of blood had stained the carving. Banyon examined more closely the female figure. His recent whittling had transformed it from being as solid and curvaceous looking as Iris to being as short and plump-looking as the Indian woman who'd sold him groceries at the reservation store. 'That dark, Injun look,' said one of the indistinguishable voices in his head, 'must favor the mother who used him for fishbait.' Banyon pushed the carving a few inches down into the soft dirt, which apparently filled in a fair-sized hole, between his legs. He padded the soil down with his palm, then sprinkled pine needles over it. He stood up, holding his switchblade. Lacking a pocket to put it in, he gripped the knife in his right hand as he stealthily approached the building.

Five feet from the window he squatted down, then walked to it the rest of the way on his haunches. He raised up enough so that his eyes came just above the ledge. He inclined his head forward, stopping when his nose touched the screen. He faintly smelled Iris; her essential odor, heightened by one of the perfumes he'd more than once delighted in watching her, after they'd showered, dab onto her neck, wrists, bosoms, spine where it disappeared into her bottom, abdomen above her pubic bush. Finch, he realized at that moment, had no essential odor; his smell, like his looks, varied, in Banyon's mind, with the occasion. In the darkness beyond the blowing curtain he could make out nothing, not even the shape of the bureau he knew he was facing. Beads of sweat fell from his brow onto the ledge. The curtain softly scraped against the screen. The ceiling fan's aerodynamic whir, the vanity clock's ticking reached him. He put his right ear where his nose had been and, to block out the noises behind him, a finger in his left ear. He distinctly heard the steady rise and fall of breathing.

He backed away from the window. He folded his knife and started back through the woods to the cottage. Now he tried to remember anything particular about the breathing noises and couldn't. It occurred to him that when asleep all large animals – human or otherwise – sound alike. The thought made him shiver. He realized he had no idea who – or what – he'd heard. He ran the remaining ways to the cottage. He locked the door to keep from leaving without knowing it again. He crawled into bed and buried his head beneath the covers. He thought he heard a door slam at the motel. He understood with a start that the mysterious breathing he had heard had been coming not from someone or something in Finch's room, but from himself outside of the room. He pictured the Indian store clerk backing away from him as if he were a diseased dog. His dreaming when he closed his eyes felt to him like fast driving. He had the impression the Rottweiler was hunting him. He opened his eyes, in darkness still. He suddenly remembered the Newport's unmistakable roar as he'd glimpsed it hours earlier, under the direction of a thief he couldn't see, speeding out of the lot onto the westbound highway, toward the Indian lands.

He got out of bed, washed out in the bathroom sink the cut on his hand – it wasn't deep – bandaged it, then chugged a beer. Sitting on the front stoop afterward, he drank another beer more slowly. He counted four falling stars, three birds landing loudly on the water, twenty-eight seconds between each time a coyote made a series of six yaps. To stop from thinking about things he didn't want to think about he periodically pinched himself until it hurt. He kept half an ear out for the Newport, praying it would return while he was listening for it, but if it did he didn't hear it.

Eighteen

He opened his eyes punching wildly at the string attached to the ceiling light above him. The bare bulb snapped on. Its weak glow added nothing to the light coming from outside. Still breathing hard, he reached up and snapped it off. In one motion he jumped out of bed and, responding to a feeling of danger from a threat he couldn't isolate, began dancing and jabbing at the room's shadows. He danced to the window, making his punches stop a fraction of an inch from the screen, overcome, suddenly, by the memory from the bottom of that farm pond of death, not stopping just short of him, but hitting him flush, and of gazing up through the water at someone's eyes gazing down at him.

Whose eyes?

In his mind he saw the albino's eyes and heard a voice say that half-blind son of a bitch wouldn't know an Indian from his own self.

Melodic sounds from the woods and water reached him; Banyon imagined his fists, like a conductor's baton, orchestrating them. Beneath the rising sun the lake's surface was as flat and shiny as a just-waxed floor; the sky, already a dark blue, might have been its reflection. From between the creases in his left fist blood flew against the screen. He quit punching.

The sounds kept coming. The red drops rolled down the window to the floor. Banyon looked down to where his clenched fingers had opened the scabbed-over cut on his palm. Some bastard, he remembered, had stolen his car.

He bandaged his palm, pissed, brushed his teeth, shaved, cupped water in his hands, dumped the water on his head, slicked his hair straight back from his temples, then smiled, scowled, frowned, sneered at himself in the bathroom mirror.

He stripped naked and flexed before it.

He counted the separate ridges of muscle, suggestive of the combined peaks in a mountain range, running from the bottom of his abdomen to his chest. If he had an ounce of fat on him he couldn't find it. He smashed his fists into his rock-hard belly. He winked at himself. He told himself, 'Hello,' and 'Watch out, now.' He peered hard at himself but couldn't find in himself anyone he recognized. The thought of going up to the motel suddenly terrified him. He didn't feel like going down by the lake either; or going anywhere outside at all.

He walked to the refrigerator, got out a quart of orange juice, and returned to his bed. Reclining on the mattress, he drank the juice, studying first on Iris's drawing of HOME, then on the words and letters carved into the wall. When the juice was gone he played solitaire. Finch appeared in his mind as a one-eyed jack. He took out his switchblade, carved a tiny, nearly imperceptible slice in the one-eyed jack of spades's lower-left corner. He shuffled it in with the rest of the cards and dealt them out face-down to see if he could pick out the marked one; he did and did so again on twenty subsequent attempts; with each success he felt a little more confident, a little more like himself. After putting away the deck, he got into his sweats and did forty-five minutes of hard calisthenics on the cottage floor. He completed the workout by performing fifty rapid, one-handed pushups with each arm. Then he went into the bathroom and stood before the mirror again. He saw exactly who he'd hoped to see. He showered, put on his work clothes, and went up to the parking lot.

The Newport sat where he'd turned it off the day before.

In the clear morning air sounds reached him with a distinct clarity; a room door creaked open on rusty hinges: two young kids splashed in the pool; songbirds sang; squirrels chattered; a horn honked near the diner; coming out of an open window on the L's long side a man's voice demanded, 'Where's my fucking shaving cream, dear?' Banyon's pulse made an insistent rapping noise in his head above a voice which told him, Get the hell out to the road and hitchhike gone from here, and, in response to it, another voice which said, Fuck you and fuck him too if he thinks he can make Nat Banyon believe Nat Banyon didn't see what Nat Banyon saw.

Experiencing the sort of anxious euphoria that used to hit him every time a social services vehicle came to take him from one house in one town to another house in another town, he slowly circled the car three times; examined from his back its undercarriage; looked under its hood; pushed down on its trunk to make sure it was securely shut; tried each of its doors to be certain it was locked as he'd left it. He found no outward indications the car had been driven. He pulled its key from his pants pocket. He unlocked and opened the driver door. Before climbing inside, he glanced at the office.

He thought he saw the window curtain move. He pictured Finch's camera peeking out through the fabric at him.

He smelled something in the car as he got into it that he hadn't smelled in it the day before. He wasn't sure what: the faint residue of some odor not unfamiliar to him.

His jacket, one of his sweat-stained bandanas, the few

221

cassettes he owned cluttered the shotgun seat; some candy wrappers and soda cans he'd tossed on that side of the floor appeared not to have been disturbed. Everything he'd put in the glovebox, and nothing else, was in it. His cooler sat as it had yesterday on the floor before the backseat. A bloodstained rag lay as if it had been casually or inadvertently dropped in the indentation rear of the stick shift. Drops of blood dotted the floor in front of it.

A number of small, black particles lay atop the rear seat cushions. Banyon pinched a couple of the particles – now they looked like hairs – between his right thumb and index finger; he brought them up to his face. Pubic hairs was his first thought; they aren't coarse or curly enough to be his second one. The hairs he could see were straight and soft as fur. Banyon peered again at the bloody rag. He sniffed the familiar, predacious scent in the air. He gazed down once more at the scattered black hairs. He felt incapable of moving, of even breathing, as if he'd been frozen, with his immediate surroundings, in a block of ice.

Feeling the gush of his own exhale he got out of the car. He instantly went from one extreme state to its opposite: now his breathing struck him as being exaggeratedly loud, as if it were being broadcast over a microphone, the day painfully bright, the area's general odor – a combination of chlorine, pine trees, daffodils, exhaust, lake mud, and drying paint – overwhelming. He locked the Newport and leaned, gasping, against it, facing the pool. He watched the two kids dive for coins their parents had tossed into the water until, after an indefinite interval, his breathing somewhat modulated and his senses returned to near-normal.

Aiming to talk to Iris, or at least to see her, he walked to the diner, where an especially heavy breakfast crowd filled every seat but for a counter stool on which he perched, nursing a cup of coffee in a miasma of cigarette and fryer smoke, between a county highway worker reeking of fresh tar and a lumberjack covered in wood chips. A guy in buckskins and a raccoon hat came out of the gift shop, allowing Banyon a peek through the open doorway at enough browsers to tell him it would be no go with Iris. A mean-mouthed countergirl named Velma asked him what he wanted besides coffee. To drink it in peace, answered Banyon. Velma told him to take it to church with him in a foam cup so a paying customer could sit down. Banyon handed her a five-dollar bill and told her to keep the change. Then he thanked her for the service and split.

Back at the motel he found Finch sitting on a lawn chair before the office, pulling burrs from the Rottweiler's coat.

Finch tossed a handful of the prickly balls into the trash receptacle to his right. 'He was covered in 'em nose to tail.'

Banyon, to keep from falling down, steadied himself with one hand on Finch's Caddy. Then he half-sat on its hood. With its eye closest to him, the dog followed his every move. 'I've had him inside with me the last two hours' – Finch patted the back of the Rottweiler's head – 'cleaning him up.'

Banyon kicked a pebble across the concrete; in trying to give his entire attention to the skittering path it made to the grass, he felt the Rottweiler concentrating on him in the same way; and he remembered a beast, just out of his sight, casting first a two-legged, then a four-legged shadow while it stalked and chased him through the woods as if Banyon were one more helpless fawn come to drink in the water-hole it had staked out.

'What a story he could tell if he could talk, Nat.'

'What story?'

Finch shrugged. 'You know.'

'I don't know much of anything. And not near what you act like I do.'

'I just meant if he could talk he could tell us 'bout his last four weeks.' Finch frowned. 'He'd unravel the mystery for us.'

Banyon for the first time noticed that the Rottweiler's and Finch's eyes were the same dark brown. In response to a silent voice that told him get yourself ready to fight or run he pushed himself away from the Caddy. 'How'd you figure where it was at, Herman?'

'Figure what?'

Banyon nodded at the Rottweiler. 'To go and bring it back.'

'I didn't go and bring it back.'

'Who did if you didn't?'

'Dog was setting out here when I got up this morning, Nat' – Finch smiled – 'like he'd never left. I'd say he finally found his own way home.'

'From over fifty miles away it did?'

'Over fifty miles from where?'

'From where Earl got washed up at.'

Finch looked at Banyon curiously. 'What's Earl got to do with Dog?'

'What are you trying to make me believe, Herman?'

'Make you believe how, Nat?'

'I stood and watched my car leave here without me in it last night.'

Finch looked at the Newport, then back at Banyon. 'It's here now, Nat.'

'Whoever brought it back while I was asleep brung your dog back with it.'

Finch shook his head. 'I ain't got keys to your car, young man. 'Sides, I drove it all I wanted to thirty years ago.'

Banyon took a step toward the office and stopped when a low growl erupted in the Rottweiler's throat.

Finch patted Dog to make it quit growling; it did, but kept staring at Banyon. Banyon wordlessly turned and walked to the Newport. He pulled out his keys, opened the driver door. He glanced back at Finch. Finch separated his hands in the air before him as if to indicate he was as puzzled by what Banyon had claimed to have seen as Banyon was. A doomed sensation hit Banyon. He imagined himself, as he'd often done when he was a boy, as the only person at a magic show who didn't know how the tricks were performed, who'd not been tuned into how things — even families and memories — could be made to disappear before one's eyes. He climbed into the car. Only fragments of black dirt and a few pine needles lay on the backseat. Banyon picked up the bloody rag, wadded it into a ball, and, for no reason he could name, stuffed it into his front pants pocket.

He backed out of the Newport. He looked again at Finch, who had a hand buried in the rottweiler's fur, creating the illusion that the hand was attached to them both as if they were parts of the same creature. His words sounding more like a plea than the accusation he'd intended them to be, Banyon said, 'Somebody stole my car last night, Herman, or I'm not Nat Banyon.'

Nodding as if he was considering one or both of those possibilities, Finch finally replied, 'At least you got yours back if somebody did, Nat.'

Banyon couldn't think how to answer him, so he didn't. He slammed shut and locked the Newport's door. Saying nothing more to Finch, he walked behind the motel. In the clear morning air a bald eagle glided high above the woods. Banyon felt slow and exposed beneath it. At the storage cottage he tossed the rag he'd taken from the Newport into a garbage bin. He gathered together his tools and paint. Lugging them back to the lot he passed the albino, pissing with his back to him on a tree trunk. Not even glancing over his shoulder at Banyon, he called out, 'Is that the Indian painter?'

Banyon put down his equipment and walked to him. 'How'd you know it was me?' he asked.

The albino squinted up at him. 'I heard all them cans and shit you were carrying clattering.'

'Why do you keep calling me an Indian?'

'I don't know what you're talking about.'

'Twice now you've called me an Indian.'

'I ain't never called you an Indian. Are you one?'

Banyon brought out his dick and started pissing next to the albino. 'When I was a kid I heard some people say my mother was one, but I never met her.'

'That'd make you half a one.'

'I heard them same people say she tried to drown me too, and sometimes I half-remember her doing it, but I'd like to meet her and hear it from her. If she gave me a good enough reason to I'd maybe forget about it just to know her.'

'She couldn't come up with a reason good enough.'

'You don't think so?'

'Hell no. And no use trying to forget it neither, 'cause you won't no more than I will that every bat in the world sees better than me.' The albino shook his dick dry and secured it in his pants. Scarcely aware he was doing so Banyon reached out and clapped a hand on his shoulder. Apparently mis-interpreting the gesture the albino said, 'Don't tell me I pissed on my new brogans?'

Banyon checked it out for him. 'No.'

'See ya later then. I'm gonna go down and smell the water.' The albino started stumbling toward the motel with his hands out in front of him. Banyon turned him around and headed

226

him at the lake. A minute later he retrieved his tools and paint. He carried them out front to find Walnut and Petersen seated with Finch in a semi circle around the Rottweiler. Petersen aimed and shot an imaginary rifle at him. 'Saturday's 12-to-1 favorite,' he said.

Banyon halted on the near side of them. 'Who says I am?'

'Every shit-for-brains in the area making book on it.' Petersen blew chimeric smoke away from the end of his index finger. 'Least every shit-for-brains Walnut and me have checked with.'

Walnut leaned back in his lawn chair and farted.

Finch took off his hat and waved it at the air between him and Walnut.

Petersen reached out and plucked a burr from the Rott-weiler, which sat as regally before the three men as a bronzed, muscular statue. 'I don't personally get why, though.'

Banyon didn't say anything, just put down the stepladder digging into his shoulder.

'I mean here's Herman by his own account been through wars, more fights than any ten men, a slew a car wrecks, a bunch a marriages – and that's just in this lifetime – and here's you, who looks good with your shirt off.'

'I'm putting my life savings on Herman,' said Walnut.

'Fuck the odds, then. I'm with you, Walnut.' Petersen threw the burr out into the parking lot. 'Nothing personal, Nat, but something tells me you're gonna crack under all a what Herman's gonna throw at you. I'm guessing it'll happen in about the third round.'

'What will?'

'Crack' – Petersen pointed the finger he'd pantomimed blowing smoke away from at Banyon's head – 'Crack.'

Banyon was half-certain Petersen had just warned him to go down in the third round Saturday if he didn't want to go down forever like Earl and that shot woodchuck in the meadow across the road. Finch said, 'I already told ya about Petersen's mouth big enough to fall into, didn't I, Nat?'

Banyon didn't say if he'd told him about it or not.

Petersen opened his mouth wide, showing Banyon how big it was.

Walnut spat tobacco juice onto the grass bordering the concrete.

Banyon had the sensation of being nudged through a tunnel toward a place he'd been before but couldn't remember. 'Way I got it, Herman,' he said, 'I weren't gon' be fighting no assholes day after tomorrow. Only you.'

'No assholes, young man, no big mouths, no tobacco spitters, no bookies. Just Herman Finch.' Finch turned to Walnut and Petersen. 'Didn't I say you'd never rattle Nat Banyon? Didn't I say him and Herman Finch come from the same cloth?' He threw an uppercut from his waist as if to emphasize the point. 'Now zip that thing, Petersen, 'fore a bird shits in it.'

Petersen slowly closed his gaping mouth into a tight-lipped smile at Banyon; he drew a forefinger across it. Walnut spat again. A hay truck trailing chaff went by out on the highway. Banyon picked up and started carting his ladder past the men. Finch said to him, 'Guess you feel like you've 'bout buried Herman Finch's old motel.'

Banyon stopped walking to look at Finch, wondering, but not sure he wanted to know, what new topic they'd moved on to.

Finch whistled shrilly, prompting the Rottweiler to stand instantly and trot three steps to him; it sat down again, laid its head in Finch's lap, and peered up at Banyon with eyes so identical looking to Finch's that Banyon had the feeling Finch was seeing him twice at once. 'And went and built your own brand-spanking-new one.'

Banyon said, 'I feel like I made the same one darker's all.' He shifted the ladder to his other shoulder, wishing the dog or Finch, or both, would stop looking at him.

'I don't forget, Nat, was you first suggested going that route.'

'Only to make it easier to cover up what was already on her.'

'I wasn't sure you were right first, young man.' The terrifying thought struck Banyon that Finch's brain registered what the Rottweiler's eyes saw, that through them Finch had witnessed not only its kidnapping but, on more than one occasion, Banyon and Iris disappearing together for several minutes into a Deepwater room, and maybe even, had Dog been watching them through a window, fucking each other. 'Now I am.'

'She looks closer to what she is in it,' agreed Petersen.

Walnut tongued his chaw from one cheek to the other. 'A damn sight more'n she did in that candyass yellow.'

Finch lifted his hand from the Rottweiler's back fur, which was now nearly free of burrs, and, wiggling a thumb and pinkie at Banyon, reminded him of the number of days he had to finish the job.

Banyon responded to him only with a nod.

'You a pork eater, Nat, or a fish eater?'

'Why?'

Finch closed his fingers into a fist. 'We're gonna do barbecue the afternoon of the fight.'

'Pork, I guess,' said Banyon.

Petersen took from his shirt pocket a pad and pencil. Writing onto the pad, he said, 'Pork for Nat.'

'Dinner'll be right here round three,' said Finch.

'Free time or whatever after that,' Walnut told Banyon, 'till you two get it on at my place at eight sharp.'

Banyon waited several seconds for Finch to say more to him, but Finch, though he continued – like the Rottweiler – looking at him, evidently was done talking to him. All day while working, even as Iris, passing to his rear, whispered at him to come to her room at nine, Banyon felt those eyes – the Rottweiler's and Finch's common set of eyes – glancing, from wherever they were, at, into, and straight through him.

He entered the pitch-black bedroom through the window and walked at the breathing coming from on or near the bed; unaccompanied by audible footsteps, the rustling of clothes, the creaking of the floor, the breathing began moving parallel to him near the far wall. 'Iris?' he whispered.

He didn't receive a response.

Turning away from the bed, he hissed her name in the opposite direction. No sound at all returned to him. Then warm, damp breath touched the back of his neck as her voice whispered, 'Don't talk to or look at me.'

Her speaking at once relieved and aroused him.

Hands pressed lightly against his shoulders; they slowly made their way down to his waist. Strong and supple fingers slid around to and unbuckled his belt.

The sound of his zipper being yanked open in the quiet room brought to his mind the noise thick paper makes when violently torn from top to bottom. His pants and underwear were wrestled down to his ankles. He was brusquely turned from his hips in a half-circle toward the hands. Looking straight ahead, Banyon couldn't see a body, not even a hint or shadow of one.

Still, he closed his eyes.

He couldn't smell a fragrance on her. He couldn't, he suddenly realized, smell her at all. He said as much. The voice answering him out of the blackness near his waist made him think of the whooshing of a bat winging through the night. 'I'm not wearing no perfume is why, no deodorant, no powder, no clothes, no jewelry, not even a diaphragm. I'm naked, Nat, as the wildest animal you can name.'

Banyon swallowed and it rumbled in his ears like a landslide.

The hands abruptly stopped touching him as Iris just as suddenly quit talking.

Abandoned by his senses, Banyon had only his faith and his memory to tell him that she still was or ever had been kneeling before him, that she'd ever been flesh and blood to begin with, that she, and not someone or something else, was exhaling onto his genitals.

A warm, wet tongue probed his scrotum. A tremor bred equally of fear and titillation moved through him. Teeth nipped at his testicles.

He suppressed a terrified scream, while squelching an ecstatic yelp. Salacious lapping noises. His erection was engulfed. He heard a deep growl, unsure if it had come from him. He opened his eyes. He looked down at the top of a head of thick, dark hair.

He snarled and groaned simultaneously.

He was pulled down onto the floor and mounted. A mouth covered his, giving him back what it had just coaxed out of him.

Out in the woods the Rottweiler barked.

Shivering, Banyon felt himself grow smaller and smaller.

'It's just his dog, Nat.'

Banyon slid completely out of her. 'It's got your color hair,' he said.

'What?'

'And his color eyes.'

Iris propped herself up onto her elbows above him.

In the three-quarters dark he couldn't distinguish her features. Her eyes and mouth appeared to him as two gaping holes above a knife slash. He accused her, inside or outside his head (he wasn't sure which), of knowing the Rottweiler was no more just a dog than Finch was just a man, the Newport just a car, she just a woman. Her index finger crooked forward, tapping his temple like the beak of a giant bird. 'You let him get much deeper into here, Nat' – he imagined her words floating through the window on the same breeze as the Rottweiler's bark – 'and he won't have to throw a punch to beat you Saturday. You won't be able to see or think but what he wants you to.'

Then she was gone.

Lying alone on the disheveled sheets, Banyon stared up at the shadowy blur made by the revolving ceiling fan, not certain if he'd just awoke or if he'd just become aware of being awake. He heard a scratching sound, then wordless piano music that was scarcely loud enough to overcome the fan's relentless whirring.

'Iris?'

'At our house in Maine, Nat' – her voice came out of the darkness to the left of the bed – 'we'll have a CD player and music on all the time.' He felt a weight depress the mattress near his feet. 'That is if you like listening to it as much as I do. And you still want to go there with me.'

Banyon reached a hand down toward his knees and found her again. With a relieved sigh he located her hand and interwove their fingers to let her know that yes, he loved, if she did, listening to music and of course he still wanted to run off and make a new home with her, or else why was he even there.

'I was thinking, Nat, you could catch and sell fish.'

Banyon fought once more not to let his suspicions of her defeat his love for her.

'I hear it pays good and there's oodles of 'em up there.'

'If I could catch 'em from shore, I guess.'

'I don't know if you don't have to go out in a boat after the big ones.'

'I'll make do with the little ones then.'

Though he'd never told her of his fear of the water, Iris's next words convinced him, to his joy, that she'd now intuited and accepted it as a part of him. 'Don't catch any of 'em, Nat, if you don't want to.'

'You wouldn't mind?'

'I'd likely, anyhow, get tired of their stench being on you.'

'Tell me anything to do on land, Iris, and I'll do it.'

'You could cut down trees. What I saw they might have more of 'em up there even than fish.'

'I wouldn't mind that, 'specially after all of 'em I've planted.'

Iris lay back on the bed and rested her head on his shoulder. Banyon wished he could confide in her, tell her about the strange happenings, coincidences, and dreams he'd encountered of late that had led him to say the accusatory things he had before she'd turned on the music, but he was afraid that if he did he would reveal a secret about himself – he wasn't sure what – that might scare her and the Banyon she was in love with away forever. Instead he asked her to describe to him again what the bedroom in their beachhouse would be like.

Iris placed her mouth directly against his ear and in the near dark whispered, 'It'll have a bathroom with a hot tub and two sinks right in it – that's called a bedroom suite – and a king-size bed with a skylight over it, a built-in closet and bookshelf for each of us, and an easel where I can paint. The front window will look out at the ocean and the back one at the stone cliffs behind our backyard.'

'Tell about the backyard.'

'A huge vegetable garden will take up a lot of it. What we don't eat we'll sell or give to our neighbors. There'll be lots of flowers too. Maybe we'll tether a cow in it, you know, to give us fresh milk, only I never have milked one and I'm not sure I'd want to. Have you ever, Nat?'

Banyon shook his head.

'We could, if we wanted, have a horse instead of a cow.'

'I'd love to see you on one, Iris. A horse.'

'I'd like to ride one. On the beach especially. I only did in a circle at a county fair one time, but I liked how it smelled and felt.' Iris laughed, softly but as loudly as Banyon had ever heard her laugh. 'Just one would probably be lonely so we'll have another one for you, Nat, and as many more as we have kids, if you think you'd like to have them someday – with me, I mean.'

'You'd only have to tell me when, Iris.'

'Probably not for a few years. Unless we get lonely sooner than that.'

'A few years after we get the horses?'

'A few years from when we get there.'

Banyon tried to picture them together, or even either of them alone, in a few years and couldn't. The concept of that much time passing and him and her, or the world, existing still wouldn't register with him, particularly as he wasn't sure when any part of it, including Iris, might dissolve or turn into something else.

'What if we don't get there?'

'Don't get hold of our inheritance, you mean?'

'Would you still want to get someplace with me?'

'On foot and broke?'

'If I beat him we'll go in the Newport with my purse money.'

'Even if you beat him, Nat, you and me won't beat him long's he's still alive. Don't you get it?'

'He told me I'll be free and clear of him if I do.'

'*You*, Nat. You'll maybe be free and clear of him.'

'Way he said it, Iris, sounded like he meant both of us would be.'

'He'd step aside and give me to you, that's what you think?'

'He said he'll be just an old, lonely man in my rearview mirror if he loses and if he don't I'll have to haul ass – alone – with nothing but what I come with.'

'What did you say?'

'I nodded my head.'

Rolling up onto her side, Iris exhaled a warm, misty breath into Banyon's face. 'If he found out about us, Nat, how come he put us in his will instead of killing you?'

Banyon didn't have an answer for her.

Iris laid her head back on the pillow.

'There must be about a thousand ways to kill someone and make it look like you didn't, least on purpose.'

'Doing it with your fists in a crowded room's probably 'bout the hardest way you could name.'

'Want to talk about another way?'

'I don't know as I could do it any way at all, Iris. Not in front of myself.'

'Not in front of yourself. Who am I talking to if I'm not talking to yourself?'

'I mean I don't know as I could do it while knowing I was.'

'How could you do it and not know you was?'

Banyon didn't say. He held up his hands and studied on the dark shapes they made, the left one marred by the outline of the bandage on his palm. His mind tried to move him away from where he was, to the night before when he'd been cut, but he fought against it. He squeezed his fingers into fists, involuntarily envisioning, as he felt the wound's residual pain, the knife blade penetrating his flesh.

'You could convince someone else to be you for a while,' said Iris. 'I'd be in bed – I am before him anyway – and this other fella, for what's in the till maybe, could walk into the office late tomorrow night, ring the bell, conk Herman over the head or jab him when he comes out, rifle the register and his wallet while you're as sound asleep as me.'

Banyon turned his head toward her, but saw only her shape, steadily rising and falling with the sound of her breathing. The thought struck him that he could no more murder Finch than he could murder himself or than Finch could murder him, that Finch's fate and his own were as entwined as the fibers of a rope; how, why, or in what ways they were he didn't want to know. A panicky feeling came over him. 'He'd see it coming,' he said.

'How would he?'

'It's like he's in my head sometimes.'

'You can push him out of it if you try. I've about pushed him out of mine.'

'What if he's been in it all along and what he wants is all that matters?'

'You believing that is exactly what he's counting on.'

'Did you hear him go out in my car last night?'

'I didn't hear anything. I was asleep. Why?'

'Somebody not me left in it. It was back this morning and so's his dog.'

'This is maybe our last night together, Nat, unless we figure out how to make it not be, and you're talking about his dog.'

'It ain't no normal dog, Iris.'

Iris didn't say anything.

Banyon imagined her staring in the dark toward him, thinking odd, frightening thoughts about him. 'We'll be all right long's I beat him,' he assured her.

'What?'

Banyon lay a hand on her thigh. 'I'm a good fighter, Iris.'

'That's your whole plan for our future, Nat? To beat him up?'

Banyon told her, 'I don't think I could find nobody like who you said.'

'Like who?'

'That fella you mentioned.'

Iris rolled over onto her stomach. 'Put your hands on my bottom, Nat. One on each side.'

Banyon did. Iris flexed her buttocks. 'Rub me, okay?'

Banyon massaged her bottom, the cheeks and the crevasse between them, as Iris tensed it and gently humped the bed. She began to softly moan. Banyon felt the heat and moisture rising from her. He pushed a thumb into her bottom. Seconds later he slid two fingers into her beneath where his thumb was. He moved them in and out of her. Iris moaned louder. She got onto her knees. Banyon raised up behind her. She backed slowly into him. When he was completely buried in her she stopped moving. Banyon did too. To the world looking in they might've been a single statue. What the world couldn't see was her relentlessly tugging at him from the inside, slow, then fast. Banyon was nearly passing out from the ecstasy of it. He couldn't have escaped her grip if he'd wanted to and he didn't want to and she wasn't about to release him until she'd used him up and left him hardly able to move.

As he sat on the edge of the bed later, pulling on his clothes, she asked him if he was sure he couldn't locate a fella who might be willing to walk in his shoes for a few minutes the next night. The question made Banyon tighten up physically, as if his skin were shrinking around him. He walked over to the window. He looked out at the moon. He imagined a needle-sized sliver of it plunging down through the clouds and the treetops, directly toward his brain. He went back to and stood silently before Iris. Iris kissed him and said, 'If you can, Nat, tell him I'll be sound asleep, dreaming of our future, by ten-thirty tomorrow night.'

Nineteen

He woke in the grip of a single thought: Finch and he had both come back from the dead, which accounted for why they now seemed so familiar to each other.

He closed his eyes immediately after opening them to see if darkness would erase the thought. It didn't. He tried to trace it back to it origins. He couldn't. An internal voice informed him that by all rights neither Finch nor he should be alive and that at least one of them maybe wasn't. Surging blood hissed in his ears. He started to sweat profusely. The voice told him that if he opened his eyes he would see what was in front of him, but that if he kept them closed he would see what was behind him, which would be far worse.

He opened them.

A fat, brown spider crawled toward his face down a string dangling from a web, which hadn't been there when he'd gone to bed, covering half of Iris's beachhouse painting.

Where's that other fella?

Don't nobody live in this cottage but me.

The one she wants you to find by tonight. Same guy what took off from here in your car night 'fore last.

Nobody left outta here that night!

And come back bleeding, missing his clothes, and stinking like a dog.

Banyon unleashed a series of upward jabs at the spider, chasing it back up to the ceiling. He leapt up onto the mattress and ripped down its web. The spider lit out for the far wall. Banyon didn't bother chasing it.

His rhythmic pummeling of the heavy bag fifteen minutes later lent, in his mind, a beat to the warbling, chattering, whistling, croaking, peeping, screeching, quacking, buzzing assailing him from the woods and water. He started to derive a rhythm in all that noise. He imagined it flowing together in the clear, warm air like tributaries into a single, powerful stream; each of his punches made the stream stronger, its course narrower. Soon it was a river, its song drowning out in his head every voice, thought, and memory, its sole focus the dark blue sea, huge and endless, toward which it moved.

He lay on shore later, facing a sky striated by cirrus clouds, his hands tingling, visualizing himself taking his gym bag out to the road and hitchhiking away from the Deepwater, back up Highmore Mountain, to where he imagined he'd left the real Nat Banyon, of whom he had occasional fond memories, standing near a fox run down by a Cadillac. Then he thought of Iris, whom he craved as much as he guessed all addicts craved their addictions, and of the strong feeling he had that he couldn't outrun his fate and of an even stronger feeling that told him Finch and he were destined in this place and time to settle something.

The death he remembered going through felt as close to him as his sweat.

Hopeful turkey vultures circled above him. Needles sporadically rained onto him from the canopy. He absently tossed into the air and caught a pinecone. 'Nope,' he said, 'nuh-uh,' and didn't know why. Frantic quacking struck him as being more than that.

He abruptly sat up.

Halfway across the water, a handful of ducks or coots were noisily lifting off from the silvery surface a scant breeze was making undulate. A creature, too fat for a duck and too small for a goose, paddling just beyond and directly at the spot had apparently spooked them. Watching the determined swimmer coming at him Banyon got a fluttery sensation in his stomach. He gazed down, into the shallows nearest him, at swirling bits of sediment, barely moving fish, dark shapes revealed in rays of penetrating sun as rocks and fallen trees on the mud bottom. He heard the thing splashing. He looked up to see that what he'd taken to be the entire animal, which was now less than a hundred feet from him, was just its head and that the rest of it was submerged but for the tip of a black tail protruding from the water three or four feet behind its ears.

Banyon leapt into a standing position.

The Rottweiler barked at him or at his movements.

Banyon ran along the bank to where he'd left his gym bag, pulled his knife from the bag, and hurried back to the piece of shore the Rottweiler was just reaching. After stepping over the rocks at the water's edge, the dog bounded up the bank; it halted ten feet from Banyon. Banyon stood facing it on the needle-covered dirt, holding his knife open in a defensive posture. The Rottweiler pricked up its ears; cocked its head; shook itself. Banyon decided if it came any closer he'd slit its throat.

The dog sat down. It looked directly into Banyon's eyes.

Banyon's hand holding the knife began to tremble; now his other hand did; now both of his arms; now his legs; now his entire body as if he were atop a vibrating platform. He couldn't stop it from happening. Nor, as much as he wanted to, could he avoid the dog's eyes, as he felt them entering his head; they peered into every crevasse, peeked behind every closed door, found and stared straight at every part of himself – even the parts Banyon wasn't consciously acquainted with – and he couldn't turn away from them.

The dog stood up and took a step toward him.

Banyon began shaking so hard his vision was wavery. He pictured Finch, through the dog's eyes, watching him fall apart. Even as the dog approached him its eyes kept probing him. Banyon was powerless against them. He imagined them putting their owner's memories into his head. He recalled a muffled scream, someone's hand flailing out at his hand as he pushed forward the same knife he was holding now, causing its blade to puncture his other palm; then finding himself bleeding from the same palm and nearly naked under a tree before Iris and Finch's bedroom window with no recollection of the hours since he'd fallen asleep in his cottage earlier that night.

He dropped his knife and fell, shuddering, to his knees. The Rottweiler rushed forward, stopping inches from him. Vigorously shaking its head, it shed more water from itself, acting not in the least winded from its swim. 'What in God's name have you done?' Banyon asked it.

The dog nudged him in the chest with its nose. Now Banyon realized its eyes were not clones of Finch's eyes. Still, he recognized them from somewhere. Then he remembered the eyes he'd seen staring up at him out of the lake, eyes he'd at first believed had belonged to a dead man; the eyes in the face that had spoken to him, eyes an exact match for the eyes he was now looking into.

The Rottweiler inclined its head to the forest floor and picked up in its mouth then dropped before Banyon a small stick. Banyon seized the stick in one hand and stood up. He threw the stick as far out over the water as he could. The Rottweiler visually followed it until it landed; then, barking once, it rushed down the bank into the lake and started swimming out after it. Banyon grabbed his knife and gym bag and ran up to the cottage.

He reclined on his bed with a quart of orange juice, wondering if a part of him, without telling the rest of him, could have gone off and lived chunks of his life of which only it had knowledge or a memory. The thought caused him to glance furtively into the room's corners, for who or what he was afraid to ask himself. Aware of something falling toward him, he reactively swiped at it; inches from his face, his hand snatched the spider out of the air; in nearly the same motion he flung it up, bounced it off the ceiling, and caught it again. He placed it onto his chest. The insect appeared disoriented. It ran a couple of inches one way, then the other, before it rolled onto its back and kicked its feet in the air. Banyon gave it a ten-count. Then he catapulted it with his index finger into the far wall.

He showered, dressed, and walked to the diner, where he took the only available seat, at the counter, next to Joe Littlefeet, who, reeking of Thunderbird and dried piss, inquired of him, 'You ready for it, little warrior?'

Banyon just looked at him.

Littlefeet flapped his pinkies like a tiny bird's wings aside his ears. 'Are you carrying the spirit of the sparrow' – he growled – 'or the mountain lion?'

Banyon didn't say which, if any, spirit he was carrying.

Littlefeet made his palsied hands into fists and flailed them weakly at the air before him, accidentally knocking his cigarette out of his lips. He got down from the stool, picked up the cigarette, put it back into his mouth, and retook his seat. He sucked the cigarette down to the filter. He squashed it out in his coffee cup saucer. He lit another one. He said to Banyon, 'You gonna kick ass tomorrow, kemosabe?'

Banyon wordlessly got up and went into the men's room.

He stood before the mirror, staring into his eyes, at once hoping and fearing they would reveal to him something about himself he didn't consciously know. They only gazed blankly out at him, though, as if they were meeting him for the first time and weren't sure yet whether to trust him. Banyon blanketed his face with his hands. He peeked out several times through the cracks between his fingers, trying to catch his eyes off guard in the glass, but they were too quick for him. He decided to skip breakfast and go directly to work.

He reached with his brush a foot or so above his head onto the outside of Iris and Finch's back bedroom wall, then painted slowly toward his waist; immediately in front of him, from within the dwelling, came a gasp, then a muffled crash, as if he'd knocked someone in there down.

Banyon reeled backward, kicking over his ladder.

He looked at the swathe he'd just completed. He thought he'd made it straight, but saw now that he hadn't; the dark blue line had tiny wriggles in it, like the body of a sleeping snake; it began pulsating, then erupted into a red stream flowing from a deep wound, and Banyon's paintbrush was a bloody switchblade.

He closed his eyes. He heard only the rustle of the pines behind him. He tried to envision the memory portion of a brain; he settled on one of those black boxes that carry an airplane's flight data, picturing his own box as having large blank spaces on its recording.

He heard a voice call his name.

He opened his eyes to see Finch snapping a camera at him through the open bedroom window.

Banyon flinched as if in anticipation of taking a bullet.

'I'll label that one,' said Finch, 'the man caught with his hand in the cookie jar.' He lowered the camera. 'Who'd you kill out here?'

Banyon, not answering, feared he might dissolve like groundwater into the earth.

Finch smiled, maybe at Banyon's expression or maybe at his silence. 'I heard a crash is what I meant.'

'What?'

'Like something fell.'

Banyon waved at the downed ladder, then past Finch, at the bedroom's interior. 'A noise in there startled me into kicking it over.'

Finch nodded, not saying what the noise might've been. He gazed around at the near-perfect day (even the humidity had lessened), a day that suddenly struck Banyon as a mask over a scarred, pockmarked face. 'Been sleeping all right, Nat?' He looked back at Banyon. 'Or, like me, you been having prefight nightmares?'

Banyon eyed him suspiciously. 'Don't know nothing about the ones you been having,' he said.

'Last night I had one 'bout that kid again. The one that was drowning?' To hide his expression from Finch, Banyon reached down and picked up the fallen ladder. 'Dumbass me went in tried to save him, and I did too – got him onto a log headed for shore, you know – but doing it I went under myself somehow and died.' Banyon placed the ladder upright next to the building. 'Terrible thing, Nat, watching yourself die, even in a dream. Makes you want to keep pinching yourself to make sure you didn't really, know what I mean?'

Banyon heard himself say, 'Did we know each other 'fore we met on that mountain, Herman?'

Finch acted not at all surprised by the question. 'Not that I can put a finger on as to a date and place, Nat. You think we did?'

'I can't remember it neither.'

'Guess that don't mean it ain't so.'

Banyon didn't say anything. As clearly as if he was staring again down into the lake at it, he saw in his mind's eye the ravaged, blank-eyed face that had talked at him. He closed his eyes and inwardly grimaced at it until it went away. When he opened his eyes Finch was eyeing him almost paternally. Not sure why but convinced he ought to, Banyon told him, 'I ain't gonna stop by your place tonight, Herman.'

'Hadn't heard you'd planned to, Nat.'

'To wish you good luck, whatever.'

'Every fighter's got their own way of readying themselves to do battle, Nat. If that's yours, I understand.'

'Somebody does come by it won't be me.'

'I won't look for you then.'

'Anybody rings your bell saying it's me is lying.'

Finch half-smiled. 'Thanks for the warning, young man.'

' 'Ccount I'll be in bed early,' said Banyon, 'with my door locked.'

Finch gave him an inscrutable look. 'Finally come back to me what I missed most about fighting, Nat. Not the getting in shape or the competition but that feeling as you climb between the ropes that you and the guy across from you will be the only two people in the world for however long it takes for there to be only one of you.' He drew his head back into the bedroom and disappeared.

Banyon turned back to the wall, feeling again as if he was just coming to. The wall appeared to him like any primed wall with one swathe of fresh paint on it. He resumed working. Hours he was not conscious of and would never recall beyond the consistent, monotonous movement of his right arm as it transformed light into dark passed. The squawking, chattering, buzzing, croaking in his ears might have been coming over loudspeakers for all he was aware of the creatures making the noises. He completed a stroke around two o'clock and realized the job was done. He stepped back and looked at what he could see of it. He couldn't remember the building being any color other than what it now was. He had the sensation of having at long last arrived at the actual Deepwater motel that had been hiding, until he'd unmasked it, under a sickly yellow veneer.

He carried his brushes around back, washed them out in the hose, then put them and the leftover paint away. He walked to the portico. The albino sat facing the lot in a lawn chair before the soda machine, smoking a cigarette while listening to soft country tunes playing on Banyon's transistor radio near his feet. 'That's my radio,' said Banyon.

Peering at him through wraparound sunglasses, the albino said, 'Indian painter?'

Banyon told him, 'I ain't no more.'

'An Indian?'

'A painter. I'm done with her.'

'Feel good?'

'All right. Not's good as I thought, though. Listen. That's my radio. You been in my cottage?'

'Finders keepers, Indian. That radio was setting down by the lake.'

Banyon scratched his head. 'Maybe I left it there after working out this morning.'

'Maybe you did and maybe you owe me an apology.'

Banyon bought a lemonade. 'You can listen to her but I need her back.'

'Soon's my shuttle out to the casino comes in about five minutes you can have her.'

Banyon leaned against the post right of him. He saw Iris step off the woods trail into the lot and head for the office. He waved to her, but she acted as if he were thin air. Finch greeted her at the door. A yellow and green van turned off the highway and made for the portico. The albino stood up, telling Banyon, 'Don't let on I'm near-blind.'

'Far as I know you ain't,' said Banyon.

The van pulled up before them and a pint-sized Indian kid got out from behind the wheel and opened the rear passenger door for the albino, who asked him if he had a license.

The driver said that he did.

Climbing into the backseat across from an old liver-spotted couple in matching baseball hats, the albino cautioned the driver, 'Just remember, I can see better than you think I can.'

The driver, grinning to himself ear to ear, shut the door. He got in the van and it left. Banyon bought another lemonade and sat down in the seat vacated by the albino. He drank his lemonade and listened to a Rosanne Cash song. He closed his eyes. He opened them when he heard a newscaster announce, '. . . the mother of two children was last seen two nights ago in the grocery store she owns and operates beneath her home on the Onondaga Indian Reservation . . .'

Banyon bent down and picked up the radio. A voice from it said, '. . . there's still tickets for the rotary square dance this Saturday night . . .'

Banyon switched off the radio. His chest hurt and his vision was tremulant. He turned the radio back on. A Patty Loveless song was playing. He turned off the radio again and carried it over to where the Newport sat before the office. He unlocked the car and got in behind the wheel, throwing the radio onto the passenger seat. He started up the car, which backfired loudly. He saw Finch and Iris looking out at him from the office window. A plume of gray exhaust came out the Newport's back. Banyon turned her around and steered her onto the highway. She ran rough, was skipping badly, and lacked power. Turbid, black smoke spewed out her manifold. It took him ten minutes to cover the three or four miles to the back road to the reservation. He turned onto the road, went a half-mile or so up it, and, still nine miles from the reservation border, heard an awful grinding sound from the Chrysler. Then it died. Banyon got out of her. Half of him wanted to light a match and drop it into her gas tank. His other half told him just get the hell away from her. He left her there and started hoofing back down the road to the Deepwater.

He got there a little after seven, sweat-drenched and parched. He walked directly to the office to find it unmanned and a sign on the front desk saying:

Out to dinner. To check-in please write in the register your name, address, make of car, license plate number, method of payment you intend to use (no personal checks), and take any of the available rooms, 8 to 12. Keys are in the wall rack. You can pay your bill in the morning.

Thank you,
The Management

Banyon pulled from a metal tray atop the desk, then read, a pamphlet about a nearby cavern, where eighteen dollars bought a person a glass-bottom-boat ride on an underground river and a look at rock formations with Indian names.

Big deal, he thought.

He put back the pamphlet and through his soaked T-shirt scratched an itch in his chest. The itch moved lower down, to his belly, but even scratching the skin above it he couldn't relieve it. He imagined someone else's hand clawing at his insides as he raked at his outsides and an unreachable place between them where the itch was. He studied on some business cards of local fishing guides and tour-boat operators stuck under the desktop glass around a snapshot of Finch holding up a giant bass. What looked to be the same bass was mounted on the wall behind the desk. Dust swirled in slivers of dying sunlight coming between the slats in the front door blind. The wall clock made a monotonous tick. Banyon pictured space frozen around him; or him frozen in the middle of it. The desk phone rang. He picked it up.

'How far you from the reservation?' inquired a man's voice.

'Why you asking me?' said Banyon, immediately suspicious.

'I'm coming up there to gamble and I don't want to drive all over God's creation to have to.'

'Makes you think I'd know anymore 'bout getting there than the rest of the world?'

'You work at the goddamn motel, don't you?'

'I changed her color, that's all.'

'What?'

'And put her pool back in shape.'

The line clicked dead.

Banyon's hand was shaking. He took out from beneath the desk the phonebook and, remembering seeing MOLLY's RESERVATION GROCERY on the front of the Indian's clerk's store, found in it the store's number. He dialed it. He listened to ten rings. 'Pick it up,' he said. His whole arm started to shake. The phone kept ringing.

Son of a bitch, you.

He counted six more rings.

I ain't shutting my eyes again!

Good luck.

Could be she's just closed the place up for the night.

A harsh laugh from his own mouth startled him.

Banyon slammed down the phone.

He put back the phonebook, then reached above it and took Finch's camera from its hook. He turned it toward him and peered into its long, tubular eye at a face's distorted reflection. He pushed a button behind the lens and heard the shutter snap. 'Got ya,' he said.

He moved the film forward, walked behind the desk, and pointed the camera at the mounted bass. He photographed the fish. He went over to the window, pulled back the curtain, saw a round, buttery Chinaman walking hand in hand toward the pool with a knife-shaped black lady. He snapped three shots of them and two more of a gangly long-hair routing in a car's trunk. Then he returned the camera to its hook, went around behind the residence, and, in the receding light, crawled through the window into Finch and Iris's bedroom, where he was hit by odors so familiar he imagined he'd been smelling them for longer than he'd been alive, feelings so intensely intimate his head swooned, a sense of being watched so overpowering that he spun a paranoid circle in the shadowy room hearing as he did so a voice whisper, 'Ain't a thought in your head I can't see as clear as if you was living it.'

Banyon collapsed onto the bed, envisioning all of his terror, hope, confusion, half-recollected memories, anger with roots he wasn't consciously aware of and the potential of which petrified him pouring out of his head onto a table beneath a set of dark, probing eyes.

'Who 's it?' he panted.

No one answered him.

He could divulge only the outlines of the room's familiar furnishings: headboard, beveled posts at the bed's corners, bureau, circular mirror screwed into a vanity table, two straight-back wood chairs, linen chest, a few hanging pictures. To see deeper into the room he would have to get up, but doing so suddenly struck him as impossible. He felt as if he'd been anesthetized and paralyzed at once; not only that, he had the sense that things were being done to him out of his sight, that, in places he couldn't see, hands were being laid upon his body. Drops of moisture formed on his face; the drops rolled down his cheeks into his mouth. He couldn't understand why he wasn't acting more frightened, then realized that he was unable to, that he had no way, short of blinking, of making anyone looking at him aware of how terrified he was. He closed his eyes and saw a hand-held scalpel severing a human body from head to crotch and realized the body – now bodies – were his. He tried to scream, but couldn't.

Through the window into the mostly dark room the moon and a few stars cast a corridor of dull light. Banyon's blood coursed with adrenaline; his heart pumped hard as if he'd been running. For several moments after his eyes opened he lay listening to his exercised inhaling and exhaling, as if it was coming not from him, yet was coming from the room's sole occupant. Where that left him he wasn't sure, only that he wasn't entirely on that bed and that wherever the rest of him was he didn't feel able at that moment to bring himself back from it.

Feeling as if the space containing him was moving steadily forward under its own power and carrying him with it he stood up and strode to the window. Gazing out on the lake's silvery, flat surface he abruptly realized that he was not where he remembered being last, but in his own cottage.

He brought his hand up to scratch his head. The scant light showed his fingers to be covered with soil. He looked at his other hand; it was as black as the first one. He gazed down at his body. He was naked. His knees were stained with dirt, as if he'd been on all fours in it.

His open jackknife, his sneakers, a small carving lay amid a cluster of wood chips on the floor near his feet.

A memory of walking over a familiar, dark terrain, of being the most dangerous animal about, of bearing a heavy weight clouded his thoughts. He picked up the carving. He recognized the small pine stick from which he'd created, before burying it, the Indian grocer's likeness. Only now it didn't resemble her. Recent whittling had made it into the shape of a thick-bodied man.

He jerked his watch up to his face. One-ten: nearly five hours since he'd closed his eyes on Iris and Finch's bed.

A compulsion to change his appearance hit him.

He longed to be back asleep.

Then he swore to himself he'd never sleep again.

He flung the carving out the open window. He pictured it rolling down the hill, getting larger and larger until it was a full-sized man with a shock of white hair and infinitely alive eyes tumbling into the lake.

He looked around for his clothes and couldn't find them.

Avoiding seeing himself in the mirror, he went into the bathroom, squatted next to the tub, turned on the cold water, drank deeply of it directly from the nozzle, then switched on and stepped under the shower. His head bowed under the cool stream, he watched the water carrying the detritus from his body circle and go down the drain as if it were not comprised of countless drops, but was a single, transparent serpent endlessly slithering off him. He sat down and, as the jet hit him in the chest and belly, wondered how many lives he'd lived while he was living this one, how many hours he'd wandered unaware through, how many nights had been made darker by his presence.

He stepped out, turned off the water, and dried himself. He stood before the mirror with his eyes shut. After several seconds he summoned up the courage to open them. He frowned, smiled, flexed his biceps. For close to a minute he fixed his reflection with a challenging, closemouthed stare; his reflection didn't react to him. It did everything he did. He told it that he was an honest, hard worker who had never hurt anyone not looking to hurt him.

His reflection didn't argue with him.

Banyon went into the other room and put on a pair of boxer shorts and a T-shirt. He ate a sandwich, drank a beer, returned to the bathroom and brushed his teeth. He came back out into the main room. He double-locked the door, closed and latched the window, then reclined on his bed with the lights on and his eyes wide open, determined not to look backward, forward, or anywhere but at the moment he was in. The spider he thought he'd killed – or another one – scampering across the ceiling was his last conscious sight before the morning sun streaming through the window.

Twenty

Gratitude at finding himself alive and in a familiar body was tempered by his suspicion that he really wasn't alive, that he was only in a vacuum of perceptions making him think he was.

He wished the motel wasn't painted so he could occupy his mind working. Then he thought, No. First he had to get his mind back from the spell that had been cast on it at the Deepwater, a place he'd woken up viewing as a geographical dead spot in which the present never moved beyond the past. He glanced up at Iris's drawing of HOME. His mind's eye saw the two of them galloping on horses along the beach. He told himself that everything but them together and him painting the Deepwater had been a dream. He got out of bed, feeling as if he'd wriggled through a crease into the space he now occupied and wondering, with a nervous, twitchy sensation, what he'd left behind in the space he'd escaped from.

An awful fear came over him that much of what he'd washed from his body the night before had not been fresh dirt, but fresh blood and that his failure to perceive it as such had been one more manipulation of his senses by whatever force had hold of him. He also chillingly recalled a splash in the lake too loud for a small carving to make.

He stared hard at a blank piece of wall.

He pictured in it a set of eyes, at once as warm as a mother's and as cold as a killer's, the eyes he'd caught looking at him again and again out of different faces – the Indian store clerk's face had those eyes and, yesterday afternoon, Finch's eyes – since they'd gazed complacently down at him through the pond that had drowned him. It wasn't me they watched drown, he inwardly railed, or else I'm not here now! So why did he recognize the eyes and feel the sensation of drowning? And if it hadn't been him, then who?

Banyon took another shower, sensing he couldn't get clean enough. Now he conceptualized the Deepwater as a place where people with intersecting histories, people such as Finch and him, encountered one another again after they, or anyway a part of each of them, had met sometime in the past.

Back in the kitchenette he gulped down some orange juice. An intuition visited him that he and Finch had been at war for years. Banyon was petrified to think about how come they had been, or about why suddenly a part of him felt an affectionate longing for Finch even as another part of him was terrified of seeing him. He put on the one shirt and only pair of jeans he could locate of the three sets of clothes he'd come with to the Deepwater, assuring himself that nothing from yesterday's world had changed on his account.

He opened the door to find the Rottweiler perched on his stoop as if it had been waiting there for him. Banyon reached down, patted the dog's head. The Rottweiler looked up at him, wagging its tail. Their eyes met. They had the same eyes.

Not quite trusting that the air was as clear as it seemed, that the birds were making music as beautiful as what he was hearing, that the lake and sky were the matching dark blue his eyes divulged to him, Banyon, followed closely by the Rottweiler, headed up through the woods.

★　　★　　★

He walked out of the trees into the parking lot just as the Newport was entering it from the highway.

The car circled before the building, then pulled into the space at the top of which Banyon, flanked by the Rottweiler, stood watching it. Walnut gunned her engine, then turned her off. He stepped out, tossed Banyon the keys, said, 'You're tempting thieves leaving 'em in her that way.'

Banyon gazed past him at the high grass across the road, where the cicadas droning suddenly became to his ears louder and more chaotic, as if the insects were abruptly turning on one another or, on the contrary, massing to attack a common enemy; dandelion pods and pollen swirled over the field; on the shoulder nearest it a sweatsuit-clad woman strode hell-bent for town.

'Finchie called me last night after he'd passed her on his way back from the casino and asked me to put her 'hind my tow-truck this mornin' figurin' she'd need it, but son of a bitch' – Walnut made as if to turn a key in the air – 'she didn't turn over for me on a single crank 'fore running like a dream.'

A metal detector a bandy-legged little Mexican guy was playing over the grass behind the pool started beeping.

'You just felt like walking, did ya, boy?'

Banyon, remembering how his car had died the night before like the bodies of the souls he was now sure possessed it, didn't say what he'd felt like. He didn't say anything at all. He watched the Rottweiler trot to and start sniffing at the Newport, behavior that heightened his desire to get away from the vehicle. 'Don't bother thanking me,' said Walnut.

Banyon didn't.

'You gone mute, boy?'

Banyon wordlessly put the keys in his pocket. Not sure what prompted him to do it, he snapped his fingers, and the Rottweiler, surprising him only slightly, left the car and,

257

facing Walnut, sat down next to Banyon in the way it customarily positioned itself next to Finch. Appearing perplexed by what he'd just seen, Walnut looked from the dog to Banyon. He slowly ran a hand over his face. He tugged at his crotch. Banyon's silence worked on Walnut like an odorless poison. Walnut jerked his head at the Newport. 'Maybe shoulda hauled her right to my place, save me havin' to after Herman puts your lights out later.'

Banyon, not intending nor trying to, grinned at Walnut. Walnut backed up a step. 'Finchie ain't up yet?'

Banyon, powerless not to, just kept grinning. Walnut glanced nervously over his shoulder at where his Eighty Eight was slowing down to swing off the highway into the lot. 'I got a thousand bucks down to make me twelve says you won't beat him this lifetime.'

Banyon's grin broadened.

Walnut backed up farther. 'You know something I don't?'

Banyon didn't say.

'What's to smile about?'

Banyon didn't answer him beyond how he already was doing so.

Walnut spit. He looked unsure of himself. 'Fuck you,' he said.

The Rottweiler made a low growl. Walnut, betraying slight alarm, moved farther away from it. Banyon placed a hand on the dog's head and it shut up.

Walnut wheeled away from them, toward the approaching Olds. The car halted next to him. Nudging his wife into the passenger seat, Walnut got in behind the wheel. 'We'll see who's smiling tonight,' he said to Banyon.

Banyon heard himself boldly laugh.

'What's that?' Walnut asked, looking at Banyon as if uncertain that what he'd just heard had come from Banyon.

Banyon turned his back on him and walked toward the motel.

He heard the Oldsmobile drive away as he entered the office.

Iris was assuring a beer-bellied woman eating a cruller from a continental breakfast tray on a table left of the desk that the cavern was well worth visiting, that some of its natural rock formations looked closer to being real people than did most of the sculptures she'd seen at museums or in parks.

Laying eyes on her, Banyon instantly felt more one with his own body and less connected to another person's ghost. He desired to feel her, smell her, taste her, with every one of his senses to prove to himself that they both were flesh and blood. He smiled at her.

She didn't smile back, only pushed with four fingers at her hair, which was unfettered. 'My pay here?' Banyon asked her.

She nodded to the mail slots on the wall behind her, telling the woman, whose bottom in a pair of glittery red bermudas made Banyon think of a freshly painted barn door, that heat rising from the caves had led to their discovery by a dairy farmer curious as to why snow never collected on a section of his pasture above them.

Banyon walked to and pulled his pay envelope out of its slot. Putting it in his shirt pocket, he returned to the food spread. He picked up a jelly donut; as soon as he looked at it he knew he could no more eat it than he could eat a piece of road kill. He tossed it back in the box. He poured himself a coffee, the cup shaking in his hand, its contents dribbling onto the table. Iris informed the woman that the local Indians believed time was frozen inside of the caves, that a person while in them was at once a newborn baby and a thousand years old.

'Goodness,' said the woman.

Banyon sat down in one of the plastic spoon chairs facing the desk. He imagined every tick of the wall clock tweaking his brain in an effort to make it remember – or maybe forget – more. He took out his pay envelope; he tapped it against his forehead in time with the ticking. He tried to catch Iris's eye. She'd have no part of it. Beneath a powder blue, sleeveless shift, her arms were bare. Banyon pictured their bodies joined together like planes refueling in midair, everything in his emptying into hers. 'But will my little ten-and eleven-year-old monsters be bored?' asked the woman.

Iris said, 'There's a glass-bottom boat.'

Banyon placed the envelope back in his pocket, removed it again, unsealed it with an index finger. He emptied the envelope into his lap. A hundred-dollar bill, three fifties, two twenties, a ten, a five – a hundred dollars more than he'd figured on – and a folded paper slip came out. Banyon drank some of his coffee. He sat his cup on the floor next to him. He took out his wallet, slipped the cash into it, put the wallet away. He finished his coffee, tossed the empty cup in the trash bin to his right. He glanced down at the paper. He heard the woman tell Iris, 'Well, you talked me into it.' He picked up and unfolded the paper. His killer's dark eyes stared up at him from its center as they had stared down at him through that pond, while the voice he had heard the night before whispered to him, 'It's not over. It'll never be over.'

Banyon screamed.

He suddenly couldn't remember a time when he hadn't been screaming; he felt he had been doing so for the length of his memory; yet, no one seemed to be hearing him or they weren't reacting to him if they did. He might not have been in the room period for all the notice Iris and the woman took of him. Even while screaming he heard Iris caution the woman to bring a sweatshirt with her as the caves had a constant temperature of fifty-five degrees, which, in combination with the windless air and lack of any natural light in them, added to the Indians' belief that time never moved there. 'You ought to be a guide for them,' the woman told her admiringly.

'I've just always liked old, mysterious places and things,' said Iris.

Finally Banyon realized that only a part of him was screaming, a part without access to his lungs. Another part of him was sitting quietly in a chair, drinking coffee, drawing strength from a vision of a hand pulling a blade hard across a series of human throats, stopping the bloodflow to his killer's eyes, once, twice, however many times it took, as if the eyes were weeds that kept coming back from being macheted to the ground.

'Excuse me.'

Banyon looked up to see the beer-bellied woman side-stepping his feet on her way to the pastries. She picked up half a dozen crullers, wrapped them in napkins, stuffed them in her purse. A vision of Finch, with his girlish giggle, clapping Banyon on the back, saying, 'A young man reminds me myself at his age,' came over him. An urge suddenly hit him to undream his worst dreams, to kill the part of him that had hatched them, to see Finch standing in front of him. He watched the woman head for the door. He looked into his lap at the slip of paper. Beneath the eyes, which were actually lead sketches of eyes, Finch had written,

For putting her into the shape I knew ya would when I hired ya, young man, we're even.

Banyon heard the door open, then shut. He raised his eyes and through the door's rectangular glass pane watched the beer-bellied woman's huge red bottom undulating as it moved away from him through the parking lot. He refolded and slid the paper into his pocket.

'Where is he, Nat?'

He slowly turned to her.

'I know he's not invisible.'

'He is when he wants to be.'

She looked at him as if she'd never seen him before. 'He wasn't supposed to be moved.'

Banyon stood up.

'The whole point was for him to be found – out here – and the cash drawer empty.'

Stay up, Banyon told himself. Stay up! 'Was it?'

'It wasn't. You know it wasn't.'

'Now I do.'

'What do you mean?'

'I believe everything you tell me, Iris.'

Iris continued looking at him as if he was a stranger in off the street. 'If he's not found, to the law he's only missing.'

Banyon walked at her.

'As long as he's just missing, Nat, we get nothing of what's his.'

Banyon stopped before her, on the desk's near side. 'I ain't seen him, Iris, since yesterday afternoon.'

Iris put a hand to her chest as if she was having trouble breathing. 'I saw your shadow go by my window around eleven, Nat, then I heard the bell ring – just like we talked about.'

Banyon blinked hard. 'I was asleep at eleven.'

'Okay then' – Iris's lower lip started quivering – 'I seen and heard the fella who took your place do those things. And when I came out an hour later – no him and no Herman, only the bloody mess I was close to an hour cleaning up from the floor behind here – and this morning, still no Herman, and both his vehicles are here. So you ask him, Nat, you ask that other fella – where's my husband at?'

Banyon had the sensation that an army of flesh-eating ants was chewing its way out of his stomach.

'Are you telling me he got up and walked away after, Nat?'

Banyon moved his eyes wildly around the room, half-expecting to encounter another set of eyes looking back at him. 'You've called around for him?'

She looked at him with alarm. 'Called around? Called around to who?'

'He could be anywhere.'

Iris backed up a step. 'Anywhere?'

Banyon shook his head to clear it.

Iris's face was flushed. She looked as close to breaking down as Banyon had ever seen her. He reached out to touch her arm, but she shrunk away from him. He told her, 'I'll go up check his study.'

'Check his study for what?'

'See if he's in it.'

'In it how?'

'He's got to be somewhere.'

'How in God's name, Nat, can you not know where he is?'

Banyon's only answer was to stride past her through the residence door.

His desk swivel chair stood at a half-turn toward the corridor as if in his invisible mode he'd just spun around in it to greet Banyon. On the desk sat an open newspaper, a porcelain coffee mug, a bitten-from bagel on a napkin. A neat rack of balls atop the pool table invited the start of a game. Sunlight funneling through a glass porthole in the facing wall, the room's sole window, landed in a yellow bull's eye on the rug beneath the speed bag, now dangling from a ceiling hook. Finch's gloves lay under the bag as if after working out he'd peeled them off and just dropped them.

Banyon shut the door.

He walked over and picked up the gloves. He slipped his fingers a ways into them. Surprised to find them wet still with what could only be Finch's sweat, he yanked them off. He tied their laces together, hung them on the closet door handle. On the wall left of the closet, among the shots of various landscapes he remembered from his previous visit, was a framed black-and-white photo of Finch as a young man jumping rope before a lake reflecting a bright sunrise. Banyon abruptly recognized the pictured setting as the lakeshore behind his cottage. Then it dawned on him that Finch wasn't the person jumping rope; he was.

Struck by a disturbing feeling that half of him was alive only as a dead kid's anger, Banyon squeezed shut his eyes. He imagined a tug of war occurring in his head between someone else's past and his own present. He envisioned Finch observing the battle from the surrounding air. He saw a mother's eyes watching him suck in water and die – no, not himself, his second self, but now it felt like him – and he saw the Indian store clerk and Finch looking at that part of him out of the same eyes.

He opened his eyes and saw only the room.

He decided that the jump-roper in the picture in fact was Finch, looking like him. He blinked again and thought, no; it was him looking like Finch when Finch was his age.

He walked over to the desk to look above it at the snapshots of the boxer and the Army private he recalled seeing when he'd been in the room with Iris. The snapshots were no longer there. In their stead was a framed photograph of a young guy in sweats jogging along a roadside in a rainstorm, which once more Banyon could only say for certain was either of himself or of Finch three decades earlier. Now Banyon wasn't sure if the Finch of thirty years ago and himself of today were truly physical twins, one and the same person, or if he'd just lost his ability to tell them apart. A remorseful feeling came over him, though he wasn't sure for what or for who he was experiencing it.

The thought suddenly occurred to him that every photograph he'd ever seen of Finch – in this room or anywhere – was of the current Finch or of Finch at around Banyon's age, if indeed there had ever been such a Finch. He gazed down at the desk.

Bagel crumbs dotted the newspaper. An inch of coffee sat in the mug. Banyon impulsively reached out and pressed a finger to the mug, at the same time feeling on the back of his neck a prickly sensation that might have resulted either from his heightened apprehension at finding the mug to be warm or from someone touching his neck exactly as he was touching the mug. He made a one-hundred-eighty-degree turn toward the opposite wall.

He saw no one, but found the study looking slightly altered from a minute ago, as if items in it had been subtly rearranged, though he couldn't point to any that had been. Then he noticed the speed bag was swaying gently back and forth. Banyon had a vision of Finch imperceptibly hurling punches at the bag before Banyon convinced himself he'd bumped into the bag on his way past it to where he was. He again faced and looked down at the desk. Now he saw that the newspaper, the *County Weekly*, was opened to the local page on which appeared a number of single paragraph articles, including one headed, 'Foul Play Feared in Disappearance of Reservation Grocery Store Proprietor.'

You believe me now?

Banyon picked up the paper, straining to keep his brain in a mental vise he hoped would prevent it from wobbling. According to the article blood had been found behind the counter of the store owned by Molly Two Trees, who, ironically, was recently profiled in the paper's personality page for what more than a few grieving people in the area claimed was her faculty for communicating with the dead, an ability Mrs. Two Trees told the reporter she practiced without charge for any bereaved individual who asked her to as partial atonement for the terrible sins, including infanticide, her dreams informed her were committed by an earlier incarnation of her soul.

Banyon collapsed into the desk chair.

There you go.

Banyon put his fingers in his ears for all the good it did. He spun the chair in a fast circle, feeling on one hand more alive than he ever had and on the other as if he existed only in the memory, and at the whim, of a long since drowned boy.

I'm saying we didn't make a mistake's all.

Banyon kick-stopped the chair, facing the desk again.

'Bout what was in them eyes.

I didn't see nothing in 'em but a nice lady selling groceries!

That's 'cause it weren't you they was looking at.

How many more like her, wondered Banyon, walking around in this world, pregnant with the danger of someone from another? Or like himself, enslaved to a murdered person's fear? He yanked open the desk's middle drawer, finding in it pencils, pens, paper clips, notepads, staples. He shut it. He drew out the higher of the two deeper, side drawers. A dozen or so upright photo albums filled the space. Banyon pulled out the album closest to him, started flipping through it, seeing shot after shot of men, women, children;

going into and out of the Deepwater's rooms, crossing its parking lot, climbing from cars, heading to the lake, diving into the pool, petting family pets, scratching themselves, toting luggage, laughing, talking, arguing.

Banyon returned the album to where he'd found it; he removed and glanced at four or five others. He encountered in them more of the same: anonymous people forever frozen in what should have been passing moments in their lives by a flick of Finch's finger. Banyon imagined Finch's camera stealing a part of everyone he secretly snapped it at and them never knowing it beyond their periodically waking in the night to a panicky feeling that a piece of the world they'd gone to sleep in had dissolved into thin air through which they were endlessly tumbling.

He put back the albums and shut the drawer. He opened the lower drawer; several legal-sized manila envelopes stood in it. A person's name topped each envelope; under each name was a column of hand-written numbers fronted by dollar signs next to dates and boxes containing or not containing a red X. Tim Boyer's name was there. And Earl's, with a line through it. And Banyon's. Though nothing appeared under his name: not the amount of his debt, its interest rate, a payment schedule. It was as if Nat Banyon was the entire transaction. Banyon pulled out the envelope, turned it upside down over the desk; from it fluttered another photograph of Finch or of himself, a 3-by-5, black-and-white snapshot showing one of them at the wheel of the Newport when it was brand-new. Banyon peered inside the envelope for anything else. Thin air.

He was suddenly aware of the silence in the study. He wondered if its walls were soundproof. Then he realized no noise was coming from within them either. He didn't count the breathing his body seemed to be doing separately from him. He understood he'd never had a solitary, unguarded moment; at the same time he felt as if he was in the emptiest room in the world. The prickly sensation increased on the back of his neck. He turned to see the door to the corridor open, as he heard Iris say, 'People are going to start wondering where he is soon.'

He watched her step into the study.

'I don't know how to answer them. How to act at all.'

Banyon faced her. 'He's out for a walk.'

'A walk?'

'Far as you know, right?'

'You know what I know, Nat. I just don't know what you know.'

'He could have gone for a walk.'

'It's nearly eight-thirty. People come back from walks.'

'Maybe he will.'

'Maybe he will until he doesn't and then what?'

'He's lost maybe.'

'It's me, Nat' – Iris pushed shut the door – 'the girl who loves you.'

Banyon visualized her as the winning shell in a shell game, the only one with a coin beneath it. 'You ain't got to tell me, Iris. I'd know you anywhere.'

'Talk to me then.'

'I'm saying things and you're saying things back, so I must be.'

'Everything was for the two of us, Nat, so why aren't you here with me now?'

'Can't you see me, Iris?'

'What?'

'Do I look like someone else to you?'

'You're frightening me, Nat.'

'How am I?'

'This.'

'Herman you mean?'

'It wasn't s'posed to be this way.'

Banyon walked to her.

'Only I don't even know what way it is' – Iris pushed at her hair, looking at him in a way he couldn't read – 'because you won't tell me.'

Banyon handed her the snapshot. 'Who do you see there?'

Iris glanced at the picture, then at Banyon. 'Him, fifty pounds and 'bout as many years ago.'

'Look again.'

'I've seen him too much already. I don't want to see him no more except at his funeral.'

'Maybe you only saw what you was expecting to see.'

She looked more closely at the picture. 'It's him still. He ain't gone nowhere.'

'You sure?'

'Course I'm sure. I can't stop seeing him. Who do you see?'

Banyon didn't say.

'Where'd you get it from?'

Banyon nodded at the file cabinet. 'Was in an envelope with my name on it.'

Iris turned back to him. 'Something in whoever he was back then' – she nodded at the picture – ' 'fore he became what he did later, he saw in you, Nat. Right from the start he did. It's why he put you in his will, I think, and at the same time wanted to beat you up in a fair fight in front of me and the world. It's like he loved and hated you at once.'

He couldn't have even been born when the eyes he's half-possessed of and that keep multiplying watched their owner drown her baby boy, whose memory of it somehow ended up in my head, he told Iris; silently though, so not to scare her.

'I shouldn't a pushed you to it, Nat. I should've seen that you being of two minds about him it'd work on you after.'

Banyon aimed an index finger at the photograph of the jump-roper hanging left of the closet. 'Who's that?'

Iris took two steps toward the photograph and stared at it. 'You know's well as me who it is.'

' 'Nother words you got no idea.'

'I hope to God I do.'

'But you ain't.'

'The sweet guy I thought it was wouldn't scare the living bejesus out of me this way!'

'That don't tell us who it is.' Banyon walked to the pool table.

'It don't make him your father, Nat – or anything special at all – just 'cause he hung a few pictures of you.'

Banyon picked up a cue. 'You want to play a game of pool?'

Iris didn't say.

'While we're waiting.'

'Waiting for what?'

Banyon didn't have an answer for her.

'I guess in your mind, Nat, I've ruined everything.'

Banyon quashed an urge to tell her to stop right there, that Finch was watching them and listening to every word they said.

'That you blame me for it and so think less of me now.'

Banyon leaned over the table, addressing the cueball, seeing only it, its virgin white surface filling half his brain, while his muscles refused to follow the command from his other half to pull back his stick and smash the ball. 'I could never think bad of you, Iris.'

Her breathing at his back could have been anyone's. 'We can't just pretend it didn't happen, Nat.' Banyon felt his arm,

270

as if of its own accord, arc slowly back, then thrust forward. 'People, real soon, are going to start asking after him.'

Banyon watched the balls career about the table, ricochet quietly off its cushions. 'Was he happy with the job I done?'

'What?'

'On the motel.' Banyon swiveled his head toward her. 'Did he say?'

Iris's look at him suggested to Banyon that she was totally reassessing her feelings for and about him. 'That's why he gave you the extra hundred.'

'I wish he'd of told me himself.'

'Without a body, Nat, we're no better off than we were before.'

'I'd be more surprised than anybody, Iris, he don't show up anytime now making the joke on us.'

'I'm willing to play it any way you want me to, Nat. I just need you to tell me.'

Banyon put his eyes back on the table. Iris's silence behind him started him wondering if she'd left the room; or had never entered it to begin with. Suddenly he couldn't envision her; couldn't remember what she looked like at all. Or himself. Or Finch. Or the store clerk. Their fleshly forms became as elusive to his mind as ghosts; as ephemeral as dreams. At the same time the study felt crowded with the essences of them.

'I can only figure he got up before me this morning, Nat, and went for a walk.' Banyon lined up his stick on the cueball, aiming it at the seven. He could feel a single set of eyes watching him from every corner of the room. 'That's how I'm going to tell it then.'

'Is your hair up in a bun, Iris?'

'What?'

'Or flowing down your back.' Banyon tapped the cueball into the seven ball. 'I can't remember.'

Iris didn't answer.

Banyon watched the seven ball roll slowly across the table into the corner pocket, in his mind's eye seeing two blood-spattered T-shirts and two bloody pairs of jeans he thought he'd lost disappearing on consecutive evenings into a hand-scratched hole in the ground where a small carving had been buried. He dropped his cue onto the table. Breathing heavily, he peered into the pocket. 'If he isn't back by midday,' he heard Iris say, 'I'll call the police and tell them the same thing.'

Banyon turned toward her. Her hair was down and flowing wild around her shoulders, but he could see by the look on her face that she'd glimpsed in him someone who, when she had time to reflect on him later, would scare her past the point of shaking and change her mind about ever wanting to live in a dream house with Nat Banyon or even to spend another moment alone with him. 'Before it comes to that I'll figure the fight's off,' he said.

Not exactly replying to him, Iris said, 'I've got to open the gift shop.'

'And since he ain't got me owing him nothing on it that he'll want me to keep the Newport.'

'You ought to leave separate from me, Nat,' she said, turning to the door. 'It wouldn't do for us to be seen coming out of the house together.'

Her departing without kissing or even touching him left Banyon feeling melancholy and unjustly abandoned, as if the mere sight of him had chased off a beautiful animal he'd happened upon in the woods. He tried to recall what he'd said that might have spooked her; not a word, only the gist, of their just completed conversation came back to him. He attempted to picture her still standing before him; all that he could see of her was her frightened stare at him right before she'd left.

He strode to and smashed his fist into the speed bag.

He remembered a kite flying over a raging fire, beneath some storm clouds, at the end of its string. Then what? But that was all of it, the entire scene. He couldn't figure out, with so much of his distant and near past a blank to him, the point of remembering some doomed kite. He didn't even know whose kite it had been, if it had been flying yesterday or three lifetimes ago, or even if the memory belonged to himself or to his second self.

He tore into the speed bag. Every bone in his body, every cell in his brain screamed to the eyes watching him that Nat Banyon was still standing, still breathing.

He stopped hitting the bag.

His heart's beating exactly echoed in his mind the sound of his recent punches. He listened for a second heart pounding in the room and couldn't hear one.

The knowledge struck him like a bolt of lightning that no more had he desired to kiss or touch Iris that morning than had she apparently desired to kiss or touch him, that his incessant craving of her, that maddening, tingling passion that no amount of lovemaking had diminished and that had felt like a ticking bomb inside of him, had vanished as if he'd spent himself in one exhaustive orgy he now couldn't remember.

He returned to his game of pool, alternating hard, wild shots with deft, accurate ones; grimaces at the snap of the colliding balls with cool stares at the directed paths he sent them on.

An anxious, though not unfamiliar feeling – he sensed he'd experienced it whenever he'd finished a job and had known it was time to move on – came over him. He reracked the balls, then replaced as he'd found the other items he'd disturbed in the study, except the snapshot from Nat Banyon's file, which he put in his shirt pocket. Not viewing again the photographs in the room nor looking at anything more in the residence not in his direct path, he went downstairs and, envisioning himself as a black smear being brushed onto a living, three-dimensional painting, exited into the woods through Iris and Finch's bedroom window. Unsure which of his selves was guiding him, he walked to a large pine tree facing the building under which pine needles partially obscured a patch of overturned dirt. After kicking enough more needles onto the spot, which was the approximate size of a table setting, to make it indistinguishable from the earth around it, he went down to his cottage.

He packed into his gym bag his jump rope, switchblade, playing cards, toiletries, boxing gloves, running shoes, underwear, Bible, the weasel carving and miniature teepee he'd bought from Iris. Standing up on the bed, he took down her birthday present to him. After putting it back in its frame he lay it in the bag, beneath his sweats. He zipped the bag, got from the refrigerator a quart of orange juice. Reclining with the juice on his bed, he gazed up at the piece of ceiling slightly whiter than that which surrounded it where Iris's and his dream house had been. He placed the juice box on the floor. Tears filled his eyes. 'Shit,' he said dejectedly.

He dozed off.

He dreamed a body was floating to the top of the lake.

There's stones anchoring it.

Banyon opened his eyes.

Enough to keep it there till the fish eat it.

The spider – he was sure only one lived in the cottage – peered down at him.

Other hand, it's risky, that Newport just setting there.

Banyon rose to his knees on the mattress.

'Fore long she'll be calling out to anyone's got a nose.

274

Banyon leapt up, grabbing at the insect. He caught it in his right hand. He could feel its papery limbs flailing in his palm, its puny head and body pushing at the bottoms of his cupped fingers, its itty-bitty lungs gasping. He took it outside. He flung it down hard onto the cement stoop. He returned to his bed, got his gym bag, carried it back out front to see the Rottweiler, soaking wet, running at him from the lake with something in its mouth, still acting as if it and Banyon were on the same wavelength. 'We ain't friends!' Banyon told it.

The Rottweiler sat down before him, trying again to lock eyes with him, to enter his head, to implant in his brain more memories of its own atrocious deeds.

Avoiding its eyes, Banyon looked down at the stoop. He watched the spider hobble back into the cottage. He heard the Rottweiler's jaws open. He saw what they'd been grasping fall at his feet. An intuition told him he was nearing the worst of it; soon his thoughts would start to coalesce, his brain would begin to heal, his awareness of now would sink to the deep, dark bottom of his mind. He reached down and from the ground where the Rottweiler had dropped it picked up Finch's Stetson. Barely looking at the drenched hat, he whipped it over his shoulder through the open doorway. The Rottweiler rushed inside to fetch it. Banyon slammed shut and bolted the cottage door. He headed with his belongings up through the woods into the parking lot.

The Newport's rear fenders were a quarter of the way down over its hubcaps.

He remembered the day he'd driven over the mountain, the store clerk telling him, 'I don't know who you are,' and asking, 'Are you past it now?'; the way she'd slid out from behind the counter; how she'd nearly run down the aisle away

275

from him; her wary look back at him as if at an animal foaming at the mouth.

He reminded himself that the Newport's shocks were shot, that it had been sitting low on them since he'd bought it.

He unlocked the driver door, opened it, threw his gym bag into the passenger seat. He relived in a split-second a panicky, Jesus-Christ someone's-coming sort of feeling; a what-do-I-do-now? sort of a feeling; a get-this-mess-out-of-sight-and-the-hell-gone-from here sort of feeling.

He turned away from the car, then leaned against it, panting, watching a big porker of a guy cannonball into the pool to the handclaps of three other fatsos waiting behind the diving board to follow him in.

A woman and two young boys stood before a minivan a few spaces to his left, arguing about how to spend the day. The littler kid wanted to play miniature golf. The bigger one wanted to go to a movie in town. The woman, a ropy-legged bleached blonde, wanted to do anything the two boys could agree on. Catching Banyon looking at her, she threw up her arms. Banyon's mind's eye showed him a squat female body being rolled up inside of a canvas tarp and tossed next to a tire jack. A terrified feeling came over him that he'd been put in jeopardy by someone else's behavior. He recalled a dream he'd had about a fast drive he'd taken.

The woman asked if he was all right.

Banyon tried to smile at her.

'For a good-looking guy,' said the woman, 'you look like hell.'

Banyon asked her if she'd been to the caverns where time stopped.

'No. Is it worth seeing?' asked the woman.

'They got a glass-bottom-boat ride,' said Banyon.

'Can we go, Ma?' asked the smaller kid.

276

'Can we, Ma?' said the bigger one.

The woman shrugged as if to say going beat the alternative, then good-naturedly told Banyon, 'Maybe you want to come with us, mister, since it was your idea.'

Banyon said, 'Being 'neath the ground scares me.'

'Too bad,' said the woman.

Banyon watched them get into the minivan and drive away. He walked to the Newport's rear. Above the pines' masking scent, he smelled the growing odor of rotting flesh coming from the trunk. He had a sad intuition that he would forget all of the good things and good people he'd encountered here. He thought of the pancakes he'd eaten nearly every morning since he'd eaten in front of Finch two stacks of them, the best pancakes he could remember having tasted. His mouth watered to taste them one last time. He got into the Newport and drove to the diner, parking near the road, away from the building and from the couple of cars before it.

'I wouldn't mind you being my mother.'

Pam cocked her head at him in a curious way as if, perceived Banyon, she was mentally measuring him to see if she could fit him into an odd-sized box; he tried to appear to her the same as he always had; he was mostly guessing at how he'd looked to her in the past though. 'Just through breakfast.'

Pam wiped a rag over the place he was sitting before. She poured him coffee. She told him the same hawk she had rescued after it had flown into her patio window weeks earlier had flown into it again, broke its neck, and died that morning. 'I had a husband killed at the pulp plant and two divorce me and none of it made me as angry. Poor, dumb, beautiful thing mustn't have listened to a word I told it.'

Banyon asked her for a double order of pancakes. 'Your competition ain't been in yet this morning,' said Pam.

Banyon glanced at the gift shop. He pictured its door opening and Finch and Iris coming hand in hand out of it into the room. To stop from picturing it he looked down into his coffee. In its blackness he saw Finch's eyes, in the moment they'd recognized the truth in Banyon's eyes, open wide at him in a look of incredulity; he saw the store clerk frown as if she'd known since the day she'd watched him halve that apple he'd be back.

'You seen him?'

Banyon poured and stirred cream into the blackness. 'A Boy Named Sue' played on the jukebox. 'Not today I ain't.'

'You still planning to tonight?'

Banyon only looked at her.

Pam nodded through the front plate-glass window at his car.

'I'm taking a little ride's all,' said Banyon.

Pam wrote down his order. Behind her, ascending fryer smoke made ghostly gyrations; at the counter an Indian with gray hair to his waist chain-smoked hand-rolled cigarettes three stools from a backpacker around Banyon's age reading a paperback. Pam said, 'I'm just a good old girl, stud. A few minutes laughs while you eat is all.'

Banyon emphatically shook his head. He felt like crying.

' 'Sides, I wouldn't want to be nobody's mother gives me the kind of unmotherly thoughts you do.'

'I'd like to remember you when I'm gone from here though.'

'I hope you do.' She leaned down and kissed him on the cheek. 'What would make you forget me?'

'I don't know. Something.'

'Give it a name.'

'I can't.'

Banyon had the unsettling sensation that while looking at

him Pam was seeing a smashed hawk too blind or stupid not to know a glass wall from thin air. 'It's happened to you before – forgetting people and things – you think?'

'I get a scared feeling it has.' Banyon's mind's eye showed him a switchblade being moved by a large hand in a continuous, powerful, side-to-side cutting motion like a mechanical arm that won't quit until it's shut off or its batteries die. 'More times than I can stand to know.'

He pictured the remote road he'd driven over the mountain west of the reservation, its sheer cliffs dropping off into secluded, scarcely visible valleys. He had a premonition of the Newport plummeting into and burning with its contents at the bottom of the deepest of the valleys and of himself hitchhiking off the mountain, looking for work someplace in the far west's wide open spaces. 'I got a theory,' said Pam, 'you only forget what you're afraid of.'

'Maybe.'

'You ain't afraid of me, are you?'

'Not sitting here now I ain't.'

Pam laughed and left to put in his order. A few minutes later she returned with his pancakes. She sat across from him while he ate them, smiling wryly at this appetite. Under her warm gaze Banyon imagined himself as an infant in a good mother's arms. 'You ought to paint a picture, whatever,' he said.

'Do what?'

'Onto your window, so birds'll see what it is and to steer clear of it.'

Pam nodded musingly. 'A big, black grim reaper maybe.'

When he finished eating Banyon wiped his mouth and thanked her for the pancakes and conversation. Pam stood up, kissed him again on the cheek, and whispered, 'Don't get yourself backed into no corners tonight, child.'

279

Banyon assured her, 'I'll keep moving.'

Shortly afterward he went outside, climbed into the New-port, and drove west, toward the mountains, never glancing in his rearview mirror until he was miles gone and worlds away from the Deepwater.

A NOTE ON THE AUTHOR

Matthew F. Jones was born in Boston and raised in rural upstate New York. He has written four other novels, all of them critically accalimed, including *Blind Pursuit* and *A Single Shot*. He has, among other things, practiced law and taught writing. He lives with his family in Charlottesville, Virginia.

A NOTE ON THE TYPE

The text of this book is set in Bembo. The original types for which were cut by Francesco Griffo for the Venetian printer Aldus Manutius, and were first used in 1495 for Cardinal Bembo's *De Aetna*. Claude Garamond (1480–1561) used Bembo as a model and so it became the forerunner of standard European type for the following two centuries. Its modern form was designed, following the original, for Monotype in 1929 and is widely in use today.